The Lyons Orphanage

Charlie King

Published by New Generation Publishing in 2017

Copyright © Charlie King 2017

First Edition

The author asserts the moral right under the Copyright, Designs and Patents Act 1988 to be identified as the author of this work.

All Rights reserved. No part of this publication may be reproduced, stored in a retrieval system or transmitted, in any form or by any means without the prior consent of the author, nor be otherwise circulated in any form of binding or cover other than that which it is published and without a similar condition being imposed on the subsequent purchaser.

www.newgeneration-publishing.com

Chapter 1

When growing up in an orphanage, there are only so many things a person can do to entertain themselves, especially when school's out for the summer and they are left inside over the holidays. Luckily, I was born with a power that has given me plenty of amusement over the years. It is also a power that means drama surrounds me constantly.

"I'm going to kill him!" says one voice.

"I shouldn't have done that," says another voice.

"Why is this happening to me?" asks a third voice.

"Should I have chicken or pork tonight?" asks another. This is why I read the minds of people less and less these days. Mind-reading sounds like fun and it can be sometimes but there are so many minds filled with hate, regret, sadness and other things that are just plain boring. Therefore, it is better for me just to block it out. Now, whenever I read minds, I'm doing it purely for my own or someone else's advantage rather than just being nosy. I do get a sense of well-being knowing the troubles of the other orphans in here and being able to help them; I mainly help myself when it comes to school and the work that comes with it.

I'm usually reading a book that the owner Mr Lyons lets me take from his personal collection to pass the time. I like to read these books rather than some of the old comics that are strewn about the orphanage which the other orphans prefer to read. The owner of the orphanage, Mr Lyons, along with the nurses who treated me, said I cried much more than a normal baby. That was probably because I had no filter on the thoughts I was reading, a baby would cry a lot if it had hundreds of people talking to it every single minute.

I could hear the office door of Mr Lyons open and he came downstairs into the main open area. It was impossible not to hear him coming downstairs with his slow movement and the creaky stairs a complete giveaway. This gives us time to hide things or stop certain actions that Mr Lyons may frown upon so we hardly ever got told off, not that Mr Lyons was prone to anger, at least not with me he wasn't. Still, he was intimidating enough if you were caught in the glare of his big hazel eyes. Mr Lyons appeared downstairs in one of his custom-made suits to fit his rather large frame. In the last few years, Mr Lyons has always appeared wearing a suit whereas before he usually just stuck to a smart shirt and smart trousers.

"Good morning, Sam," he said to me.

"Good morning, Mr Lyons," I said.

"What are you up to today?" he asked.

"I'm still reading through this book you gave me," I said as I revealed the book cover to him.

"Ah, Of Mice and Men," he said. "The book's a classic and I think you're old enough and mature enough to handle all of its themes."

"I'm enjoying it so far," I said.

"What's your favourite thing about it so far?" asked Mr Lyons.

"Well, I think the relationship between George and Lenny is interesting, they seem to have an unbreakable bond," I replied.

"They do indeed," said Mr Lyons. "That's why I recommend this book to every orphan who has come into my care who has an interest in reading."

"Why's that?" I asked.

"Because George and Lenny aren't brothers and yet they travel together like a family chasing the American Dream," he said. "I think this book gives hope to everyone without a family because if you have a strong enough bond, a strong enough friendship, that connection is more important in an individual's life than blood, I hope you remember that," he told me as he walked back up the stairs. I wondered why he even came down in the first place. It seems like he just wants to check on us every now and again to make sure we haven't killed each other and then resume whatever it was he was doing before. He never really talks to the other orphans though unless they are doing something wrong right in his eye-line.

Mr Lyons has always been kind to me and it is advice like that which makes me view him as a father figure. I always have to ask Mr Lyons to explain what he means because for some reason, he has a mind which I can't read and this only occurs with a few people. I have a theory that it is because I have made such a strong connection with him that my brain is somehow refusing to let me see into his mind simply out of respect. In truth, I do respect and admire Mr Lyons so I wouldn't want to be constantly reading his mind because he is happy to express so much to me himself.

However, Mr Lyons has never told me the details of my parents' death and that's the one reason I wish I could read his mind. He says I'm old enough at thirteen to be reading more mature literature and yet I'm not old enough to handle the truth behind the death of my parents, all he lets me know is that they died before I was twelve months old.

The orphanage itself is a bit dilapidated but it's still in one piece and I know Mr Lyons does all he can to look after the orphans and keep the orphanage running. The orphanage is a big, old building that hasn't seen much change in the twenty five years since Mr Lyons bought up the property which he has owned and managed ever since. We have the kitchen and dining area, bathrooms, dormitories and a general open area for all the orphans to gather, read, converse and play games most of which require imagination other than card games. There are broken sinks in the bathroom, wonky seats in the dining area and loose fixtures on the wall but at least there's everything you need in life to survive. The open area is very basic; there are individual seats scattered around and a couple of tables to rest things on. That's where I spend most of my time reading while the other orphans enjoy each other's company.

The orphans have their own little friend groups. Even though I help these other kids out when I can, having the ability to read their minds makes it too awkward for me to try and form close friendships, so instead I just make passing conversation with them. Therefore, the groups I talk to will change daily and I'll be their tag along for that day. I like it this way. It means I'm usually doing something different each day and talking about a different topic whereas each group is stuck with each other all day, every day. No matter how much they get on with each other, anybody who spends so much time with the same people is bound to get bored or frustrated on certain days.

Some orphans feel compelled to stick with their group even though I can see it in their mind that they are tired of the same old conversations. For example, one group will always talk about football, another will talk about what games they could invent to amuse themselves while others just mope around, complaining about school life and the orphanage. I get the sense that the dull or irritating days are worth it for the sake of being part of a group; after all, each group has found common ground through the discussion of certain topics and it's nice for them to have that constant in their life, given all that has gone before.

No orphans can really be considered lucky but having a brother or sister orphaned with you must be a major help when growing up here. Gareth and Natasha Wade are twins, who are my age, and as anyone would expect, they look very similar. They always seem to be together at every point of the day, eating together, playing together. I envy them and I know the other orphans do too.

Their relationship is pretty close so they don't gravitate towards the other orphans very much, except for a boy named Ben who I regularly see playing with them. I think that Ben felt alone when he joined the orphanage and it was the twins who looked after him like a younger brother but the twins are quite shut off from the rest of the orphans. This trio are one of the main groups who rely on their imagination for fun. They usually chase each other round the orphanage either hiding, fighting or trying to 'kill' each other with a number of weapons they have invented. The closeness of their relationship is clear to see for anyone but with my mind-reading ability, I can see how deep their bond lies. Whenever they decide how they will entertain themselves on a certain day, they seem to come to the same conclusion in their mind although only one of them will say it.

"After this, we should go ask Natalie for permission to go out the front of the orphanage so we can play football," thought Natasha. At that moment, Gareth stopped running and started panting, bringing a halt to whatever game they were playing this time and Ben stopped right behind him.

"I'm bored of this now," said Gareth out loud. "Let me catch my breath and then we should go see if Natalie will let us play outside today." I knew Natasha was thinking the exact same thing so I'm always curious to see how they react to each other's similar thoughts but it never seems to faze them, not even a slight change in expression. Then again, with such a nice day outside, it was a logical conclusion to jump to.

"Sure, that's a good idea," said Natasha. Football was the one uniting factor amongst the orphans. Those who had no interest in talking about it and watching it were always keen to play it. It may simply be because going outside for anything other than school is quite a rarity and people want any excuse to have a change of scenery from the grey brick walls that make up the whole orphanage.

It's also a rarity to have so much free time during the day and any sunlight you get in British weather has to be made the most of by us otherwise we'd never get out of the orphanage. Most people aren't very good at it but that doesn't stop them enjoying themselves. The only problem that arises is a few of the most competitive and talented orphans like Natasha have the tendency to get annoyed very easily while Gareth tends to stay quiet. On one hand, almost everybody comes together to play and all the groups mix but the negative behaviour of people while playing just increases the gap in communication between the different groups afterwards.

"Ben, go see Natalie and ask her if she can let us outside," demanded Gareth.

"Okay," said Ben timidly. Ben was comfortable around Gareth and Natasha but he was very nervous around the other orphans as well as the adults in the orphanage. I could see the anxiety in his blue eyes, same colour as mine, as he edged his way towards the steps. I could see in his mind that he was nervous simply at the prospect of talking to someone alone.

"Hey Ben," I said.

"Yes?" he asked.

"I'll come with you to Natalie's office," I told him. "We'll go talk to her together."

"Oh, well, thank you," he said. I walked up the stairs side by side with him. Ben was struggling to hold his nerve simply talking to me so he might have crumbled left alone with adults. It was strange to see because when I look at him playing with Gareth and Natasha from afar, he seems a completely different person, with the ability to express himself and say anything that might come into his head.

We walked up to see Natalie, the assistant manager of the orphanage who has been in this role at least since I first arrived here. She is not as approachable as Mr Lyons but I can tell she cares about the orphans and the orphanage almost as much as Mr Lyons does. We had to walk past Mr Lyons' office to get to her office. The window on the door and surrounding the door are all blurry so when you walk past, all you can see are the vague outlines of objects and people sitting in there. Every time I walk past, I always have a look even though I can't see anything.

As we walked past, I looked in and I could see two figures in there and judging by their outlines, Natalie was in there with Mr Lyons. If it were one of the kitchen staff, there would have been an outline of a hat on there and it couldn't have been the caretaker Mr Thompson because he was a short, old man. The outline next to Mr Lyons was a tall, slim one with hair going down to the shoulders. We decided to wait by the door for Natalie to exit. You can only hear murmurs through the walls, unless somebody is raising their voice.

The whole first floor corridor is plastered with framed newspaper cuttings regarding Mr Lyons. It's not hard to spot them, especially if you are waiting around on the first floor. The biggest frame is reserved for an article which signifies the start of the orphanage. The headline reads *'RICH ORPHAN SELLS HIS BUSINESS TO FUND NEW ORPHANAGE.'* dated January 1991, twenty five years ago. It explains that Mr Lyons had a retail business which sold every type of item you could imagine which he then sold for the purpose of running an orphanage. I like to read it from time to time because it reaffirms my respect for Mr Lyons. A quote from Mr Lyons reads:

'I have loved every moment of running this business, I started it up by myself and it is now a global force but I feel the need for a new challenge. I could have sold this company and retired at the age of thirty but I want to help with something that is close to my heart. I was orphaned at a young age with my brother and if it wasn't for an orphanage, I wouldn't be where I am today. Therefore, I want to give orphans the same chance in life I have been given. I have purchased an old factory on Brighton Road which I intend to make into an orphanage. It saddens me that the number of orphanages in the country is dwindling but I intend to make this orphanage stand out from the rest.'

The other articles praise Mr Lyons' philanthropic work within the Croydon area and his continued dedication to this orphanage. He has all this money and all he wants to do is use it to help the less fortunate and help us, the orphans. Other cuttings show his support for charities specifically targeting disadvantaged children. The older cuttings show a thinner, dark-haired man in stark contrast to the big figure of Mr Lyons with thinning, grey hair. Most of the more modern articles on display refer solely to his work with the orphanage; there are less examples of his charitable work in recent years. I think Mr Lyons means well but I think he has seen the state of the orphanage and decided he needs to put all his focus into this. I'm sure he helps out where he can but right now, his money needs to be going into the repairing and upgrading of the orphanage.

Mr Lyons seems to thrive under this attention; at least it seems like that from what I've seen. He seems to take more time out of the orphanage these days to make media appearances; he is quite the local celebrity due to his generosity. He looks to get as much attention as possible for the orphanage so that people can make any donations they want. He insists he doesn't need it but it still helps. He's very open with me in explaining the reasons why he may not be at the orphanage for an extended period of time and relaying to me what he feels the benefits are of his decision. He doesn't need to explain it to me but he does anyway. I suppose he feels he has to be truly honest with me due to our close connection, to reassure me that he puts his all into keeping the orphanage running and trying to find ways to improve it.

We turned round from the frames to see Natalie moving towards the door. We made sure to keep our distance from the door as Mr Lyons gets agitated if anyone is standing too close when the door opens; going into his office is strictly prohibited unless he invites you in. We decided to stand on the opposite side of the corridor so that Natalie could see us as soon as she left the room but letting her know that we were no threat to try and enter Mr Lyons' office. The person who lets someone else in the office is as much at fault as the child trying to get in; at least that's how Mr Lyons sees it. Natalie opened the door looking a little bit flustered which is easy to spot as her usually pale face becomes reddened when it's not covered by her blonde fringe. She was always well-dressed like Mr Lyons, with similar attire if you just swap Mr Lyons trousers for a skirt and add a small amount of make-up. She let out a huge sigh and then looked up to see me and Ben waiting for her.

"Oh," she said as if she was caught off-guard. "Hello Ben, hello Sam, is there something I can do for you?" I had gone completely blank because I was too busy trying to look into Natalie's mind to see what was troubling her before I realised that I needed to respond. All this time waiting, Ben had looked towards me as I stared blankly at Natalie who covered up the left side of her cheek. She may have thought I was staring at the blue vein that is quite visible on the surface of her left cheek and I should have considered that; I know from reading her mind that she is self-conscious about that.

"We...we would like to ask...if we could go outside and play football soon?" asked Ben timidly as he decided to interject himself into asking while I snapped back to reality.

"I'll let Mr Thompson know you guys want to go out and he can let you out and keep watch over you, thanks for coming to me first, Ben," Natalie said.

"Thanks Natalie, I thought I'd let Ben ask you because he wanted to prove he was getting better at communicating," I said. Usually I wouldn't want to take advantage of a situation like this but I'd had been staring so awkwardly for so long that I had to make an excuse that made both me and Ben look good.

"Okay then, you two head back downstairs and the caretaker will be down shortly," she said as she wandered off to her office.

"Bye!" shouted Ben down the corridor to Natalie. She looked back, gave a smile and waved. Natalie isn't always as approachable as Mr Lyons despite the fact that she allows us to call her Natalie. She can sometimes seem cold in her responses, taking everything seriously and not saying anymore than she needs to. Mr Lyons is more lenient with the orphans while Natalie sticks to tight schedules and rules. She still puts plenty of effort into the orphanage from its operations to the orphans themselves which is why she took delight in Ben's response. Knowing all that Mr Lyons has done for the orphanage and knowing that the orphanage is almost always on the mind of Natalie, I think the orphanage is in good hands for many years to come.

"Well done, Ben," I said. "I'm sorry about putting you through that and claiming it was my own idea."

"But it was," said Ben. "Gareth and Natasha wanted to send me up here when they knew I wasn't comfortable meeting adults alone but you came along to support me."

"Well, I was going to ask Natalie myself but I was just distracted by one of Mr Lyons' framed articles," I told Ben.

"It's okay though, when I looked at you not responding, it made me realise that was what I would look like a lot of the time, I need to start speaking to adults soon otherwise how can I be adopted?" said Ben. I didn't expect Ben to read so much into it, I certainly didn't, but if he thought I'd deliberately planned it to go that way, I wasn't going to be the one to tell him otherwise. He seemed to get a bit of a confidence boost out of such a simple conversation.

"Ben, you'll be fine," I told him. "I've seen you when you're comfortable with people like Gareth and Natasha; you just need to show that side with more people."

"You're right, there's a couple who have come to the orphanage a few times and they seem to like me, I just hope I can show enough that they won't think I'd just be silent if I went with them," he said.

"At least you get a chance to meet the couples," I said as I put my arm round his shoulder and walked back downstairs with him.

"You mean to say that you don't get to see them?" asked Ben.

"No, I don't know why but that's how it is, don't worry about it," I told him.

With those words, Ben fell silent. Now all we had to do was wait for the caretaker. As we got downstairs, I went back to my book as Ben wandered back over to Gareth and Natasha.

"Well, what did she say?" asked Gareth.

"She said Mr Thompson will come and let us out soon," replied Ben while almost every orphan stopped what they were doing as they awaited the news.

"Oh, knowing Mr Thompson, that could be anytime," moaned Gareth as he turned to Natasha who just rolled her eyes at him. Gareth slumped up against the wall and began slowly sliding down it. He and Natasha seemed to take it in turns to be the talkative one. The three of them have a strange relationship, they all communicate differently from one another and yet somehow it works for them. I think Ben knows the twins sometimes use him to do the things they either don't want to do or can't be bothered to do but he is grateful for the attention they have given him since his arrival.

The different groups of orphans gathered as they set out their teams in preparation for getting outside and playing football. There was no need for a change of clothes as nobody really had anything specifically suited to playing sports. Most of our clothes are the result of donations and we don't get too much to eat so most orphans walk around in baggy clothes. My collection of clothing contains the same plain t-shirts in different colours and either grey or black tracksuits; the girls weren't given anything different to wear.

I'd consider myself a decent enough player that the groups are interested in me joining them but generally I just try to choose a new group each time so that I save face with all groups. There are some people who I would never hear speak if it wasn't for the prospect of football. It dominates everyone's conversations once they know it is happening until Mr Thompson arrives to let us out.

We could hear the rattle of the keys against the entrance doors; it was the caretaker, Mr Thompson, coming in from the outside. For most of us, there was nothing more exciting than hearing that sound. It was the equivalent of an excitable dog hearing the unmistakeable sound of its lead being picked up. I don't like to think about it too much but the caretaker pretty much just performs the role of a pet owner to us. He lets us out, he ushers us towards the dining room for meals, he cleans up after us and he locks us in at night so that we can't go anywhere. Mr Thompson immediately locked the door behind him which led to a number of groans from the orphans. Mr Thompson went to his cupboard to get a couple of balls. Even though the cupboard is always open, we are not allowed in there because that's where he keeps his dangerous work tools. He then walked with the balls towards the main entrance to open it back up again.

"Right you lot," he said as he began to turn the key in the door. "You'll get a couple of hours out the front and I'll be watching you the whole time so there can be no funny business." Mr Thompson had no interest in conversing with the orphans; he just wanted to do his job. I've seen in his mind that he feels that all he needs to do is keep us alive so he can get paid. I'm not sure how I feel about that but as long as he is motivated by something to look after us; I know he will continue to do so. He opened up the door and the one beside it; there was a large cheer as the sun shone through the orphanage. At that point, Natasha came running right to the front.

"I'll take that," she said as she snatched the balls away from Mr Thompson and led the kids outside, rushing past the caretaker.

"Go careful!" he shouted as the children ran past him. "You're all going to get out and play, you're all going to get two hours, there's no need to rush."

"Yeah, yeah," said a voice among the crowd of children as they continued to stream past the caretaker. When the crowd had died down, I passed Mr Thompson on the way out who looked fed up.

"Little buggers," he thought to himself. That gives an indication of his relationship with the orphans but in this case, I can't blame him for being annoyed. His lack of communication with us doesn't make him an authority figure in the eyes of the children; he was simply the man who had the keys to let us out. The children knew he was unlikely to complain to Natalie or Mr Lyons about something so minuscule like being slightly brushed against by onrushing children.

Chapter 2

We exited through the front doors of the orphanage to bask in the warm glow of the sunlight that had struggled to pierce the grimy windows of the orphanage. Summer represented the chance to break up the same old routine; the rest of the year, we'd be in school on a day like this. This gave us the chance to add a bit of colour to our skin, although the only other colour we got was bright red from sunburn; there was no in-between.

Everybody gathered with their group of friends which always left me, Natasha, Gareth and Ben standing by ourselves waiting to join one of the teams for today, much like at school where there is always the remaining few to pick from. The only difference here was that Natasha and I are very competent players. Ben isn't very good but that made him popular with the teams because they knew they could take him and put him in goal, where nobody else wanted to play. Natasha is very good but her competitive nature can rub people up the wrong way which makes teams hesitant to recruit her.

Gareth looks like he would make a good sportsman in the future but I'm not sure football is his thing. The twins are both lanky and tower over the rest of the orphans, including me, but Gareth had the look of someone who could be a future athlete. His pace, rather than his ability, made him a popular choice for some teams. As for me, I like to play in defence. They say defenders need to be able to read the minds of attackers to tackle them and prevent them from scoring and that's my specific skill. It may technically be cheating but I doubt anybody will call me out on being a mind-reader. A couple of groups had already made gestures to Gareth and Natasha so they made their way over to the respective groups.

"Sam, would you like to join us this week?" asked Owen, who is a member of the group that is obsessed with discussing football along with Reece, Kris and Nathan. The orphans had worked out I had a system of switching teams each time we went out to play so they knew when it was their time to ask again.

"Sure," I said as I moved towards the crowd.

"Who needs a goalie this week?" asked Ben which brought laughs from the different groups. Ben seemed confident enough now to speak out loud and laugh at himself, realising that was the main reason people picked him.

"Yeah, we'll take you," said a voice which came from my team. The teams were now all set. Like always, we'd managed among ourselves to set up four teams although they weren't all equal in number but we didn't care about that, we just wanted to play. Any old clothing or objects we'd find were goalposts but there was no real layout for separate pitches, after all, we were all playing on concrete with no markings on it. This can make it a bit messy when it comes to separating out into two pitches, especially when the ball from one match enters the designated area of the other. For us, this was a kind of chaos that we welcomed. Everything about orphanage life is a routine where we follow specific rules but when we go outside and play football, we are left to our own devices; Mr Thompson is only there to make sure no fights break out or to check on any child if they fall and injure themselves.

"Give us a whistle, Mr Thompson," said Natasha. Mr Thompson gave a short sigh before making a whistling sound with his hands and mouth to start the kick-off. A traditional kick-off would start in the middle of the pitch but it usually started for us when somebody throws the ball really high in the air which is usually an accident waiting to happen straightaway. The first match Ben and I faced was against the team Natasha had joined. She took it very seriously. She tied up her usually wavy, chestnut brown hair into a ponytail so there was no chance of her hair obscuring her vision at any point. Not many of the boys have that same problem with their hair; I certainly don't with my short, black hair. She immediately ran forward as her team had the ball but they then quickly lost it.

"What the hell was that?!" Natasha shouted at her teammate who had lost the ball. She was always vocal throughout the entirety of us playing football outside but most of the time, this just consisted of frustrated noises rather than showing specific aggression to a single player. The ball came to Natasha and she ran directly towards me. "I'll fake a pass left and take it past Sam the opposite way," thought Natasha. Knowing exactly what she was going to do, I took the ball off of her.

Playing against my team caused her the most frustration because I was often there to stop her and her team as they attacked. However, when I read somebody's mind, it can slow my reaction time right down because of the amount of focus I need. That means that although I know what somebody is about to do or where they are about to go, I don't always react quick enough to prevent them from doing it. I guess there needs to be some balance of the good and bad with my mind-reading capabilities.

Sometimes, I choose to switch it off as much as I can so that I can just play football like a normal person and make things a bit fairer. After I intercepted another ball, I decided now was the time to switch off from it, I wanted to see how much I could actually achieve from instinct and knowledge to get a true judge of how good a defender I actually am. I think even that initial spate of mind-reading sets me up well for the rest of the match because I know what to look out for in terms of body language as to what they might do next. It became much more even between Natasha and I as the match went on as she dared to enjoy herself playing the game, whether her team was winning or losing.

The ball was kicked by one player into the overgrowth of plants and bushes that covered one side of the orphanage. I decided that I would go to retrieve the ball.

The ball going into the overgrowth was a common occurrence and usually the person who kicked the ball that way would go retrieve it but I was closest so I volunteered to get it. The first problem was finding the ball amongst the overgrowth, there's no telling how deep into it the ball has gone. This involves a lot of trial and error; for each area you look in or each branch you pull back, you're bound to come into contact with the stinging nettles there, which is what happened to me on this occasion. As I searched, I saw a dirty, old saucepan deep in one of the bushes; I didn't really know what to make of it. I eventually found the ball and tossed it back onto the pitch as I made my way back. As I walked back, I looked towards the other match and just saw a flash of short chestnut brown hair as Gareth began running full speed with the ball.

We'd all lost track of the score so it was agreed that the next goal would win and this applied to the other match as well. Natasha was running towards me with the ball at her feet so I went to tackle her but missed. Natasha took the ball past me to shoot directly at Ben, who saved it with his foot. The ball bounced off his foot right up to the other end of the field where Owen scored just a few seconds later. There was a cheer from my team while there was a look of frustration on Natasha's face. The team ran over to Ben to pick him up to celebrate his save which had won us the match, in part. Natasha's glum expression changed significantly upon seeing that, she was now smiling as she looked on at Ben who now seemed more confident than ever. I now had another match to play for around an hour having to deal with the irritations caused by the stinging nettles which left red patches on my arms.

Mr Thompson had been standing at the front of the orphanage the whole time. He hadn't been reading a newspaper or anything like that, he was simply watching us. He didn't offer any encouragement and he didn't smile at any of the goals, he just watched on like a robot. I saw Natalie emerge out the front with Beth, a member of the kitchen staff. Beth was a short, old member of the kitchen staff with greying blonde hair and she always had a sour look on her face. They had brought a small table poking slightly out the front doors where they began to fill up cups of water for us to drink. Most of the time, we would just play for the two hours with a few short breaks or until everybody dropped out from exhaustion. Natalie always wants us to spend as much time outside as possible, even when there's bad weather, I think she realised how much happier we are to be doing something different, to not be trapped inside the orphanage or inside a school all day.

"Come and get your drinks, everyone!" she shouted. Everybody gingerly made their way over to the drinks table, trying to catch their breath. The orphans sat outside on the floor in their teams with their drinks as they rested after the first match. There were taunts from the winning teams to the losing teams as we sat but it was all in good spirit. It was now set for the two winning teams to face off as the two losing teams faced each other.

The table was moved back inside but not before it was bashed against one of the front doors as they tried to move it. The impact of the table hitting the door had turned one of the two lion-head knockers on that door on its side; yet another thing falling apart at the orphanage. Even after all the drinks were finished and the cups had been returned, Natalie remained outside. As we were set to begin the second match, Natalie whistled to signify the start of play and it was she who chucked the two balls up in the air.

Natalie was watching both matches, making comments, clapping and cheering which was a huge contrast to Mr Thompson who had also remained outside but stood silently. Ben made another save in goal.

"Well done Ben, keep it up" said Natalie from afar. Ben looked up at her and smiled.

"Thanks Natalie, I will," said Ben. Everything about today helped Ben with his confidence; he was now talking to me, Natalie and the rest of our teammates shouting instructions to them up the pitch. We won this match quite comfortably, even without the use of my ability. Ben was the centre of attention at the end of the two matches and he seemed to be relishing it. He was getting praise from all groups; he conversed with our team for a while before eventually returning to Gareth and Natasha. Natalie had left a little bit early which left Mr Thompson to bring us back inside. His dreary tones brought about the realisation that we were now going back in as he took back the two balls and ushered us in.

The next few days were basked in glorious sunshine so the same pattern followed. Ben insisted upon asking Natalie himself about going outside, Mr Thompson let us out, Natalie would appear and then we would head back in and Ben was growing in confidence. All the while, the more I talked to Ben, the more I talked to Gareth and Natasha over the next few days. This cycle continued until the weekend where the rain took over British summer time once more. I had heard there would be some adults visiting the orphanage over the weekend with a view to fostering or adopting orphans but Mr Lyons insisted I could not meet any of them and that instead I would be confined to my room, as always when potential foster parents come to visit, I wish I knew why.

I was sitting in the boys' dormitory reading through my book when I heard the sound of the front doors opening as Mr Lyons greeted the adults who entered. Now, I just had to simply wait until I heard footsteps heading outside. I was still engrossed in my book so I hadn't really kept track of time to see how long I was waiting but it seemed like a longer visit than usual.

"Good luck with everything with your new home and family," I heard Mr Lyons tell someone as he closed the front doors to the orphanage. That explained why the visit was longer, one of the orphans was leaving for a new home. I guess that meant I was now free to leave the room but then again, it's not as if I would be doing anything differently other than reading a book in a different part of the orphanage. The only motivation for me to head back to the main area was to see who it was that had left, if I even really knew them in the first place. I decided I may as well wait until dinner time to leave the room.

The only reason anyone looks forward to dinner here is simply because they're hungry and they need to eat it. In years gone by, the quality of ingredients used in the meals has declined to the point where every meal tastes of the same blandness. There was a time where the meals here were better than the school dinners but now even that has surpassed us. I would suspect Mr Lyons is trying to save as much money as possible having funded the orphanage for over twenty five years by cheapening the cost of our meals, which I can understand. Still, being here as long as I have means I have had a taste of more luxurious food and I have seen the orphanage in a better kept condition than on offer now. I almost wish I'd never experienced the nicer meals so that I wouldn't know any better than what we were offered now. Mr Lyons never had to give us expensive meals but he did it anyway, he wanted to provide us with as many luxuries as possible until he realised it wasn't sustainable.

I walked into the dining room to see almost everybody sitting along the wide table with their food already, all sat in their respective friend groups. I walked up to Beth, who was serving the food today, with my plate at the ready.

"Today is mash, sausages and peas," said Beth in a low, husky voice.

"Okay," I said as she placed the food on my plate. There's nothing more you can say than that in all reality, it's not like you can moan and change the decision to something more exciting. Then again mash, sausages and peas would be a good choice for a meal if there was some kind of sauce or gravy and if the mash wasn't cold and lumpy and if the sausages actually had any flavour to them. Sometimes, it's the simple things like that which annoy me. I shouldn't expect luxury meals but surely they can manage to not make the mash lumpy and produce some kind of sauce for the meal. There are three members of kitchen staff; Beth, Stephen and Ryan. These three are all relatively new to the orphanage as they came in a few years ago to replace the previous staff, which produced the higher quality meals. A quick read of any of their minds shows me their hearts are not in this at all which explains why they seem to struggle with making basic meals edible.

At dinner time, I usually prefer to be alone but it's hard to do when everybody sits on one long table so I usually find a seat in a small gap between two groups which means I occasionally get dragged into their conversation. I want to eat my food as quickly as possible just to be done with it; it's bad enough eating the food but seeing dozens of plates with the same food as well is really unappetising. As I walked towards one section of the table, I could see Gareth and Natasha sitting with each other in almost complete silence. Both had a sombre look on their face as they slowly picked apart the mash with their fork.

I could have read either of their minds to work out the problem but I felt compelled to talk to them as we had bonded with each other in the last few days during football, mainly due to our mutual friendship with Ben who was the link between us. I also recalled Mr Lyons' words to me while I was reading Of Mice and Men, which became more and more prominent in my mind over the last few days with Ben. He had told me that making strong connections with people is important and that connection doesn't have to be linked by family, you can make that connection yourself.

The main reason I avoided getting too close to people was the awkwardness of reading their minds but if I can develop a relationship as strong as the one I have with Mr Lyons then I should feel less inclined to read their minds simply out of respect. I don't know how long that trust and respect has to be built up for though because for as long as I can remember, I have never been capable of reading Mr Lyons' mind.

"Anyone sitting here?" I asked, gesturing towards the empty seat.

"No, you can sit there if you like," said Natasha calmly.

"Are you two okay?" I asked.

"Why wouldn't we be?" asked Natasha.

"You two seem a little down to me, are you getting withdrawal symptoms from a lack of football today?" I asked jokingly.

"Yeah, that must be it," said Natasha who almost cracked a smile before looking back down at her food. There was a pause in the conversation. I was seriously considering looking into their minds to see what was really bothering them.

"Ben left today," said Gareth as he looked up from his plate.

"Oh," I said. I had intended to say more but at that point, I just reflected on the reality of Ben leaving. It all made sense now. They were holding back on telling me about Ben because that was the news that upset them and left them moping around. "I know he said the other day there was a couple who came to see him a few times before."

"Yeah, well today's the day the couple decided to take him," said Natasha. "They were worried at first about his communication skills but he had been getting better and on today's visit, they saw enough to convince them that he would be capable of communicating with them comfortably."

"We should be happy for Ben," said Gareth. "But selfishly, we wanted him to stay here longer; we thought we still had more time with him while his confidence grew."

"But at least you two always have each other," I told them.

"Having each other is great but it's nice to talk to other people as well, to prove you're capable of talking to people who you have no link to," said Natasha.

"And besides, we are obviously both very similar in terms of likes and dislikes and our ideas of fun so it's nice to talk to somebody else who thinks differently, who adds variety to conversation and activities," said Gareth.

"If that's the case, why didn't you make more friends other than just Ben?" I asked as I decided to finally begin tackling my food.

"When Ben came into the orphanage, we were fairly new so we decided to talk to him," began Natasha. "We could tell he was very quiet and nervous but he had a great sense of humour when he did speak and that's the side only we saw."

"Because Ben was so quiet, it unsettled many of the orphans here and they wanted to avoid talking to him thinking he might be a bit weird," said Gareth. "We knew the other orphans didn't want to make friends with him so we didn't make friends with them, it was as simple as that."

"We weren't going to sacrifice our relationship with Ben for the sake of having more friends, so we settled in this small group of three," said Natasha. I was shocked. I never realised there was such a deep bond between them. Sure, when I have read their minds in the past, it suggested they were fond of Ben but it isn't until now talking to them that I can actually see the depths of their emotional connection.

Mind-reading only gives you the headline of what people are thinking; portraying an emotion and giving a reason for it. Their detailed explanation about their grievances gave me a lot to think about when it came to how much importance I place on mind-reading and how much I can truly learn from one person without speaking to them. As I said, I mind-read less and less often these days for a few reasons but I think this one tops the rest of them. It's not even as if I had to work hard to get them to talk. I simply asked them what's wrong and they told me soon after. Their openness with me makes me less inclined to feel the need to read their minds. I understood now that I could make friendships work based on this trust, openness and understanding.

"So, what do you want to do after dinner?" I asked them, sensing a chance to bond with them some more. They looked at each other and gave a wry smile.

"Like we said, we get tired of doing the same thing over and over again, I think you should suggest what we do next," said Natasha.

"But don't say 'read a book'," said Gareth jokingly. Now I wished I hadn't promised myself that I wouldn't read their minds because I had no idea what we could do and I wasn't sure what they liked. I recalled that, with Ben, the games they played consisted of a lot of running around the orphanage so I just had to come up with an idea based around that. I also remembered that like most of the other orphans, the only time I saw Gareth and Natasha reading was when they were reading comic books.

"Well, my game involves a book," I began. "It's a game I call Anyone vs. Anyone."

"Anyone vs. Anyone?" said Natasha quizzically.

"Yeah, you choose any book character, like somebody in the comic books, and pretend to be them as we fight each other," I said. "So, if you can fly, that's your main power and you'd have to work out how you could use that to your advantage."

"So, we'll have to tell you when we're flying and tell you that we flew out of the way of your attack, for example?" asked Gareth.

"Exactly, you'll need a bit of imagination for this to work though," I chuckled.

"We can handle that, didn't you see us day after day chasing Ben with our ray gun?" asked Natasha.

"I'm sure it will go just fine then," I said. It was nice of Natasha and Gareth to agree to play along, I'll admit it wasn't a very creative idea but they could see I was making an effort.

"But who are you going to be?" asked Natasha. "You never read any of the comics; you don't know any heroes or villains." I realised I now had the perfect opportunity to make up anything I wanted.

"Don't be so sure," I said. "There's this character in Of Mice and Men called Lenny who is gigantic with superhuman strength and he has a gun that temporarily turns people into mice," I told them.

"Okay then," said Natasha. The look in her eyes suggested she didn't really believe me but they had no interest in reading the book to find out if I was telling the truth, after all, they trusted me now. We exited the dining room to the open area and began to play. I didn't really pay attention to which character they picked, they all seemed to be strong, able to fly and be immune to each and every thing I made up. A couple of hours later, we ended the game as we were all worn out from constantly running around and knew there wasn't too long until it would be time for bed.

"That was more fun than I expected," I said.

"Yeah, it was good, we'll have to do it again some time, you can teach us more about Lenny each time so that we won't ever have to read the book," said Gareth.

"Don't go telling Mr Lyons though, he might have some follow-up questions about the book that you won't be able to answer," I said.

"Speaking of Mr Lyons, what is he doing over there?" asked Gareth. From where we were sitting, we could see Mr Lyons, Mr Thompson and Natalie, who was carrying a clipboard, all talking to each other. Natasha was paying particular attention to them before turning her eyes to us.

"I know the code to Mr Lyons' room," whispered Natasha. "We should check it out."

"I don't know, what if we get caught?" I asked. "There would be no explanation as to why we'd be in there besides being nosy and what do you expect to find anyway?"

"Well, there are a few things we might find, one you might be interested in, in particular," said Natasha. "Maybe there's something on your file that explains why he won't let you meet the foster parents, wouldn't you like to know what you can change to get yourself out of here?"

"Well...," I began.

"Then it's settled," said Gareth as he interrupted me. He and Natasha stood up and began to walk upstairs.

"Wait," I said quietly as I took another look at the three adults conversing with each other. By that point, Gareth and Natasha were already halfway up the stairs so I decided to follow. To be honest, part of me was curious about the things Mr Lyons kept from me like the cause of my parents' deaths and why he won't allow me to see potential foster parents. Another part of me didn't want to lose this newly formed friendship already for the sake of something which is essentially harmless. I caught up with the two of them just before they reached the top of the stairs.

"Nice of you to join us Sam," said Natasha.

"How come you have never told me the code?" Gareth asked Natasha.

"I only learnt the code a few days ago and I knew I wouldn't be able to use it until all the adults were downstairs out of the way," she said. "So now was the perfect time to reveal it and if they come back up, we'll easily hear them with the creaky steps."

"Are you sure about this, you two?" I asked.

"Of course we're sure," replied Natasha.

"It's just that I really don't want to get into any trouble with Mr Lyons for the sake of a few files," I said.

"Nothing bad can happen when we go in there; we look around to see if we can find any files on us and if not, we leave," said Natasha.

"If we hear footsteps, we leave," said Gareth.

"Either way, we're going in," said Natasha as she turned to face the keypad.

"So, what is the code?" asked Gareth.

"I'm not going to tell you, it would spoil all the fun," said Natasha as she began entering the code while blocking our view of it. Natasha typed in the first two numbers and then we heard an alarm sound. We panicked and ran downstairs immediately.

Chapter 3

"I told you to leave that room alone," I said to Gareth and Natasha as we ran down the stairs.

"It's Natasha's fault, she put the code in wrong, and she was too busy trying to hide it from us rather than focussing on what buttons her fingers were pressing," said Gareth.

"Calm down, maybe nobody will notice," said Natasha. However, as soon as we reached the bottom step, we saw Natalie who apprehended us.

"What have I told you?" asked Natalie as our faces sank. "When there's a fire alarm, you have to move slowly otherwise you could trip up, fall down the stairs and injure yourself leaving you helpless." In our blind panic at hearing an alarm when trying to open the door, we didn't realise that it was the fire alarm that we were used to hearing. Although for all we knew, both alarms could make the same noise.

"Sorry Natalie," said Gareth as the three of us walked past her, relieved that the only thing she suspected us of was being lousy at following standard fire alarm procedure. We immediately blended into the crowd of orphans as if we hadn't been anywhere else; we knew we got away with something that on another day could have gone horribly wrong.

"Everybody, stop what you're doing, leave everything where it is and head out the entrance," said Natalie. For the urgency there should be when a fire alarm goes off, the building was being evacuated very slowly. Orphans tried to get out of the orphanage as fast as they could and all the adults, including the kitchen staff, were waiting to get out the front doors as well. We'd be in real trouble if the fire spread to this room anytime soon. Some orphans in the crowd were getting very nervous about the slow movement ahead.

"Hurry up," said a voice from the middle of the crowd.

"Everyone stay calm and take your time," said Natalie. Mr Lyons was present but he wasn't saying a word, he was letting Natalie do all the talking and all the ushering while he watched from the back of the crowd with Mr Thompson. Mr Lyons looked calm, almost disinterested, about the whole event. Eventually, all the orphans exited out the front and the adults followed soon afterwards. We finally got to go outside today as well but we had to stand in the pouring rain and wait around in the cold as the light faded. We stood around outside for around twenty minutes while everybody was accounted for; it always is a tedious affair while you wait for your name.

"Sam Watkins?" asked Natalie as she read out the list of names from the clipboard she was holding.

"Here," I replied.

"Okay everyone, that was just a drill, you may go back inside," said Mr Lyons. There was the same crowding problem for getting back inside as well; there was lots of pushing but little movement. As I looked round, I could see Natalie in deep discussion with Mr Lyons. She didn't look very pleased with him about something. I'd never caught a glimpse of any kind of conflict between Mr Lyons and Natalie; they are usually very measured in their speech whatever the situation. Natalie's arms were flailing as she spoke while Mr Lyons was using hand gestures to Natalie which suggested she needed to calm down. Their apparent argument seemed to end as Mr Lyons simply turned away while speaking to her. He looked round to see me and I instantly looked away from him and headed back inside to the open area of the orphanage.

"That was a shambolic fire drill," thought Natalie. "Howard's going to run this place into the ground soon; I need to make him see that." If I could've read Mr Lyons' mind as well, I would have done but Natalie's reaction is all I have to go by. It was clear that Natalie was angry with the slowness of the evacuation which I had picked up on as well. I understood Natalie's point but I couldn't see anything more that Mr Lyons could have done to speed up the process. I felt sorry for Mr Lyons that Natalie had put him under some pressure, apparently to make changes to the orphanage, perhaps to suit her. Natalie was staring at Mr Lyons as he walked up the stairs towards his office but Mr Lyons hadn't looked back at all. The kitchen staff trudged back towards the kitchen and they also looked annoyed.

"If it wasn't for that fire drill, we'd have been out of here by now," thought Beth. So, the kitchen staff and the caretaker don't like being here and yet they remain in their jobs. Natalie may have been harsh to Mr Lyons but at least she has passion for the orphanage which, I guess, was always bound to lead to arguments about how things are done around here.

"Okay everyone, I want you to head to your dormitories soon," said Natalie. There was a collective groan from the orphans.

"But we still had another hour and we lost a lot of that due to this stupid fake fire drill," said Natasha.

"I'm sorry about that but the fire drill isn't stupid; it is an absolute necessity for us to do this now and again to make sure all of us are prepared for a real fire," said Natalie.

"Well, I rate my chances of survival but I'm not sure about the rest of you," said Gareth. "I can power my way to the front and you'll all be left behind, you're all doomed." Although Gareth's words sounded sinister, everybody saw the funny side of the point he was trying to make and everyone erupted with laughter, everyone besides Natalie. Natalie looked to the caretaker who had been standing in the corner and made a gesture to him and he nodded. Natalie looked round at us, opened her mouth as if to say something before closing it as she headed upstairs. Natalie was usually one for discipline and part of that was making sure that orphans never had the last word when it came to orphans challenging adults on a certain topic. All the orphans turned round to Gareth as they tried to stop chuckling, they all look impressed with him.

"You are going to be in so much trouble tomorrow," said Owen.

"She knows it's the truth, that's why she didn't answer back," said Gareth.

"All right, you lot, you heard her," said Mr Thompson. "It's time for bed." There was another collective groan from the orphans but we all accepted it pretty quickly. I could see the kitchen staff leaving with their belongings while Natalie and Mr Lyons had gone up to their offices. When we were all herded into our dormitories, Mr Thompson locked the door behind us.

My sleeping pattern has never been straightforward at the orphanage, mainly because there are so many noises from people heading out late in the evening and people arriving early in the morning. There is no set time Natalie and Mr Lyons stay for until they leave for their own home or for them to arrive here in the morning. On this night, the last person to leave left at one in the morning while the other left around half eleven. The caretaker lives right across the road from the orphanage so there is no adult on site during the night which is why every door gets locked, trapping us in our rooms until morning. The caretaker has a very clear time-frame he works in. He works from eight in the morning until eight at night which is the latest time we are allowed to stay outside our dormitories. This may sound like a long day for him but he often heads out of the orphanage during the day to return to his house across the road when he can. Sometimes Mr Lyons and Natalie come in earlier than him, sometimes later but there is an unmistakeable sound made by the opening of the front entrance that means whenever one of them arrives, everybody is woken up by it.

On this particular morning at six o'clock, one of either Natalie or Mr Lyons entered the building. It was a surprise to hear an entrance so early given that whether it was

Natalie or Mr Lyons, neither one of them would have had much sleep before they were back in at work today. I hadn't slept much and I turned to Gareth who also looked like he hadn't had a good night's sleep.

"You okay?" I asked.

"No," said Gareth sleepily.

"You get woken up by the noises too?" I asked.

"No, I never got to sleep in the first place," replied Gareth. "I've been up all night with my thoughts."

"Your thoughts?" I enquired.

"Yeah, I've been thinking about how Ben is settling in, in his new home," said Gareth.

"It must be worrying for you to think about," I said.

"If this was a few days ago, I would have been worried but not now, not after the week he's had," said Gareth.

"He was like a brand new Ben," I said.

"It was all thanks to you," said Gareth. "You talked to him for a day and he did so much better, he spent years with me and Natasha but all we did was hold him back."

"That's not true, he loved you two," I said.

"He did and we had a great time but we talked to him in the first place because we could see how nervous and lonely he was when he came here," said Gareth. "We made him accept his nervousness as the norm for his life because we felt better about ourselves for having him with us but you saw it, there was a lot more depth to him than that." I knew there was some truth in what Gareth was saying but I felt like I had to say something to try and cheer him up.

"You need to stop being so hard on yourself, Ben enjoyed his time at the orphanage because of you two, he would never have got to express himself to other people if he couldn't express to you two first," I said.

"When we accepted Ben as a friend, we only spoke to him and he only spoke to us," said Gareth. "We never considered that while he was with us, his confidence might have grown enough to speak to others but myself and Natasha were isolated from everyone else and he felt it necessary to remain in isolation with us."

"It's not so bad, I mean, look at me," I began. "I spend my days here dropping in and out of different conversations without feeling like I'm a part of any of it, believe me, Ben's grateful that he had two people he could always rely on."

"Yeah, I guess you're right," he said as he let out a small chuckle. "You're always right; it must be all those books you read."

"Again with the books?" I asked.

"Always," replied Gareth as we both looked at each other. We then both began to burst out laughing before realising it was still early and most of the orphans were still asleep. We covered our mouths to muffle the sound as a few orphans poked their heads up to look round before dropping their heads straight back down to their pillows.

"Shhh," I said as I covered my mouth with my finger, still trying to repress laughter. After a short while, we had finished laughing and Gareth's look had turned sterner.

"So, why don't you hang out with any of the groups?" asked Gareth changing the conversation tone to a more serious one.

"There's no real reason for it," I said. "I've never really wanted to get too close to people, to know everything about them because they could be gone the next day."

"But you've been here a long time," said Gareth.

"Yeah, I think I might have tried more if I knew I was going to be stuck here for over ten years," I said. "Mr Lyons won't let me even meet prospective foster parents."

"Why's that?" asked Gareth.

"I wish I knew," I replied.

"Well, why not just ask him?" asked Gareth.

"It's not like the thought never crossed my mind, I just don't want to make things awkward with Mr Lyons because he has always treated me really well," I said.

"You may as well ask him, the worst thing he can say is 'none of your business' and send you on your way, you may as well try," said Gareth. In truth, I had never asked Mr Lyons because I expected that very answer, especially since he won't tell me about the death of my parents, I doubt he'd tell me why he keeps me here but I began thinking I might as well ask.

"You're right, you didn't even need a book to tell me that," I said.

"Don't you start this again," said Gareth beginning to laugh.

"You started in the first place," I said also trying to repress more laughter. "I'll ask him today," I said as we both began to calm down. Gareth nodded and placed his head down on the pillow. For the next couple of hours while we were stuck in the dormitory, I sat there with my eyes wide open thinking about everything we had just discussed. There was nothing to focus on in the dormitories, no pictures or portraits, just rows and rows of beds. At least the brown wallpaper is a change from the grey that surrounds the rest of the building. I thought about Ben in his new home and the sacrifices Gareth and Natasha had made to keep themselves in isolation for the sake of Ben. Gareth seemed to think Ben could have joined any group he wanted but I wasn't so sure. I'd like to think Ben was confident to talk to others but that he chose not to so he could remain with Gareth and Natasha. I was also thinking about my own time here in the orphanage, how I'd been comfortable with one way for so long and how that had completely changed in the last few days. Now, I wanted to be good friends with Gareth and Natasha particularly because I don't know how much longer I'll be here. I thought that by keeping quiet and not ruffling any feathers, I would have been out the orphanage a long time ago but for some reason, Mr Lyons keeps me here; I was now determined to find out why.

I was relieved to hear the sound of the key unlocking the dormitory so that I could eat my breakfast quickly and head straight to Mr Lyons for a conversation. The questions had been keeping me up the last two hours so I couldn't wait any longer. I rushed to the dining room without waiting for Gareth or Natasha. Today's meal was porridge; at least that's what the kitchen staff called it. This is another instance where if I didn't know what good porridge tasted like, I'd be more grateful for the slop put in front of me. Gareth and Natasha eventually came in just a few moments before I finished my meal and headed straight over to me rather than heading for the breakfast.

"Well, someone was hungry," said Natasha.

"I just wanted to eat as soon as possible," I said. "There are things to do urgently today."

"Did you reach a cliff-hanger in your book?" asked Natasha jokingly as she looked towards Gareth and smiled.

"Very funny, life isn't always about books," I said, trying to repress a smile.

"Your life is," said Natasha. "Your life at this orphanage has been all books."

"Well today's different," I said. "Today, I have you two as bona-fide friends and today I'm going to get the answers I want from Mr Lyons." It felt good to say that out loud. I had settled into a comfortable zone of isolation and ignorance for a long time and I felt it was finally time to change it.

"So you just made two friends and you won't even have breakfast with them?" asked Gareth.

"Not today, no," I said. I could tell they were joking but I still felt like I did need to justify my early breakfast to them. After we spent a lot of time over the past week bonding, the least I could give them was an explanation.

"It's alright, that can be the theme of our friendship, we mock you about all your books and it return, you leave us behind when it's time for food," said Natasha.

"It's not like that at all," I said. "But today is a day where I need to do this, for me."

"Alright case dismissed," said Natasha who slammed an imaginary gavel.

"Off you go, we can't have you eating all the slop now, can we?" asked Gareth. I finished up the remainder of my porridge that had been untouched while I was talking to Natasha and Gareth. Despite my insistence that I had to do this urgently, I stood at the foot of the stairs for around five minutes contemplating what I was about to do. I started to think about how Mr Lyons would react. I was unsure if he would be welcoming or if he felt like I was making some kind of attack on him by asking these questions. I was hoping that my good relationship with him could stay intact and help me get the answers I want from him. I could hear movement from upstairs and saw Natalie turn the corner as she reached the stairs. I stepped to the side of the stairs and looked away.

"That man is an idiot!" thought Natalie as she came downstairs. I was really confused by this. Natalie has always been nice to everyone she has been in contact with, even if appearing a little cold, and even when I have looked into her thoughts before, they had never been filled with malice. However, this thought suggested she was angry with either Mr Lyons or Mr Thompson.

"Good morning Natalie," I said as I turned to face her as she reached the bottom of the stairs. Not only did Natalie look angry but she looked tired too.

"Morning Sam, you had breakfast already?" asked Natalie.

"Yeah, I couldn't sleep last night so I wanted to get out of that dorm as soon as I could," I replied.

"Well, I hope you're alright," said Natalie.

"I'll be fine, I'm sure I'll get a better night's sleep tonight," I said.

"I hope so," she said. "See you around, Sam." Natalie walked past me towards the dining room. I'd got out of bed today feeling completely different from anything I had felt before and it seemed like the same was happening with Natalie. There was a big contrast in her demeanour today from all the years I have known her. She had thoughts of irritation and anger towards either Mr Lyons or Mr Thompson and she had no energy in her movement or speech. I suppose everybody has their off days and maybe Natalie was due one considering how much work she has put into the orphanage to help Mr Lyons over the years.

As soon as Natalie entered the dining room, I decided that I wouldn't delay confronting Mr Lyons any longer. I headed up the stairs slowly, continuously thinking about the points I wanted to bring up to Mr Lyons and how he would react. On a day where everybody seems to be acting differently, I wondered if this could finally be the day where I would be able to see into Mr Lyons' mind to put an end to my unanswered questions about my parents and my time here at the orphanage. It frustrates me that there are only a few things I want to know from Mr Lyons but these are the things that Mr Lyons keeps quiet about. I approached Mr Lyons' door and knocked. I saw the outline of his figure rise from the desk and saw it head towards the door. The door clicked open and Mr Lyons opened it up slightly so that he could see me on the other side.

"Ah Sam, come on in," he said as he swung the door open. It was a surprise that he invited me in. Usually when people want to talk to him, he ushers them to another room to chat. His office is usually sacred ground where he keeps piles and piles of files on every one of us and it is plastered with even more framed newspaper cuttings than in the corridor. There were a lot of files around his office but they were all either neatly stacked up on the ground, table or bookshelf. The windows behind his desk were crystal clear and overlooked the front of the orphanage and I could see buildings for miles. "Please take a seat," he said as he pointed towards a chair by his desk.

"Thank you Mr Lyons," I said as I sat down. Mr Lyons grabbed his chair from the other side of the desk and brought it round to my side to talk with me.

"I don't want you to feel like you're in some kind of meeting, relax," said Mr Lyons. He had this way of instantly defusing any situation even if he didn't know a situation was about to arise. I had gone in there preparing to get straight to the point and be direct with him but his demeanour helped to calm me. Mr Lyons looked to the side of his desk and quickly lunged for a green first aid kit that had been left out, placed it into a drawer and slammed the drawer shut. "Don't need that any more."

"What happened?" I asked.

"Oh it's nothing really, just a small graze on my leg," replied Mr Lyons. "Anyway, what did you want to talk about Sam?" he asked.

"Well I've just been wondering," I said hesitantly.

"If it's about your parents, you know I can't tell you about that," said Mr Lyons. It was an answer I was expecting but it still left me disappointed.

"No, it's not that, I ask you that every time," I said. "I wanted to know why it is that I never get a chance to meet potential foster parents."

"I'm surprised you never asked sooner," said Mr Lyons.

"I was happy here and I still am so I got comfortable with this way of life," I said.

"Well, you've partly answered your own question," said Mr Lyons. "All this time you've been at the orphanage, I wasn't sure how much you would want to leave and how you would fit in with a new family." Even now, I wasn't sure how much I wanted to leave but I did know that I at least wanted a full answer as to why I've never met foster parents, why I have never had the chance to do something different.

"I like it here because I can trust you and Natalie to look after me, I get food, shelter and I get to read books but that's because I seemed to accept from an early age that me not meeting foster parents was the norm so I made myself comfortable here," I said.

"I was worried about you that since you've been here, you've kept yourself isolated from the rest of the orphans," he said. "In the early years, I wasn't sure how you'd handle communicating with family members so I kept you back but I knew there was potential because of how comfortable you are in conversation with me."

"So, if you realised that in the early years, why is it still the case now?" I asked.

"I'll admit some selfishness on my part," replied Mr Lyons. "It is great to have a kid here who was interested in the books I like, not only that but I have seen you with the other children, you may not always talk to them but you help them out whenever you can and it makes mine and Natalie's job that little bit easier."

"I just like to help out where I can," I said.

"No, it's more than that," said Mr Lyons. "It seems like you have a real understanding of people that sets you apart from the rest, I saw you with Ben over the last week or so helping him to grow his confidence."

"Ben had it all along," I said.

"Maybe so but you coaxed it out of him, you showed us that Ben could communicate with adults so it is you who helped Ben find a home," said Mr Lyons. "At the same time, you showed me that your communication skills among people your age is also improving, Natalie tells me that you, Gareth and Natasha are now good friends."

"Yeah, we bonded through Ben's departure," I said.

"You helped Ben get a new home, you filled the void left behind for Gareth and Natasha and you have shown your own communication capabilities," said Mr Lyons. "Therefore I promise to let you meet potential foster parents soon, I just need you around for a little longer." I was shocked. After all these years of wondering and waiting, suddenly Mr Lyons said it was almost time for me to go. I couldn't help thinking about how my actions in the past had actually hindered my chance of getting a new home, how if I hadn't isolated myself due to my mind-reading ability, I might already be out of here.

"Thank you Mr Lyons for being so honest with me, when I do go to a new home, there will always be a tinge of sadness about leaving you, Natalie and the books behind," I said.

"While we're being honest Sam, I should let you know that you shouldn't hold Natalie in the highest regard," said Mr Lyons.

"What do you mean?" I asked.

"You've seen her around recently, you've seen the stress and anger in her face," replied Mr Lyons. "I shouldn't really be telling you this but we both trust each other, right?" he asked.

"Of course," I responded.

"For the past year, Natalie has been trying to oust me from my position so that she can take charge of the orphanage," said Mr Lyons.

"I don't understand why she would do that, you two have worked tirelessly over the years for the orphanage," I said.

"We have but recently Natalie seems to have convinced herself that she has the only right way to do things, she can't wait to undermine me at every opportunity and tell me how my decisions are ruining the orphanage," said Mr Lyons.

"That doesn't sound like Natalie," I said.

"She didn't use to be like this but I think with all the work she has put in, she is seeking fame for running such a charitable cause, she feels she should be rewarded with some sort of celebrity status," said Mr Lyons. "The only ego-driven decision I made was to have lion-head knockers on the front doors to represent me, even though my surname isn't spelt the same."

"But you're the one who funds the orphanage, how does she expect to keep it running?" I asked.

"She wants to cut corners everywhere to save money, I know that she saved up well from her previous job so she can just do enough to fund this place for a while but if you thought I had to make sacrifices with the building and quality of food, you don't want to see what she'd do to the orphanage," said Mr Lyons. I couldn't believe that Natalie would have these intentions so I was intent on finding out the truth myself so that next time I saw her, I'd read her mind to know exactly what she was thinking. It is supported by the fact that reading Natalie's mind earlier had shown me she was angry and that apparently Mr Lyons was the idiot Natalie was referring to.

"Are you sure she's not just saying these things out of stress?" I asked Mr Lyons.

"I wish it was because then I'd understand it but that stress over the years has manifested itself in her recently to a nasty, continuous campaign of hate against me," said Mr Lyons. "Under stress, she has turned to alcohol which is why, if you saw her this morning, she looks tired and lacks energy."

"In that case, I don't understand why she's still here," I said.

"It's not so easy to replace her, despite all this, Natalie is still committed to working here and finding a new assistant would be a struggle for me right now," said Mr Lyons. "Natalie is killing herself and her relationship with me but for now, I need her to keep up the hard work while I search for a suitable replacement."

"She wouldn't leave though, you said it yourself, she's after your job," I said.

"Don't you worry about me, I'm keeping in control of everything, just let me know if you ever see anything suspicious from Natalie," said Mr Lyons. "That's why I've told you this, I trust you to use this information wisely and help you to distance yourself from Natalie so the final goodbye is far less emotional."

"Okay, thank you sir," I said.

"I'm glad we have had this chat, make sure it stays just between us," said Mr Lyons. I nodded towards him and headed out the room.

Chapter 4

I walked back downstairs still in a state of shock from what Mr Lyons had just revealed to me. I couldn't believe that Natalie would want to stab Mr Lyons in the back and take the orphanage for herself. She's always had the best interests of the orphans in mind and maybe she thinks it is in our best interest that she takes over but I can't see that to be the case. I've seen those two work closely together for so long but to know the relationship is faltering makes me worry about both of them as well as the future of the orphanage. I was trying to put this out of my mind because of the other news Mr Lyons gave me, the news that I would soon have the chance to meet foster parents and be re-homed after all these years. I could see Gareth and Natasha playing cards so I went over to join them.

"So, how did it go?" asked Gareth.

"It's good news; Mr Lyons is going to let me meet potential foster parents very soon." I said. "And you two can focus on getting out of the orphanage as well now that you don't have to worry about leaving Ben behind."

"Yeah, that would be nice," said Natasha. "Perhaps the three of us will leave here at the same time."

"Why is it now that Mr Lyons will let you leave?" asked Gareth.

"I have no idea but I wasn't going to argue with him, he made some good points for keeping me here but that's just between me and him," I replied.

"Fair enough, would you like to play some cards?" asked Gareth.

"Sure, what game are we going to play?" I asked.

"Well, when it was just the two of us, we were just playing blackjack but that gets boring after a while," replied Gareth.

"We could play Go Fish," said Natasha. Card games are awkward for me to play generally with my mind-reading but Go Fish in particular is a game where I really have the unfair advantage. It doesn't always help because the opponents will probably be thinking about a different card every few seconds but I still try and shut off when I can.

"Let's do it," I said. Natasha dealt the cards out and we began playing. Much to my surprise, Gareth and Natasha were having quite a high success rate in asking for cards and completing sets. They seemed to know the right time to ask each other or ask me so much so that I felt I had to really focus on mind-reading to have a chance of getting back into the game as my turn was up next. I gained several sets straight away and my ability took me from the brink of losing badly to winning the game of Go Fish. It can drain some of the fun out of the game to constantly guess right but nothing looks suspicious when there are only three of you playing and at least I'm not taking money off of them.

"Let's do it again but this time let's try and get a few more people involved; that got a bit boring and predictable towards the end," said Gareth.

"Well, go ask some of the others then," said Natasha.

"No, that's Sam job," said Gareth. "He's the one who is in with all the groups here."

"I wouldn't really say I'm in with the different groups, I'm usually just on the outside looking in," I said.

"That's still more than us, off you go," said Gareth.

"You'll never find a home with that attitude," I said jokingly as I stood up and headed off to see one of the groups. I figured the football fanatics group would be the most likely option for people who would enjoy card games so I headed towards them. There was a loud knock on the front doors of the orphanage. Mr Thompson headed towards the entrance with the key in his hand to let whoever it was in. It was usually only staff members and prospective foster parents who ever came into the orphanage but the foster parents would never show up unannounced. There was a sense of intrigue about who was behind the doors but Mr Thompson showed no hesitation in opening the doors up. A giant of a man walked through the doors; he was both tall and fat. There was a scar which was instantly visible upon seeing him as it stretched across one side of his bald head as he lumbered through the front entrance.

"Good morning Jamie, how are things?" he asked Mr Thompson.

"Things are fine with me, Mr Lyons, I'll let Howard know you've arrived," replied Mr Thompson.

"Mr Lyons?" whispered Natasha as she turned to face Gareth and myself.

"Good morning to all of you too!" said the man in a booming tone as he turned to face the crowd of orphans.

"Good morning," said a number of the orphans at once who had stopped what they were doing as they looked at him.

"Carry on everyone," he said sensing the awkwardness of the situation. We returned to playing cards when the man came towards us. "What card game are you playing?" he asked us.

"We just finished a game of Go Fish," I said.

"Go Fish? Howard, er, Mr Lyons should teach you some proper card games," said the man.

"Sir, if you don't mind me asking, how do you know Mr Lyons?" I asked.

"I don't mind at all, it's only natural when you see someone unannounced that you want to know about them," said the man. "My name is Nicholas Lyons, I'm the brother of Mr Lyons," said Nicholas.

"How come we've never seen you before?" I asked.

"Mr Lyons and I constantly meet up outside of here but recently I have been away and it has been hard to find a time to drag Mr Lyons from his work so he invited me here instead," said Nicholas. "Have you ever played poker?" he asked.

"No," replied Gareth and Natasha in unison.

"I love playing poker," said Nicholas. "I play it all the time with my work friends and we play with some serious money, I'll teach you while I wait for Mr Lyons but first what are your names?"

"I'm Sam, this is Gareth and Natasha," I said.

"A pleasure to meet all of you, now let's begin," he said. He began showing us how to play poker. I realised that the challenge of this skilful game, like most card games we had learnt, could be easily undermined by my ability. I chose to read minds a little bit during the practice just so I could impress him. "Sam, is it?" he asked. "You've really picked up this game quickly; Gareth and Natalie had good poker faces and you still saw right through them, I'm impressed."

"Actually, I'm Natasha not Natalie," said Natasha.

"Oh my, you'll have to forgive me; my memory has always been bad and now I've confused your name with the Natalie who works here," said Nicholas.

"It's okay, really," said Natasha.

"You know Natalie as well?" I asked

"Yes, sometimes when Mr Lyons has asked for advice about the orphanage, he and Natalie have both come to see me over the past few years, she's always been very sweet to me," said Nicholas. I couldn't tell Nicholas about Natalie's intentions and hurt his feelings but I wondered if Mr Lyons was going to tell him instead, after all, he had told me and I'm just one of the orphans. Mr Lyons came down the stairs and walked over to Nicholas who was distracted still talking to us.

"Hello Nicholas," said Mr Lyons as he tapped him on the shoulder. Nicholas turned round and hugged Mr Lyons who wasn't able to free his arms up to embrace Nicholas as well; Nicholas' height and girth made Mr Lyons look like a normal sized man. Nicholas eventually let go of him. Mr Lyons looked slightly embarrassed by what had just happened with all the orphans watching him.

"Howard, so nice to see you again," said Nicholas.

"And you, how was your trip away?" asked Mr Lyons.

"It was great, I wish you could have come along as well," said Nicholas.

"My place is here," said Mr Lyons. "Meanwhile, you're free to do everything with your lovely wife and the families of your children so you don't need me."

"Yeah I guess so," said Nicholas forlornly. I decided to look into the mind of Nicholas while the two chatted away. "It would have been great to have you with us but I know nobody can take you away from this place," thought Nicholas. If only he knew about Natalie, that she was trying to take him away from this place. It was clear that Nicholas held Mr Lyons in such high regard, even to the point that his wife and kids were an afterthought in terms of his relationship with his brother. Eventually, Mr Lyons looked over towards us as we continued playing cards although I was still distracted by Nicholas' thoughts.

"You're not teaching them poker, are you Nicholas?" asked Mr Lyons.

"Howard, it's a great game and I think you've got a natural in Sam over there, he could be a future star" said Nicholas.

"It's alright for fun and games Sam but don't take it too seriously, Nicholas probably told you he likes to play but never told you he always loses," said Mr Lyons as he chuckled quietly.

"It's still fun for me," said Nicholas. "If I could win, it would be even better."

"Thanks Nicholas and don't worry Mr Lyons, I'll just do it for fun," I said.

"Good," said Mr Lyons as he ushered Nicholas upstairs. As we heard Mr Lyons' office door shut, there were plenty of murmurs coming from the different groups of orphans.

"He was a bit odd, wasn't he?" asked Natasha.

"He seems really nice though, very excitable like a child," I said.

"And he taught us how to play poker, that's something Mr Lyons or any other adult wouldn't have taught us, I'm really enjoying it," said Gareth. We played for well over an hour with Nicholas and Mr Lyons still talking upstairs and the caretaker had headed back across the road to his house. I'll admit I was mind-reading these two to call their bluffs throughout which I think annoyed Natasha as she eventually let out a big sigh.

"Well, I think that's enough for one day," said Natasha.

"Yeah, do you want to play something else Sam?" asked Gareth.

"No, it's okay, I'll just get back to reading my book," I replied.

"Knew you'd say that," said Gareth and Natasha in unison as they wandered off. They may laugh at it but I hadn't managed to get much reading done over the last couple of days while I bonded with them. It didn't take me long to immerse myself into the book once more to the point where I couldn't keep track of time. My concentration was broken as Nicholas came down the stairs alone, his figure making the creaking steps even louder. He walked over to the front entrance but the doors were locked. The caretaker wasn't in and Mr Lyons and Natalie were the only other ones with the keys. Nicholas turned round and chuckled as he wandered away from the entrance. He began walking towards me, possibly because I was one of the few orphans sitting down at this point while the others were chasing after each other.

"Simon, how are you?" asked Nicholas as he looked at me. I looked behind me to see if there was anyone else but it was just me nearby.

"I'm fine," I said hesitantly. "But my name is Sam."

"Sam, of course!" he exclaimed. "I'm not doing well with names today."

"It's alright, I know you said you had a problem with your memory," I said to calm him down as he appeared visibly stressed by getting the name wrong.

"Do you know where Mr Thompson is, Sam?" asked Nicholas.

"He lives across the road so sometimes he heads back there and locks us in," I said.

"That's a bit strange; I didn't think Mr Lyons would allow that sort of thing," said Nicholas.

"Well, you can get Mr Lyons or Natalie to open the doors for you," I said.

"Yes but I don't want to bother them, I only just came from up there, do you mind if I sit with you for a while Sam?" asked Nicholas.

"That's no problem at all," I said as I placed my book down.

"Ah, I bet Mr Lyons has got you into reading some of his books," said Nicholas.

"He has but it's because I wanted to, I really enjoy reading and his collection of books are all classics, how about you Nicholas, do you like reading books?" I asked.

"I would like to but unfortunately with my memory, I just can't keep up which is also why I always lose my matches at poker," replied Nicholas.

"But you still like to play it?" I asked him.

"Of course, I get to spend time with friends by playing it and I have a healthy supply of money to gamble with so it's all worth it in my eyes," replied Nicholas.

"No offence but how do you have so much money available when you lose some each time you play poker?" I asked.

"Well, I used to run my own retail business, my brother and I both seemed to follow the same route as we were both successful in business," began Nicholas. "I was inspired by my brother's success to set it up but after years of being the head of a successful company, I had a stroke back in 1997."

"I'm sorry to hear that, it must have been awful," I said.

"In truth, I don't really remember it, I don't remember feeling unwell at any point before passing out, I just woke up one day in a hospital bed, that's why I have this scar," said Nicholas as he pointed to the scar on his head. "They had to clear a blood clot in my brain and one of the side effects of the operation and the stroke itself was that it affected my memory."

"In that case, you should never have to apologise for not remembering something," I told him. "You've been through all that and you still built a successful company."

"Mr Lyons helped me out immensely; he looked after the company when I was recovering and when I came back, I knew I was on limited time before my memory got so bad that I could no longer work in the business I loved," said Nicholas. "So, I built it up as much as I could and sold it on to someone else for a sum which has funded me throughout my life ever since."

"That must have been a lot of money then," I said as I realised once again how much more you can get out of people by simply talking to them rather than mind-reading.

"Oh, it was astronomical!" exclaimed Nicholas. "Even so, I never went out spending all my money; I just bought what I needed to support my wife and children, I made sure we weren't spoilt, I just kept a bit aside for poker and some for charitable donations."

"It was nice of Mr Lyons to run the company for you while you were hospitalised," I said.

"It was beyond anything I could have expected from him, if he didn't keep the company running, I'd have been in no position to sell it and he did all that while still running the orphanage," replied Nicholas. "That only helped to strengthen a bond that has been vital to me throughout my whole life."

"I saw in one of the articles Mr Lyons has posted around here that he was an orphan too along with his brother which must be you," I said.

"That's right; it wouldn't be a lie to say that Mr Lyons has helped me throughout my whole life, not just about the business but also our time at the orphanage was made a lot easier by him, he constantly reassured me that everything would be okay," said Nicholas. "He would tell me all about our parents in a way that made me happy rather than sad."

"You remember your parents?" I asked.

"He was old enough to remember our parents, I was only three but he was twelve years old, so I have no memory of them, I think that's why he didn't get along with our foster parents."

"Mr Lyons didn't like his foster parents?" I asked.

"Not exactly a dislike but he never seemed happy around them which was a strange position for me to be in because I really liked them, then again, he was probably just being protective of me," said Nicholas.

"Oh, I think that's why he really likes George and Lenny then," I said.

"Who's that?" asked Nicholas.

"They are characters in this book here," I said pointing to the Of Mice and Men cover. "Mr Lyons told me about how their relationship is so close, as if they were brothers, and how every orphan should aspire to have a friendship that feels more like a brotherhood, to have the same strong bond you two share." The last week I have had at this orphanage had completely changed my view on the importance of friendship in people's lives and helped me appreciate that it was important in my own life too.

"He is and always has been the smartest person I have ever known, it's no wonder the local politicians around here always want to talk to him," Nicholas said.

"Politicians?" I asked.

"Yes, when Mr Lyons holds or attends charity events, I always see politicians talking to him, asking him advice, I think he'd make a better politician than all of them," said Nicholas.

"Mr Lyons seems like he could do everything in the world really well," I said.

"It sure feels that way every time I talk to him," said Nicholas. "He could do really well in politics, he wouldn't be swayed by the false promises of others and I'm sure he'd take a hard stance against them."

"I've seen Mr Lyons' fierce side, although never with me, was he like that in business?" I asked Nicholas.

"He was when he needed to be, he's a very fair man but even he has his limits," said Nicholas. It was hard for me to picture Mr Lyons saying harsh words to other adults like he would the orphans. When he does get angry with orphans, it's based on his desire for them to be kept safe and help them to develop. "He's argued with politicians before at these events he attends."

"Really?" I asked.

"Yes, if he feels a politician isn't doing enough, locally or nationally, he's not afraid to let them know about it," said Nicholas.

"Well, if he can influence the thinking of politicians without having to be directly involved, it would be win-win for him," I said.

"How so?" asked Nicholas.

"Mr Lyons would still be able to run the orphanage while having a say in political matters without taking up too much of his time, I'm sure he'd have some good ideas," I said.

"I'm not sure he's ever had a bad idea in his life, all his decisions turn to gold," said Nicholas. "Although I wished he would've settled down and started a family but he's been married to this job the last twenty five years."

"Mr Lyons has sacrificed a lot, his time, his company and his money for this orphanage, I'd never thought about how that affected him personally," I said.

"Honestly, he's fine with it, almost too fine," said Nicholas. "I think he feels that I have been his only family for most of his life and he's done this well, so he doesn't need anybody else in his life, it's regretful he only sees my family every now and again because I want him to feel a part of a bigger family of Lyons'."

"He talks about the characters in his books like they're are all part of his family, a family that has the potential to give any readers a few pointers in life," I said.

"I'm not surprised you and Mr Lyons get on so well, you're both very intelligent and you both see these deep meanings in books, I think you could grow up to be very successful like him no matter what you choose to do," said Nicholas.

"Thanks Nicholas," I said. "But can I ask you something?"

"Of course!" replied Nicholas.

"Do you think Mr Lyons would keep me here longer than he needed to?" I asked.

"Why would he do that?" asked Nicholas.

"Well, I've been here a long time and we've always got along well but in that time, he has never let me see foster parents so I have always been here," I said.

"That's a strange one but I'm sure he has his reasons," said Nicholas. "I can't see any negative against you that he could bring up and like you said, you get along well so I wouldn't worry too much about it." I could see Natalie out of the corner of my eye sneaking up towards Nicholas.

"You weren't going to leave without seeing me, were you?" asked Natalie as she tapped Nicholas on the shoulder.

"Natalie!" exclaimed Nicholas as he instantly hugged her much like Mr Lyons. "Of course I wasn't."

"Good," said Natalie as she began to chat with him. One look into the mind of Natalie showed me that she was genuinely happy to see Nicholas, after what Mr Lyons said, I assumed that she may have a negative attitude to his brother as well. There was no sign of any coldness from Natalie towards him and it made me question if what Mr Lyons was saying had been true.

"I've just been having a discussion with Sam," said Nicholas.

"About poker I presume," said Natalie with a smile on her face.

"No, of course not, that was earlier," said Nicholas as Natalie chuckled. "I was telling him about my experience of being an orphan and my life beyond that."

"In truth, you should tell everyone here your story, I think it would be a great source of inspiration to all of the orphans here, don't you agree Sam?" asked Natalie.

"Yeah, you and Mr Lyons have achieved so much," I told Nicholas.

"Oh yes and Mr Lyons," said Natalie as her more familiar cold demeanour returned. "Speaking of Howard, next time you're around, I'd like to have a talk with you about Howard," she told Nicholas. I wondered if this had anything to do with what Howard told me and if it was possible that Natalie could turn Nicholas against Mr Lyons although Nicholas seems in awe of both of them.

"Of course but what about Howard?" asked Nicholas.

"Oh, it's nothing to worry about," said Natalie as an awkward silence grew between her and Nicholas. "Here, I'll let you out," she said as she grabbed her keys and headed towards the front doors of the orphanage.

"Bye Sam," said Nicholas as he headed out.

"Goodbye Nicholas," I said as I returned to my book once more. Natalie led him outside and closed the doors behind him, waving goodbye before turning to me. "You must be wondering if you'll ever get to finish that book, you've had so many distractions lately," she said as she walked away before I could respond. In truth, I welcomed the distractions; it was nice to be doing different things or talk to different people at random points of the day rather than losing the whole day in a book.

Chapter 5

It was clear that the arrival of Nicholas had certainly got the orphans talking. He was a hard character to ignore with his large frame and loud voice and the embarrassed look of Mr Lyons from being hugged so ferociously will live long in the memory. His personality came across as warm whether he was talking to his brother or complete strangers like myself, his enthusiasm alone had livened up everybody in the orphanage. Not all of it was positive though, some orphans were amusing themselves by imitating the way he walked, his memory problems and making fun of his size.

"I wish people wouldn't make fun of Nicholas," I said to Natasha and Gareth.

"Well, it was funny to see him lumbering his way around here," said Gareth.

"And when he got the names wrong," added Natasha.

"Let's just say there's a good reason for his bad memory," I said "I think his positive nature is infectious, we never see much emotion from anybody else around here so it's nice to have a breath of fresh air, particularly from someone who is another orphan."

"And his mannerisms, quirky as they may be, has given everybody a laugh," said Gareth. There was a brief moment of silence as we reflected on Nicholas' visit.

"I wonder if we'll see more of Nicholas," I said.

"I hope so, I want him to teach us more about poker," said Natasha.

"He might know some other card games as well," Gareth added.

"He really seems to have left a lasting impression on you," Natasha said to me.

"Well, he told me a lot about his life and, while I won't disclose his personal story, it's a very uplifting tale," I told her.

"People just seem to gravitate towards you, don't they?" asked Gareth. "Mr Lyons has always liked you, Nicholas gave you his life story and Natasha and I have joined you."

"It wasn't always like this," I began.

"Except for Mr Lyons," interrupted Gareth.

"Except for Mr Lyons," I repeated. "That one I can't explain but everything else has been coincidental; we bonded through the absence of Ben and Nicholas was interested in us as a group because we were the only ones playing cards."

"But you said you had a personal conversation with him," said Gareth.

"I did, all I had to do was ask questions and he chose to answer them otherwise you can just sit there and stare at people trying to work out what they're thinking with little success," I said.

"Well, it works for us two," said Natasha. "Between us, we can pretty much work out what the other is thinking eventually so we've never really focussed on anyone else."

"And after all our chats in the past few days, you haven't opened up to us," said Gareth.

"Like I said, all you have to do is ask questions," I told them. There was a wry smile on Gareth's face as he pondered what to ask. I began preparing myself for the types of personal questions they might ask. We were sat in silence for over a minute while Gareth thought of a question which never came so Natasha decided to intervene.

"We've told you why we have so few friends here, why don't you tell us why you've isolated yourself during your time here?" asked Natasha.

"Fair enough," I began. "In all honesty, I never thought I would be here this long, I didn't want to become too attached to people so that's why I'm always on the outskirts of the groups here, I can join a conversation or activity to fill my day and then leave them to it."

"And when you realised you weren't leaving any time soon, you realised you were in the middle of nowhere having not made any close friends?" asked Gareth.

"I guess so, I thought I was doing everything right by staying quiet and staying out of trouble but Mr Lyons told me that he didn't think I was suitable to leave for a foster home because of how isolated I had become," I replied.

"But then, how did you and Mr Lyons become so close?" asked Gareth.

"I can't explain it really, for as long as I can remember Mr Lyons has been really nice to me and he was always interested in how I was progressing but for some reason, he never told me sooner that my isolation was holding me back." I said.

"Yeah, you'd have thought that Mr Lyons would have let you know or even offered some gentle encouragement," said Natasha.

"I think it's because Mr Lyons wants to see how children develop by themselves, I don't think he wants to make us all clones," I said.

"Even so, one bit of advice from him and you could have left years ago," said Gareth. I didn't respond. Gareth's statement resonated with me and left me wondering about what might have been. All three of us sat there in silence for a moment.

"But then, you wouldn't have met us," said Natasha as she gave me a playful punch on the arm which made me smile briefly.

"That's true," I said beginning to cheer up.

"And you wouldn't have read the books," said Gareth as Natasha looked at him disapprovingly. "Don't look at me like that, I'm actually being serious."

"Well, with the books, it's a bit of a strange situation," I said. "I'm glad I have had the opportunity to read the books but the reason I started reading them was because of the isolation."

"And what about us?" asked Gareth gesturing towards himself and Natasha. "Our friendship is the result of that same strange situation, are you glad that you met us?"

"Of course," I said. "It's ironic that just as I make friends after all this time, I may now leave soon."

"Now we know what Mr Lyons looks for, it shouldn't take us too long," said Gareth.

"And hopefully we will stay nearby and in the same school, that way we could continue to see each other," added Natasha.

"That would be good but would you decide against moving to a new home with foster parents you got along with for the sake of staying at the same school?" I asked.

"To be honest, no," said Natasha. "But I would hope we could remain nearby."

"If we get offered a family and they're not crazy, we're going to take it, no questions asked," said Gareth. "Once we find parents who are willing to take us both together," said Natasha.

"At least you two are family, I don't think it was just your association with Ben which isolated you, I think people here are envious of you two," I said.

"You really think so?" asked Gareth.

"We may be family but we are an incomplete one," said Natasha. There was a short silence.

"So, do you two remember your parents?" I asked. They looked at each other briefly before turning to me and nodding.

"Mum and Dad were always great to us, they let us do the kind of things we do here," said Gareth. "We run around, make a lot of noise and we make fun of each other but they were always there when we needed them."

"We were given plenty of food and toys, if anything, they probably spoilt us particularly judging by this place," said Natasha.

"That's ironic because I felt spoilt at this place when I first arrived having seen what we have had in recent years," I said

"How so?" asked Gareth.

"When I first arrived here, the place was cleaner and the meals were nicer, I think Mr Lyons really went all out on giving us the best," I said. "But then in recent years the quality of food and cleanliness declined, I'm not sure if I would have rather have had the rubbish food to begin with or not, is it the same with knowing your parents?" I asked. Both Natasha and Gareth look confused.

"What do you mean if it's the same?" asked Natasha.

"Would you rather have never known your parents and your previous home because it's such a contrast from your life now?" I asked.

"God Sam, that's a bit heavy, isn't it?" said Gareth.

"Well, we wanted to get into the deep questions, didn't we?" asked Natasha. There was no answer from either twin; they just sat there thinking about it. Even though I asked the question, I wasn't going to read either of their minds to get their answer as I realised the magnitude of the question I had asked.

"Well, let me ask you this Sam," said Natasha breaking the silence. "Would you rather have known your parents?" she asked.

"I'm not really sure I could give an answer until I see my life as part of a family, I can't compare foster parents to my real parents so I'll never know if my life is better or worse, I have no set standard for foster parents which at least means I can't resent them based on my previous life," I said.

"That's a good answer, unfortunately in our eyes, foster parents have a lot to live up to," said Gareth. "For their sake, it would be better if we didn't know our parents but for us, we love the memories we have of our parents and couldn't imagine never knowing them," Gareth paused briefly before turning to me. "Oh, sorry."

"It's okay," I said. Mr Lyons appeared out of the corner of my eye as he walked downstairs and headed over to us.

"You all look deep in thought," he said.

"We've just been talking about potential foster parents," I said.

"Oh, so no doubt you've built up this grand image of being whisked away to a mansion," said Mr Lyons chuckling away.

"Don't worry sir, we know it's not like that," said Natasha. Natasha looked like she was going to say more but stopped, realising that she didn't want to say something about life at the orphanage that might disrespect him.

"We were thinking more about the personality of the parents and how we might view them," said Gareth.

"Well, everybody's different so you won't all have the same experience," said Mr Lyons. "It's best not to think about it too much, you'll either worry yourself or disappoint yourself by analysing hypothetical homes and parents but you can't really have a clue until it happens." That's the kind of advice he would constantly give me and I was pleased to see he involved Natasha and Gareth in the conversation.

"Thanks for the advice sir," said Natasha.

"It's important to live in the here and now, you can't change the past and you can't see the future," said Mr Lyons as we looked on in deep thought. "Anyway, I am heading out for a short while, is Mr Thompson here?" asked Mr Lyons.

"No, he's been out for a while now," I said.

"Damn," said Mr Lyons under his breath before clapping his hands together. "Okay, well Natalie is still upstairs if you need anything," he said as he wandered off. He didn't seem happy that Mr Thompson was away as it left just one adult at the orphanage but I suppose he had to go.

"He's really going to leave us here when it's just Natalie?" asked Gareth.

"I'm sure he has his reasons," I said. Natasha gave a small chuckle as she turned to face me directly.

"That seems to be your answer for everything to do with Mr Lyons," said Natasha.

"What do you mean?" I asked.

"You never question him or call him out on anything, the only time you do, you accept the simplest answer," said Natasha.

"I don't think he needs to be called out on anything," I said. "I asked him a couple of questions and got my answers, which I will keep to myself, and today, all he is doing is heading out for a bit."

"Yeah, I think you're reading a bit too much into this Natasha, you know what Mr Lyons said about not over-analysing everything," said Gareth.

"I'm not saying he's doing anything wrong but every time he suddenly leaves or won't give you a straight answer, you let him off easy," Natasha told me.

"This has come out of the blue, hasn't it?" I asked her.

"Well, if you think he's so clean, why don't we go check out his office properly this time?" asked Natasha.

"So, that's what this is all about," I said.

"I'll be honest, I had no idea she was going in that direction and I usually suss her out quickly," said Gareth.

"I had to find a way to bring it back up again and I needed an angle to make breaking into his office even more tempting," said Natasha.

"Just don't set off the alarm this time," said Gareth.

"You know that wasn't me," said Natasha.

"You two, let's not forget how much we were panicking last time, we mistook the fire alarm for another alarm and we made a mad dash for it," I said.

"But there won't be an alarm this time," said Gareth.

"That's not the point," I said. "We panicked when that happened, what will we be like if we get caught or are on the verge of getting caught?" I asked.

"You forget that we can hear whenever anybody gets near," said Gareth.

"And don't forget Mr Lyons' advice; he told us not to worry about the future but that's what you are doing right now Sam," said Natasha as she gave me a nudge on the arm.

"Okay fine," I said reluctantly. "Let's see if we can find anything." I knew they were going to do it anyway so I saw no point in trying to convince them otherwise.

"That's the spirit," said Gareth. Like before, we headed upstairs to Mr Lyons' room. "So, are you going to tell us what the code is this time?" asked Gareth.

"No," said Natasha bluntly. I decided to read Natasha's mind to fulfil my own curiosity. "2404," thought Natasha in her head as she typed the code in. A small clicking noise came from the door and Natasha pushed it open. I'd seen the office before but it somehow seemed different when we entered with no Mr Lyons in sight. The office was lit up from the sun shining through the windows so we didn't have to risk drawing attention to ourselves by turning the lights on.

"Look, actual windows you can see out of," said Gareth.

"It's clear Mr Lyons has never neglected this room, shame about the rest of the orphanage," said Natasha. I felt like Natasha's comment was unfair but I decided to ignore it.

"Well guys, we're here," I told them. "I thought you had a plan."

"We do," said Gareth. "We're going to try and find anything and everything about us and if we dig up something juicy in the meantime, then that's a bonus." There were plenty of files neatly stacked up on numerous bookshelves but there were also a lot of files spread out across the floor of the room and Mr Lyons' table.

"When I was in here earlier, everything looked a lot neater," I said.

"Maybe he was desperately looking for something which he couldn't find anywhere he looked," said Natasha.

"Or maybe he's just had too many distractions today," I said. "After all, he's had his brother in here and he had to leave us in a hurry recently."

There was no clear starting point for any of us to look; the files about ourselves could have been anywhere and the rest of the files seemed business related. Natasha and Gareth started checking the files that were neatly organised on the bookshelves.

"These files have names on the side, that will help," said Natasha.

"There has got to be every file of every orphan past and present around here, have fun looking for yours," I said.

"It would be alright if Mr Lyons could have arranged these in alphabetical order," said Gareth as he rolled his fingers along each file, checking the name on each one. I decided to head over to a different set of bookshelves to start looking.

"There you go, Sam," said Natasha. "We knew you'd be curious too."

"I'm just helping to speed up your search," I said. "Otherwise, we will be here forever." We spent what felt like a long time checking the different files with no success; we recognised no names and nothing else sounded interesting. I decided to move towards Mr Lyons' desk instead. The top file in one of the piles was a file on Ben which I picked up and took a look at.

"What have you got there Sam?" asked Gareth.

"I've found Ben's file so maybe ours are over here too," I replied.

"Well, I haven't seen anybody I know over here so it's worth a shot," said Natasha who carefully placed a file she had a hold of back into its slot on the bookshelf. Natasha and Gareth joined me round the table, I still had Ben's file in my hand.

"Are you going to take a look then?" asked Gareth.

"Do you really think we should?" I asked. "Breaking in here to read our own files is one thing but reading the files of others just seems wrong." I'd had a whole childhood at the orphanage where I would read people's minds and you soon find out you don't really want to know everything about each person you meet.

"It's okay, it's Ben," said Natasha. "We just want to get an idea of what Mr Lyons looks for in terms of him thinking we are ready to leave this orphanage."

"Let us have a look then; you don't have to be involved," Gareth told me. I reluctantly handed the file over to Gareth and decided to look closer at the newspaper cuttings displayed in his office. Just like along the corridor, many of the cuttings revolved around the orphanage, Mr Lyons and his charity work. One article stood out which was dated a couple of years back. It had a picture of Mr Lyons with the Prime Minister shaking hands outside 10 Downing Street. The headline reads *'ORPHANAGE OWNER LOOKING TO MOVE INTO POLITICS.'* I was surprised I had never heard this from Mr Lyons so I began to read the article:

"Prominent philanthropist and orphanage owner Howard Lyons has announced his intention to step into the world of politics.

The millionaire ex-entrepreneur started his own business at a young age before selling it and starting his own orphanage.

His charitable work has been praised by many public figures and it has given him plenty of opportunities to mix with the political elite at different functions and it appears as though it has given him an itch for politics.

Mr Lyons denied claims that he would be unable to run his orphanage if he took a role in politics.

"I have the utmost confidence I can keep up with both jobs, I have a hard-working assistant at the orphanage who really helps to decrease the workload and I'm grateful for her, I want to bring honesty back to politics," said Mr Lyons.' The article indicated there was more writing on the next page but there was only one page displayed on the wall.

There were two things about reading that which made me feel bad for Mr Lyons. The trust he had in Natalie a couple of years ago is a far cry from what it was like now and judging by the last couple of years, it seemed as though Mr Lyons really couldn't do two things at once. I wondered if all the supposed drama with Natalie had taken him away from a potential role in politics. From what I know of him, I think he would do well in politics. He is calm but strict when he needs to be and he has a way of putting people at ease and defusing situations.

There was another newspaper cutting on the wall which was just a headline cut out from 1996 which read *'DOCTOR STRUCK OFF FROM PROFESSION AFTER DRUG USE.'* I wondered what it had to do with Mr Lyons. It was possible that this was the doctor who had operated on Nicholas after his stroke which would have given Mr Lyons a vested interest. All this time, Gareth and Natasha were still going through Ben's file.

"Hey look at this," said Gareth picking out a piece of paper from Ben's file. "It's an evaluation of Ben's time here at the orphanage." I decided to go back towards the table having walked around each corner of the office checking out clippings.

"Let me see," said Natasha trying to snatch the paper from here.

"Careful," he said as he pulled the paper away. "We don't want to rip it; I'll tell you what it says."

"But you told us to look," said Natasha.

"With your eyes," said Gareth as Natasha rolled her eyes at him.

"So what does it say?" asked Natasha.

"I'm getting to it," replied Gareth as he cleared his throat. "Ben has progressed well during his time at the orphanage, he was incredibly nervous when he arrived, struggled to make friends, blah blah blah, he appeared confident with people he was comfortable with, we just needed to make him more comfortable around adults, blah blah blah," said Gareth. "It's all very dull and predictable, isn't it?"

"What did you expect?" I asked.

"I don't know, just something more exciting than that," he replied.

"It's probably an official report that Mr Lyons has to present to someone, I'm not surprised it's incredibly dull," I said.

"I don't even know if it's worth trying to find our files after all this," said Gareth.

"Yeah, it's not going to tell us anything we don't already know," said Natasha. Gareth and Natasha began to rearrange Ben's file so that the papers they had thrown about were all placed back together.

"Wait, does this bit of paper go before or after this one?" asked Gareth.

"I don't know, just get all the papers back in roughly the same order; I'm sure Mr Lyons will never notice," said Natasha. "I mean, look at when we came in here, everything was all over the place, if anything, we're doing him a favour."

"You're right, maybe we're trying to be too organised, he might get suspicious," said Gareth as he chuckled. While they were sorting that, I was slowly circling the table looking at the different bits of paper scattered across it. I saw an opened letter on the desk addressed to Mr Lyons. As I looked at the bottom of the letter, I could see it was written by Nicholas from a couple of years ago. I'm not sure why but I felt compelled to look at it, maybe because I wanted to learn more about Nicholas. I picked it up and began reading:

'Dear Howard,

Thanks for getting in touch. Kim and the kids send you their love. I know you said you want all business matters to be sent as a letter rather than an email so here goes.

I read about you in the paper just the other day. Going into the world of politics are you?

It's great to hear that you're going to continue running the orphanage, I know you and Natalie will continue to do a great job, she's like the sister we never had. I'm sorry to hear from you in your last letter that you have to make cutbacks in order to keep the orphanage running but hopefully when you get your role in politics, you'll be making plenty of money to keep the orphanage ticking over and then improving it.

Given the current circumstances you described, I am happy to substantially increase my donations to the orphanage in order to help you for as long as you need; I'd hate to see it collapse. Before you know it, the orphanage will be as good as new. After all, it's the least I can do. Just give me a call to let me know when you want to meet up.

Yours Sincerely,
Nicholas Lyons.'

"You two," I said to Natasha and Gareth ushering them towards me. "This letter says that Nicholas has donated to the orphanage for a long time and that, in recent years, he has had to increase his contribution to help Mr Lyons keep the orphanage running."

"I bet you feel bad about blaming Mr Lyons for the state of the orphanage," Gareth told Natasha.

"You've been complaining just as much as I have," responded Natasha.

"It explains the changes I've seen during my years at the orphanage with the decline in quality of maintenance and food," I said. "Mr Lyons was obviously spending too much on the food, I feel bad for complaining too."

"Aha, so it was Mr Lyons' fault," said Natasha. "He didn't manage his money properly and now he's down to the basics for the orphanage and begging for scraps of money."

"Well maybe but you can't fault him for his selfless effort over all these years, he could have given us the basics to begin with but he wanted more, it's too bad he couldn't sustain it as it was," I said. We began looking on the table for any more clues about how bad the situation was for Mr Lyons and the orphanage.

"What do you think you are doing in here?!" said a shrieking voice. It was Natalie, we had left the door open and Natalie had simply wondered in and caught us red-handed. We had forgotten that Natalie was already upstairs which is why there was no creaking of stairs to warn us. None of us responded. "Well?!" asked Natalie.

"We're sorry Natalie, we just saw the door open and wanted to look inside, we were just curious," said Natasha.

"I know Mr Lyons, he never leaves his office door open so you would have needed to know the code," said Natalie. "I won't tell Mr Lyons what you have done if you tell me the code." I realised Natalie wasn't angry at us for breaking in, she was angry that we had the code to get in and she didn't. If she got the code, she would try to use anything and everything in his office to get rid of him.

"You don't need to tell her Natasha," I said.

"You will tell me or I will tell Mr Lyons all about this," said Natalie. There was a long silence. Gareth and Natasha kept glancing at each other trying to think of a way out of this. I knew I had to confront Natalie with Mr Lyons' secret to get out of this situation.

"You won't tell Mr Lyons because we'll tell him that it was you who broke in," I said.

"And why would he believe you over me?" asked Natalie. I hesitated for an instant as I considered whether what I was about to say was worth saying.

"He won't believe you because he doesn't trust you, you want to get rid of him,"

I said.

"What?!" asked Natalie. "I would never think of such a thing."

"I do wish he'd leave though," thought Natalie.

"You want to take control of the orphanage for yourself so if you have the code, you can enter his room, read his emails or write fake emails, the possibilities are endless," I said. Natalie seemed calmer as she composed herself, taking in what I had just said.

"I don't know what Mr Lyons has told you but you can't believe him," said Natalie.

"Mr Lyons is very open and honest with me so I do believe him," I said.

"We do have our disagreements about how certain things should be done but I would never try to do anything so deceitful," said Natalie.

"Then why do you want the code?" asked Natasha. Natalie began to move her lips but before she could get any words out, we could hear someone coming up the stairs. It was the unmistakeable sound of Mr Lyons heading up the stairs judging by the frequency of the footsteps and how loud a noise they made. All the anger and all the questioning abruptly ended.

"We have to leave right now," said Natalie as she ushered us out the door. We quickly glanced at the table to make sure everything was how we left it before heading out the door. Natalie closed the door behind us and made a gesture for us to follow her to the outside of her office. Mr Lyons eventually made it to the top step and looked down the corridor.

"Ah Natalie, everything okay with these three here?" asked Mr Lyons. This was a nervous moment for all three of us. We wondered if Natalie was going to tell Mr Lyons what happened. Even though we planned to deny it, I wouldn't like to lie to Mr Lyons about Natalie's involvement and I didn't want to make accusations.

"No, everything's fine," she said. "We were just having a quick catch-up is all." All three of us were relieved and I don't think Natalie wanted the situation to be completely blown out of proportion.

"Good to hear," said Mr Lyons. "Oh don't forget Natalie, tomorrow is one of the hospital check up days for the boys, I need you to do the usual."

"Oh yes of course, I'll be there," said Natalie as Mr Lyons headed into his office. He briefly stood in the doorframe as he opened the door to his office making us worry that he had spotted something out of place but he soon entered and closed the door behind him.

"Sam, one day I'm happy to tell you where you've got me all wrong but for now, let's just forget about this," said Natalie as she checked her watch. "Oh, it's almost dinner time." We headed downstairs to the dining room in complete silence; we didn't know what to make of what had just happened. I told Gareth and Natasha what Mr Lyons had told me about Natalie over dinner. They were shocked by what I had told them but they knew I was telling the truth; being so close to Mr Lyons. A few hours later, we headed to the dormitories to sleep.

Chapter 6

The next morning, we were woken up by a less frequent noise to that of someone opening the orphanage doors. Instead, there was the sound of an engine which got closer and closer to the gates of the orphanage. Either Natalie or Mr Thompson had rented out a minibus and driven it here to take us to the hospital. In my early days at the orphanage, the minibus would make more appearances as we would sometimes get trips out in the summer. Nowadays, its sole purpose is to transport us to hospital for checkups. A change of scenery is always nice but having to wait in a hospital for a few hours while half the orphanage gets checked out means it's not really worth it.

On these days, breakfast was at an earlier time for those who were going to the hospital whereas the other half kept to their normal times. It was split between the boys and the girls but the trips usually occurred within a few days of each other. One of Mr Thompson or Natalie would take us with the other staying at the orphanage with the rest of the orphans and judging by what Mr Lyons said yesterday, it was Natalie who would take us today. I seem to recall that on the last few occasions for both girls and boys, it fell to Natalie to take us to the hospital. It didn't matter whether it was the turn of the boys or the girls; everybody was woken up by the minibus anyway. Gareth and I got up together for breakfast.

"I'm sure the gap between hospital visits has become shorter," said Gareth.

"No, it's the same as it's always been," I said.

"Well, it feels like it comes around quicker and quicker then," he said.

"I'm not looking forward to having to see Natalie today especially for a long period of time," I said. "Not after yesterday."

"Yeah, that was really strange yesterday, I couldn't tell if we have leverage over her or she has leverage over us," said Gareth. "I was talking to Natasha about it just before we went up to the dorms."

"I think we have the advantage, she seemed to be startled when I confronted her about her plans for Mr Lyons," I said.

"And she didn't deny it," added Gareth.

"Trust me, I know she wants to get rid of Mr Lyons," I began. "From what Mr Lyons told me, to her reaction and a feeling I have deep down, I know that's her intention."

"She might not need to replace him anyway; you remember what else we saw?" he asked.

"About the finances?" I asked.

"Yes, the orphanage is struggling anyway and those two fighting about it won't help us at all, we'll just have to hope we manage to leave here soon," said Gareth.

"Still there must be something we can do to help," I said.

"I wouldn't get your hopes up, if Mr Lyons can't raise enough money, how would we be able to do it?" asked Gareth.

"I don't know but maybe something will turn up," I said. Gareth nodded gently before focussing solely on his breakfast. I don't think he really believed something would turn up but he didn't want to sour my optimism. There were a number of problems now circling my mind. Previously, it had been my desire to learn why I couldn't leave this orphanage and learn what happened to my parents but now, to add to this, there is the threat of the orphanage declining even more and the threat of a struggle between Natalie and Mr Lyons.

At the end of breakfast, it was simply a waiting game for Natalie to have the minibus ready and make sure that every boy in the orphanage was nearly ready to go outside and board the bus. Natalie was running back and forth with bundles of documents while Mr Lyons and Mr Thompson were nowhere in sight. After a while, Natalie took a seat for a few minutes, clearly flustered and out of breath resting a clipboard against her chest. Natalie composed herself shortly afterwards and stood up while all the boys in the orphanage were scattered about the downstairs area.

"Okay!" she shouted as she knocked repeatedly on the clipboard. "I need all of you to slowly make your way out to the minibus in a nice, orderly fashion." Those words never worked. All the boys charged their way out the front doors quickly towards the minibus. Gareth and I waited for the crowd to clear before slowly heading out to the bus; we couldn't understand why everybody else was so eager to get on the bus as we couldn't see anything exciting about going to the hospital. As we got on, we realised the only two seats we could get together were right at the front of the minibus just behind the driver's seat.

"Should we find somewhere else?" I whispered to Gareth. Before Gareth could respond, Natalie made her way onto the bus.

"Take a seat, you two, there's two perfectly good seats there," said Natalie pointing to the seats at the front of the bus. We looked at each other briefly before taking those two seats.

"It's alright, it's not like she's going to make a big scene in front of everyone on this bus," whispered Gareth.

"Let's hope not, otherwise this day will be awkward for all three of us," I whispered. Natalie ran through the list of names on her clipboard.

"That's everybody," she said. "Now, be sure to keep your seatbelt on." She moved to the driver's seat and must have spent a good few minutes performing safety checks, checking and rechecking mirrors, adjusting and readjusting the position of her seat. Eventually, she started up the engine. The hospital was a fair distance away so it gave everyone a chance to relax and perhaps catch up on the sleep they missed out on due to the rude awakening this morning. Gareth and I sat quietly for the first portion of the journey almost falling asleep before a speed bump disturbed our rest.

"I don't understand why we have to leave so early," said Gareth as he yawned.

"It's because there's so many of you to get through which takes a long time even on a good day, and those days are few and far between at hospitals," said Natalie as she briefly turned her head round to face us.

"That makes sense," Gareth told Natalie. "Still, I'd rather get more sleep and wait here longer," Gareth whispered to me.

"I wouldn't want to wait any longer," I told him. "I'm always the first to be seen by Nurse Scarlett which means I have to wait around for a long time afterwards."

"I still don't understand that," said Gareth. "Your surname is Watkins and yet you go first, you should be one of the very last ones, maybe it's because Mr Lyons likes you."

"If he really liked me, he'd give me a later time," I said as Gareth laughed quietly. "There's nothing more depressing than sitting in that crowded waiting room for hours watching loads of miserable people sitting down with nothing to entertain myself."

"You could try guessing what's wrong with each person," said Gareth.

"I don't need to guess, I know what's wrong with them," I said.

"Oh, you know everyone's pain, do you?" asked Gareth. I realised that know was the wrong word to use but I did know their problems. When I'm bored in the waiting room, I read the minds of patients just to learn the story of their medical problems. Some problems are serious but others have a funny story behind them that helps to pass the time.

"Well, it's clear to see with most people, isn't it?" I asked as I decided to backtrack on how certain I had sounded. "Most people will have a visible injury and then I'll just make up stories about how they got those injuries."

"Whatever helps you through the day Sam," Gareth told me. "I wonder which nurse I'll be seeing today."

"I always get Nurse Scarlett when I get seen to," I said.

"Sticking with one nurse for each of us would make sense, I'm sick of having to repeat myself over and over again to different nurses when one of them could learn all the information about me," said Gareth.

"I think Nurse Scarlett knows everything about me, she must do by now," I said.

"I've had Nurse Scarlett every now and again, she's always very nice," said Gareth.

"Yeah, she's always very nice and always in a good mood," I said.

"Not like some of the others," Gareth began. "Don't get me wrong, they all do a good job but most of them look and sound miserable."

"Then I'm really glad I always see Nurse Scarlett, she never seems to have an off day, at least not on the days I come in," I said.

"Maybe there's a correlation, maybe you brighten her day every time she sees you and she forgets about all the worries in the world," Gareth said with a smirk on his face.

"Yeah then she sees you and her day goes downhill," I responded as we both burst into laughter. We stopped at a busy set of traffic lights where Natalie promptly turned around to face us.

"I never knew hospital trips could be so much fun," said Natalie.

"Don't mind us Natalie, we're just amusing ourselves," said Gareth who seemed in such a good mood, he had no apprehension about talking to Natalie.

"That's good to hear, you'll need to be in good spirits when they inject that needle into your arm," said Natalie.

"Needle?" asked Gareth in a worried tone. I could see from Natalie's face that she was trying to suppress a smirk.

"She's joking," I told Gareth as Natalie turned back to face the front of the bus as the lights turned green. Gareth had a relieved look on his face. I hadn't expected Natalie would have wanted to talk to us, let alone tell us jokes.

"Wasn't even worried about it," said Gareth as he shrugged his shoulders. I decided to let it slide rather than interrogate Gareth some more.

"Sure you weren't," said Natalie without turning round this time.

"I really wasn't," said Gareth under his breath. It was probably embarrassment that led to Gareth being quiet for the rest of the bus journey. After a further ten minutes, the bus arrived at the hospital as Natalie slowly parked the minibus with precision. As she shut off the engine, everybody immediately stood up.

"Okay, I know this didn't work earlier but I need you to exit the bus slowly and for you to wait by me so I can lead the way, do I make myself clear?" asked Natalie.

"Yes Natalie," said the crowd of children in a dreary tone. Natalie exited the bus first and watched as we slowly walked off the bus one by one and gathered round her on the pavement ready to be led into the hospital. Once everyone was off the bus, Natalie hit the button on the side of the bus to lock the doors.

"Okay, that's everyone, now follow me," she said waving her arm in the direction of the entrance to the hospital. We all followed her single file as we entered the hospital which drew plenty of looks from the other citizens already waiting there. The seats available in the waiting room were scattered about all over the place. "Find a seat, any seat," said Natalie as she headed up to the reception desk. The orderly line formed when we went in soon dissipated as dozens of children rushed towards any available seats. Gareth and I were at the front of the line so we got two seats next to each other quickly and easily.

"Oh, here we go," thought the old man sitting opposite me. I think he was annoyed by both the noise of the orphans and that he knew that our presence would likely increase his waiting time.

"Sorry," I said to the old man before realising that even though he was annoyed in his mind, his expression was neutral. "About all this," I added. The man didn't say anything but put his hand up near his chest and nodded. Gareth looked confused as he faced me.

"Are you going to apologise to everyone here as well?" whispered Gareth as he nudged my shoulder. I didn't respond as I sat in silence. After a long conversation with the receptionist, Natalie finally took a seat in a position where she could keep an eye on every one of us as we waited for our names to be called. I was so keen to avoid making eye contact with the old man sat across from me that I kept my eyes firmly facing the floor.

"Sam, you're up first," said a softly spoken voice from right beside me. I looked up from the floor to see the dark red hair and tanned skin of Nurse Scarlett. "Or would you rather keep staring at the floor?" she asked with a smile on her face.

"Sorry Nurse Scarlett," I responded.

"It's okay," she said before a brief pause. "Well, come on then, let's check you out."

Nurse Scarlett was her usual, happy self; it's a good job her happiness is written all over her face as she's another person I can't read the mind of.

I followed her through the maze of the hospital swerving in and out of different corridors. Despite always seeing her and the number of times I have had a check-up at this hospital, I never fully remembered the way to her room. Each time I feel like I'm mapping a little bit more of the hospital, making note of any unique signs or objects which isn't easy to do when most wards are laid out in the same way with the same faded white colouring on every wall.

Over the years, I had managed to recognise a few unique identifiers on my way to Nurse Scarlett's room. One sign directing people to one of the wards had most of its letters faded out, one corridor had a broken and disused chair which gathered more and more dust in the corner and the corridor leading to her room has a blue plaque commemorating the opening of the hospital in 1885. Nurse Scarlett opened the door to her room and I followed her in. Her room was immaculately organised with nothing out of place; a big contrast to Mr Lyons' room. Even though her room had the same colour scheme as everywhere else in the hospital, it somehow felt much more welcoming and homely.

"Please, take a seat," she said gesturing to the chair at the side of her desk. I took a seat as Nurse Scarlett began sorting through paperwork before looking up. "I don't need to look through all this, I've been seeing you since you were born so I know you have no allergies or any other medical problems to date so I'll just ask, how do you feel?" asked Nurse Scarlett.

"I still feel healthy," I replied.

"You haven't noticed anything with your own body that's different or causes you pain?" asked Nurse Scarlett.

"No, no problems have come up," I told her.

"Well, that will make this run a lot quicker," she said with a smile.

"You said you've seen me since birth?" I asked.

"Yes, I was working in this very hospital when you were born and long before that as well," she replied. "After all this time, here we still are, every time you're here, I'm here." It made me think that maybe given the fact I had seen her often since birth was the factor which stopped me reading her mind much like my bond with Mr Lyons. Nurse Scarlett has always been kind to me and Mr Lyons has always looked out for me so they would definitely be the two adults I had bonded with the most so maybe I couldn't read their minds out of respect.

"Is it coincidence that it's always you I see?" I asked.

"No," she said softly. "Mr Lyons has been a close friend of mine for a long time and he's always insisted on it being me to see to you."

"That seems a bit strange that Mr Lyons cares that much about which nurse I see," I told her. "I'd have thought it would be the same treatment regardless."

"Well, I think he feels that all three of us have a connection going back a long way because the night you were born was the night I let Mr Lyons know about you needing..." Nurse Scarlett suddenly stopped speaking as her face froze and the smile was swept from it.

"Needing what?" I asked.

"Nothing!" said Nurse Scarlett instantly as she stood up from her chair and paced back and forth remaining silent for a little while. "I shouldn't have said anything, I promised Mr Lyons I wouldn't."

"Wait, is this about me becoming orphaned?" I asked. Nurse Scarlett didn't respond but her face sunk which gave away the answer. "Oh, I see." Nurse Scarlett sat back down and put her head in her hands. After a minute or so, she put her head back up and a subtle smile returned to her face.

"Yes," she said quietly. "The night you were born was also the night you became an orphan." I kept looking straight at her, my face stayed completely still. "Your father died from cancer before you were born and your mother died during childbirth."

"I don't see why Mr Lyons would want to keep that from me; I thought he wouldn't tell me because it might involve some gruesome details," I said as Nurse Scarlett remained silent. "Thank you for telling me Scarlett." Just then, the door opened. A fresh faced male nurse with short blonde hair entered the room and headed towards a pile of files.

"Don't mind me, carry on," he told us.

"Oh Lewis, can you believe this is Sam from the Lyons Orphanage now over thirteen years on?" she asked him.

"Sam, you won't remember me but I worked here as a trainee nurse in my teens before leaving and coming back just a few years ago, I remember you back from that night..." Nurse Lewis said before seeming hesitant to continue talking.

"It's okay, I've told him about what happened that night," said Nurse Scarlett.

"I thought Mr Lyons didn't want him knowing," said Nurse Lewis.

"I wasn't supposed to tell him but I guess he is old enough to handle it," said Nurse Scarlett.

"Definitely, I've just wanted to know the fate of my parents for so long since Mr Lyons didn't want to tell me what happened to them," I said.

"I was there that night too, Scarlett told me what happened and we both treated you for a while until Mr Lyons was ready to take you into the orphanage," said Nurse Lewis.

"But, I don't think I've ever seen Mr Lyons take in any babies," I said. "It seems like children at least have to be able to walk and talk before they come to the orphanage."

"Usually yes but Mr Lyons made an exception for you," said Nurse Lewis. "Otherwise, he usually just helped us to find somewhere to home orphaned toddlers and babies."

"Why was it different for me?" I asked.

"He never said why," replied Nurse Lewis.

"I'm sure Mr Lyons had his reasons," said Nurse Scarlett. There it was again, a phrase that I've used countless times when referring to any decision of Mr Lyons, we both respect Mr Lyons enough to accept his judgement.

"What were their names?" I asked Nurse Scarlett.

"Your mother and father were Stewart and Rebecca Watkins," replied Scarlett. "I saw them both together when they had their first scan on you, unfortunately the next time around; it was just your mother."

"I can't imagine what she went through," I said.

"Maybe that's why Mr Lyons wouldn't tell you, he knows how empathetic you are and you'd depress yourself thinking about it," said Nurse Scarlett. "But you don't need to worry, your mum stayed strong throughout," said Nurse Scarlett.

"How was my mum as a person?" I asked.

"She was great; always happy and she couldn't wait to have you," replied Nurse Scarlett. "When mothers like to talk, I was happy to listen to them and still am, it can make my day." Nurse Scarlett looked like she was off in her own little world reminiscing about the past.

"Yes, she was great," repeated Lewis who hadn't really said anything about my parents.

"I'm glad to hear it," I told them.

"I don't actually remember her," thought Lewis. This is where I wish my mind reading didn't drift in and out. Lewis was trying to make me feel good about my mum but now I know he doesn't really remember anything about her but I wasn't going to hold it against Lewis. "Anyway, I'm going to set up the machine in the other room ready for the CT scan," Nurse Lewis told Nurse Scarlett before turning to me. "I'll see you in there soon."

"Okay see you soon," said Nurse Scarlett as Nurse Lewis left the room. "He's a real sweetheart; he hasn't seen Mr Lyons in a long time but he always talks to Natalie, I think he really likes her." I didn't know how to respond to Nurse Scarlett's last comment; she said it like it was a piece of gossip that I certainly wasn't interested in discussing. Nurse Lewis seemed nice but I was worried about his affiliation with Natalie that Nurse Scarlett had just mentioned. Two nice guys in Nurse Lewis and Nicholas held Natalie in high regard and I would worry that she would manipulate them against Mr Lyons especially if Nurse Lewis does have an attraction to Natalie.

"So how long have you known Mr Lyons?" I asked deciding to turn the conversation back to Mr Lyons.

"Oh, it's been a very long time," said Nurse Scarlett. "I've known him since before his brother had to be treated here and that was a long time ago in of itself."

"You mean the stroke Nicholas has?" I asked.

"I'm surprised you know about Nicholas," said Nurse Scarlett.

"Nicholas came round to the orphanage the other day and he told me his story," I said.

"I see, well yes, I operated on him when he had his stroke," said Nurse Scarlett.

"You operated on him yourself as a nurse?" I asked.

"No sorry, I meant to say I assisted with his operation," replied Nurse Scarlett hastily. "But like I said, I met Mr Lyons even earlier than that while at a hospital fundraising event."

"Mr Lyons seems to get everywhere," I remarked.

"He really does," said Nurse Scarlett. "Anyway, a lot of my friends at the hospital didn't attend and nobody else was really speaking to me so I was by myself."

"Isolated," I said under my breath.

"What was that?" asked Nurse Scarlett.

"I was thinking you must have felt isolated," I told her.

"I was but Mr Lyons came over to talk and just talk," she said. "He didn't enquire about my availability, which I was dreading particularly when you go to these events with rich people; he was his pleasant and charming self and helped to make it an enjoyable night."

"Mr Lyons seems to be good at recognising that," I said. "He sees when people are isolated and he tries to help them in any way he can, just like me at the orphanage."

"Mr Lyons is the nicest man I have ever met and he has helped me out tremendously since I have known him," she said. "Whenever I have needed help in a tight spot or just someone to talk to, he's always been there, the orphanage is lucky to have him."

"Yeah, I guess we are," I said. I wondered if Mr Lyons had told her anything about the threat of Natalie or the money problems Mr Lyons was facing but I didn't want to be the one to break it to her.

"So naturally, when you were orphaned, I looked to Mr Lyons right away; I let him know so that he could advise us on where to send you until he was ready but he took you in right away," said Nurse Scarlett. "That's just the kind of man he is."

"Mr Lyons really is a selfless man, selling his company to fund the orphanage which took all his time," I said as I began to reflect on Mr Lyons' impact on everyone around him.

"You really know a lot about the Lyons brothers, don't you?" asked Nurse Scarlett.

"Yeah, I've had long conversations with both recently and they've talked to me about their lives as they grew up," I replied.

"Seems like they want to inspire you," suggested Nurse Scarlett. "Two orphans who made huge successes of themselves." I nodded towards Nurse Scarlett as we both fell silent for a little bit as I comprehended everything we had just been talking about.

"Aren't you supposed to be going through lots of other things with me?" I asked. "After all, this is a medical check-up."

"I told you, I remember everything about you already, the only check-up we need to do is being prepared by Nurse Lewis right now so until then, we can just talk and wait," said Nurse Scarlett. Nurse Lewis entered through the door almost as soon as she finished the sentence. "Ah, speak of the devil," said Nurse Scarlett.

"Are you all done with the rest of the check-up?" Nurse Lewis asked Nurse Scarlett.

"I sure am," said Nurse Scarlett who turned to me with a wry smile on her face and gave me a wink knowing full well she was lying to him.

"Okay then, let's get Sam to the scanning room," said Nurse Lewis. "I don't know why Mr Lyons insists on it though," thought Nurse Lewis. That thought of Nurse Lewis confused me, he was about to run a test on me and he had no idea why he was doing it but still there was no harm for me in taking any medical test to prove I'm still healthy.

"Right, let's go Sam," said Nurse Scarlett gesturing towards the door. I stood up and followed Nurse Scarlett and Nurse Lewis through more of the hospital which feels even more like a maze when you get this deep into it. Eventually, we got to the scanning room. The room housed a big, circular shaped machine in the centre. At the midpoint of the machine is an open space where the scanning takes place, I had seen this machine many times before.

"Right Sam, have a lie down on the bed and relax," said Nurse Lewis. I hopped onto the fully horizontal bed near the machine and waited.

"You know the drill Sam, we'll be done in a few moments," said Nurse Scarlett as she and Nurse Lewis left the room. The bed slowly moved towards the centre of the machine while I remained motionless. I entered the centre of the machine while on the bed as bright lights shone upon me. It's a strange feeling but it's over within what seems like a matter of seconds as the bed slowly moves back out of the centre circle. I never understood the purpose of it and nobody at the hospital ever discussed the results with me, all I knew is that it was a scan. I assumed no news was good news in this case.

"There we go, nice and simple," said Nurse Lewis as he re-entered the room. "Next time you're here, Nurse Scarlett will let you know the results." I'd never had the results before but this was the first time somebody at the hospital had told me to expect feedback on it. Nurse Scarlett re-entered the room shortly afterwards.

"Right, all done Sam, let's head back to reception," said Nurse Scarlett. "We'll leave Nurse Lewis to sort out the machine."

"See you later Sam," said Nurse Lewis as he held his hand as if giving a wave without making any movement.

"Goodbye Nurse Lewis," I said mimicking his same hand gesture. I decided on the walk back to reception that I was really going to try and remember my way around the hospital. The problem with the hospital is that the first few corridors you turn in and out of make it feel like you can make a mental map of the area. This changes when you've headed into the seventh different corridor but I felt like I was keeping up with it, I'd usually give up by this point. We made it back to reception with many of the orphans still sitting exactly where they were, waiting all this time to be seen to and Natalie was still sat in her same position. Nurse Scarlett and I walked over to her.

"All done," said Nurse Scarlett to Natalie as we approached her.

"Oh good," said Natalie. "Any problems?"

"Doesn't look like it," said Nurse Scarlett. "But if anything comes up, I'll be sure to let you and Howard know."

"Good," said Natalie. "Now go on Sam, take a seat, you've got a long wait."

"Until next time Sam, goodbye," said Nurse Scarlett as she walked away.

"Bye," I said enthusiastically; Nurse Scarlett's optimism was infectious although it didn't seem to affect Natalie in any way, good or bad. There was still a spare space next to Gareth who looked on the verge of falling asleep. I went to sit next to him while his eyes were closed, I moved very quietly so that I wouldn't disturb him. I sat there staring off into the distance scanning the medical posters around the room while Gareth's head was drooping. His head suddenly shot up and his eyes opened, at which point he realised I was back sitting next to him.

"Oh, hi Sam," he said looking slightly embarrassed.

"Good sleep Gareth?" I asked.

"Yeah, it's a long old wait so why not sleep?" asked Gareth. "We all got up really early this morning but the joke's on you, you have to do all the waiting now."

"I'm used to it," I told him. "Plus I've got plenty to think about."

"Like what?" asked Gareth.

"Well-" I began before being interrupted by a nurse walking right up to us.

"Gareth Wade?" asked the nurse looking at Gareth.

"Yeah, that's me," replied Gareth.

"Come along, it's your turn next," the nurse told him.

"I guess we'll talk later Sam," said Gareth as he walked away with the nurse. On these hospital trips, I never usually had someone to talk to before so I was used to sitting alone but I couldn't wait for Gareth to get back to help pass the time quicker. Instead, I sat back and tuned into the minds of the hospital patients sitting around in the waiting area to amuse myself.

"I should have looked up from my phone, that pole came out of nowhere," thought one patient with a big bump on his head.

"It tells them not to try it at home," thought another voice from a woman sat by her two children, one was holding their shoulder.

"We really need to change that carpet; the dog just blends into it," thought a man who had his leg elevated.

"I'm never drinking again," thought a man holding his hands against his head the whole time. These are all the kinds of stories I need to get me through the boredom but I always want to keep it light-hearted, as soon as there is an element of seriousness to the cause of the injury, I switch off from their story. I looked over to Natalie and realised that she was talking to Nurse Lewis. I know Nurse Scarlett had said they often communicated with each other but I was worried that their conversation was more than a friendly catch-up. Natalie's demeanour had changed from a neutral expression to a happy expression as she conversed with Nurse Lewis. I wondered if she was turning on the charm with him to manipulate him, I decided I had to find out what the conversation involved. There was a break in the conversation which gave me my chance to focus on what they had just discussed.

"Even Nurse Lewis can see that Howard is running the orphanage into the ground and needs change," thought Natalie. "Hopefully, he can make Nurse Scarlett see that too and maybe she'll talk to Howard."

"What is Mr Lyons thinking?" thought Nurse Lewis. "He's letting the orphanage collapse and he wants to try and demonise Natalie for it, I can't believe he even spread such lies to the children at the orphanage." Natalie had discussed Mr Lyons with Nurse Lewis and how Mr Lyons told me about her apparent attempt to overthrow him. The only thing certain in my mind at this moment, undeniably, is that Natalie does want Mr Lyons to leave the orphanage so she can take control for herself; both her thoughts and Nurse Lewis' thoughts confirm it. The break in conversation seemed to signal the end of talks about Mr Lyons and the orphanage as the conversation then did turn into a catch-up chat. I had worried that Natalie would manipulate Nurse Lewis into her way of thinking, particularly if he is so enamoured with her, and it appears she's been successful in that case. The good news for Mr Lyons is that, with all due respect, I don't see how Nurse Lewis could have an impact on anything to do with the orphanage.

Chapter 7

I spent the rest of my time in the waiting area thinking about the fate of the orphanage again; its fate in terms of having enough money to keep running and the fate of Mr Lyons as the owner with Natalie plotting against him. Natalie and Nurse Lewis' small talk following their talk about Mr Lyons didn't last too much longer. Even when Gareth came back, I found it hard to start up a long conversation with him about anything; I was too focussed on the issues surrounding the orphanage so different topics we discussed would tail off quickly.

"Sam must be very tired," thought Gareth. "Ever since I got back here, he's seemed so lethargic and spaced out." This lack of flow in conversation continued through the rest of our time at the hospital and the bus ride back to the orphanage. Gareth and I both took naps on the bus ride home and it seemed to refresh me a little bit and made me worry a bit less about the orphanage.

Natalie hadn't said a word except to round us up in the waiting area and lead us onto the bus. There was something about the hospital that seemed to drain the life out of everybody, it was probably all that waiting around. The worst part about it was that we still had most of the afternoon to go when, in reality, most of us just wanted to go back to our beds. As we re-entered the orphanage, I instantly saw Natasha who was sitting against one of the walls with playing cards splayed out all around her, she looked bored as well. I guess it's not surprising when we are her only two friends at the orphanage and we had left her here all afternoon. Gareth and I walked over to her.

"You took your time," she said while trying to suppress a yawn.

"It's not like we could do anything about it and we were waiting around a long time too," Gareth told Natasha.

"Yeah but you had each other to talk to," Natasha said.

"I guess," I said deciding against telling her we spent most of the day in silence.

"Well, we were still bored," responded Gareth.

"So, anything interesting happening?" asked Natasha.

"Not at all," replied Gareth.

"Did the nurses find something wrong with you this time or is it just me who sees it?" asked Natasha in a cheeky tone. Gareth replied with a half-hearted, sarcastic laugh.

"Well, he hasn't got the scan results back yet," I said.

"Scan? What scan?" Natasha asked as she turned to Gareth.

"I don't know what you're talking about Sam," said Gareth.

"Oh you know, the big machine that has a circular opening which you get placed into under the bright light," I told him.

"I've never seen any machine like that in my life," said Gareth.

"Me either," said Natasha.

"Neither of you have seen that machine before?" I asked. They both turned to each other and shook their heads.

"No," said Gareth.

"I think it's an entire scan of the top half of the body," I told them although I wasn't actually sure myself.

"Sam, we've never had any kind of scan on a single limb before," said Natasha.

"Let alone the whole upper body," said Gareth.

"That's strange, I wonder if anyone else here has the type of scan I'm talking about," I said.

"You're free to go ask each and every one of them," said Natasha.

"No, I think that would be a bit weird to ask," I said.

"Not any weirder than you being the only one to have a scan," said Gareth.

"I'm sure it's fine even if I am the only one to have these scans." I said. "They've never brought up the results of the scan so as far as I'm concerned, the scan is giving me extra reassurances about my health."

"If you say so," said Natasha as the conversation fell silent. I looked at the pile of cards scattered across the ground around her.

"So, what have you been up to?" I asked her. "I see a lot of cards on the ground."

"Well, I was playing solitaire," she began. "That's the only single player card game I know, maybe next time Nicholas is here, he can tell us if others exist."

"How did you make such a mess playing solitaire?" asked Gareth.

"As I said, I was playing solitaire but I got bored of that as well," she replied. "So, I tried to set up a game of poker by myself trying to take everyone's turns."

"You do realise that the main part of poker is your opponent not knowing the cards you have?" asked Gareth in a derisory tone.

"Yes but I had to make do with what I had here, I'd rather practice playing poker than playing a dead end game like solitaire which you can't really get better at," Natasha replied. Gareth looked down on the playing cards before taking a seat on the floor as well.

"Well, come on then," he said. "That's enough self pity from you, let's get this game rolling, are you in Sam?"

"Sure," I said as I took a seat on the floor to the side of Gareth.

I had decided this time that I wasn't going to cheat but just simply see how well I did on my own. Now that I knew the rules of the game, I felt well equipped to play the game fairly and see if I really did have any skill playing poker. We were all quite evenly matched; I had to resist the temptation to read their minds which would have given me the edge over the other two.

"You always know when I'm bluffing," Gareth said to Natasha as he conceded one of the rounds to her.

"Well, you always seem to know when I'm bluffing," Natasha told Gareth before they both turned to me.

"And you always know when we're bluffing," they said to me in unison.

"Maybe you're just not that good at hiding it," I told them with a smirk on my face. I wasn't technically cheating because I never read their minds. Instead, I had picked up on their subtle body language gestures and nuances when they were bluffing from the last time we played. Although, it wasn't a one hundred percent success rate like the twins would make it seem.

"Surely, we're not this bad at keeping our bluffs a secret?" asked Gareth.

"Well now that you mention it, I don't think you give it away much but I just seem to know when you are lying," Natasha told him. "What about me, do I have any giveaways?"

"Not really," replied Gareth.

"Then why are we so bad at this?" asked Natasha.

"Well, you could look at it more like we are really good," I said. "We all have that feeling that someone is bluffing and we catch them out with it quite a lot even though they don't give much away."

"I'm starting to think that scan you got today was some kind of 'poker ray' which makes it easier for you to win," said Gareth.

"Really?" I asked.

"Well, how else do you explain it?" asked Gareth.

"Like I said, maybe we have a knack for distinguishing the truth from lies," I said.

"Well if we did, we'd have found out what you told us about Natalie and the risk of closure to the orphanage ourselves," said Natasha.

"Yeah, I've been thinking about it all day," I told them.

"So that's why you've been so quiet," said Gareth. "You've been worrying yourself about something out of all our control."

"Well it got worse today, do you know Nurse Lewis?" I asked them both.

"I think so," replied Gareth.

"Oh yeah, the dreamy one," replied Natasha whose eyes lit up.

"If you say so," I said feeling slightly embarrassed.

"What about Nurse Lewis?" asked Gareth.

"I saw him talking to Natalie today-" I began.

"And now Natasha will never be able to marry him," interrupted Gareth.

"Shut up you," said Natasha giving Gareth a shove on the arm. "Go on, Sam."

"Anyway, I managed to eavesdrop on their conversation and it looks like Natalie has turned Nurse Lewis against Mr Lyons."

"So, who cares?" asked Natasha. "What's a nurse going to do to bring him down?"

"They might inject Mr Lyons with something and make him disappear," said Gareth.

"I don't know what he might do but I feel like she told Nurse Lewis for a specific reason," I said.

"Maybe because they're friends and they tell each other things," said Natasha.

"And it's usually pretty easy to get friends on your side unless your friend is Natasha," said Gareth. She gave him another shove of the arm.

"It still seems like there's more to it," I said.

"Even if there is, I don't see what we can do about it now," said Gareth.

"Yeah Natalie's the main threat so if we can keep an eye on what she's doing round here, we shouldn't have to worry about Nurse Lewis," Natasha told me.

"And there's still the bigger issue of the orphanage closing down since Mr Lyons can barely keep it up and running without help from Nicholas," said Gareth.

"There must be something we can do about that at least," I said.

"Like what?" asked Natasha.

"I don't know but there's lots of ways to make money," I replied.

"Name one," said Natasha.

"Well I," I began before my mind went completely blank.

"What about a charity football match?" asked Gareth. "I bet Mr Lyons meets a lot of players at his fundraising events, heck, they probably make more money than he ever did."

"That could be worth a shot," I said.

"The footballers can play a match, make donations and the fans can pay to see it and I'll be one of the stars on the field of play," said Gareth as I gave a low sigh.

"I'm sure the fans can't wait," I said sarcastically.

"You'll see, maybe a scout will be there too," said Gareth.

"Aren't you missing an important detail out here guys?" asked Natasha who had looked like she hadn't been paying attention to our conversation. Gareth and I looked at each other trying to see if we could figure out what she was talking about.

"No," we replied in unison.

"With that plan, you'll need Mr Lyons for it," she said. Gareth and I looked back towards each other, still confused.

"Yeah, so?" asked Gareth. Natasha looked frustrated and put her hand over her face.

"So that means you'll have to tell Mr Lyons you know there are financial problems with the orphanage, something we'd only know by breaking into his office," said Natasha.

"Ah," said Gareth in a tone of disappointment. "There goes that plan then, how would we be able to hint to Mr Lyons to organise a charity match without letting on we knew about the financial troubles?"

"We wouldn't," replied Natasha. "We'd need an otherworldly command of the English language to get the idea into his head without giving it away."

"I just thought as well that surely Mr Lyons would have considered this idea among others as well especially if we thought of it after ten seconds of brainstorming," I said.

"So, we'd need a way of making money without Mr Lyons' help and without him having any knowledge of it," said Gareth.

"And even if we found a way to get the money, we would have to get it to him somehow without handing it to him and without an explanation of where the money came from," said Natasha.

"I think that idea is well and truly dead then," said Gareth.

"What about Nicholas?" I asked.

"What about Nicholas?" asked Natasha.

"If we could make money somehow, we might be able to get away with giving it to him, he probably wouldn't tell on us," I said.

"I'd hope not," said Gareth.

"Nicholas wants to see the orphanage stay open so I think he would want to help as much as possible so he wouldn't tell Mr Lyons anything," I said.

"That would be our only option," said Natasha. "But we've forgotten another thing; Nicholas doesn't know that we know about the state of the orphanage so we'd have to tell him that, maybe even the whole truth of how we found out that information."

"Nicholas strikes me as the kind of person who can see the greater good, he might be annoyed we trespassed but he'd be happy when he finds out we're doing something about it," I said.

"I really hope you're right," said Gareth. "We still need an idea to make money in the first place."

"Well, let's mull it over while we play more poker, shall we?" asked Natasha. Gareth and I both nodded and we continued to play poker. Nicholas' enthusiasm for poker the other day seemed to have rubbed off on us and I think all three of us were happy that he taught us how to play. When I thought about Nicholas and poker I came to a sudden realisation as we played.

"What if poker's the answer?" I asked Gareth and Natasha.

"What are you talking about?" asked Natasha.

"Nicholas said he likes to play his friends at poker for money," I replied.

"Which he always loses," said Natasha.

"Well, we're all good at calling people's bluffs, maybe we could help him win at poker and earn more money for the orphanage," I said.

"Correction, Natasha and I are great at calling each other's bluffs but we can never really read you while you can read us both," said Gareth. "But I think you've got a good idea going."

"Wouldn't that be cheating?" asked Natasha. I didn't respond.

"You can't cheat when you have a good intuition like Sam does," replied Gareth

"Yeah Natasha, it's just intuition," I said trying to hide the wry smile on my face.

"And Mr Lyons told you that you should only play for fun," said Natasha.

"We wouldn't be playing, we'd be assisting Nicholas," I said.

"You mean you'd be assisting Nicholas?" asked Gareth.

"Okay, just me then, I hope these people would be as easy to read as you two are," I said while not trying to hide the smile on my face this time.

"So, we basically have to admit to Nicholas that we broke into Mr Lyons' room and found out about his role here," said Gareth.

"He might not ask follow-up questions if we tell him we found it out from somewhere else," said Natasha. "If we do tell him the truth, he might get angry at us but then forget about it five minutes later."

"If he thinks it's a good idea to make money, I doubt he would tell Mr Lyons because Mr Lyons would put down the idea of me being involved in gambling in any way," I said.

"I think it goes without saying that Natalie as well as Mr Lyons can't know about this," said Natasha.

"Of course, Natalie would want to stop it but her denial would be for all the wrong reasons, she doesn't want Mr Lyons to succeed at the head of the orphanage," I said.

"If you can really read people as well as you can read us then you'd have a shot at calling the bluffs of Nicholas' friends," said Gareth.

"So not only do we have to convince Nicholas not to tell Mr Lyons about it but we also have to convince him to bring you along in the first place?" asked Natasha.

"I'm not sure what I'm worried about more," said Gareth. "Nicholas not taking you there in the first place or him taking you and you come back with no money whatsoever."

"I think I'll have to prove to Nicholas that I have an ability to read people in order for him to take me along," I said.

"Well, he saw you playing when we were sat playing poker in front of him and he complimented you on your ability then, let's hope he remembers that," said Gareth.

"I think I should tell you two that the reason Nicholas' memory is so bad was because he had a stroke a long time ago," I said.

"Sorry Sam," said Gareth. "Why didn't you say that sooner?"

"He told it to me personally so I didn't want to mention it," I said

"But now you want us to stop making jokes about him," said Gareth.

"Exactly," I said.

"Fair enough," said Natasha. We had our plan in place but the hard part would be convincing Nicholas about it when he next visited.

Chapter 8

We eagerly awaited Nicholas' next visit to the orphanage which felt like an eternity. We felt like we were losing valuable time every day we waited. Several days had passed at the orphanage until we finally heard a knock at the door. Mr Lyons was already downstairs, seemingly waiting for Nicholas' arrival, ready to unlock the doors for him. We had purposely set up a game of poker so that we could bring it into any conversation with Nicholas whenever we get the chance.

"Nicholas, good to see you again," said Mr Lyons.

"It's good to see you Howard, and all the children as well," said Nicholas.

"Well, I'm glad you're happy to see them because I'll have to leave you down here with them for a little while, there's something I just need to sort out upstairs first," Mr Lyons told Nicholas.

"Oh okay," said Nicholas in a dejected tone before looking over to Gareth, Natasha and I. "Ah, there they are."

"I'll leave you to it," said Mr Lyons as he walked upstairs while Nicholas headed towards us.

"Good morning Nicholas," I said to him.

"Good morning Sam, and...Gareth and...Natasha, did I get it right this time?" asked Nicholas hesitantly pointing to each one of us as he said our names.

"That's right Nicholas," I told him.

"Oh thank goodness!" exclaimed Nicholas. "You see, I'm not completely hopeless."

"Of course not, what brings you here today Nicholas?" I asked him.

"Just another catch up with my brother, the only time I get to speak to him these days is when I come here, he's always very busy," replied Nicholas.

"Yeah, he sure works hard for the orphanage and everyone involved with it," I said.

"Indeed, I just wish he could find a balance of personal and business life but he's never been that way," said Nicholas as he looked down at the poker game we had set up.

"Ah, I see you've all taken to poker," he said.

"We have and we've all become very good at it," said Natasha.

"But Sam's the best," said Gareth.

"Oh really?" asked Nicholas. "Well, he might give me a run for my money."

"It's funny you mention that Nicholas because there's something serious we need to discuss with you," I told him.

"Oh no, I haven't turned you lot into gambling addicts, have I?" asked Nicholas.

"No, nothing like that, it's about the orphanage," said Natasha.

"Okay, I'm all ears," said Nicholas.

"Nicholas, we know why you're here," I said.

"Yeah, to see my brother," said Nicholas.

"Not just that, we know that the orphanage is running out of money and we know that you have been helping by making donations yourself," I told him.

"How did you, well never mind, yes I have always made donations but in the last couple of years, I have had to give a lot more to help Mr Lyons," said Nicholas.

"Well, we came up with an idea to help raise the orphanage more money," said Gareth.

"I'd welcome any suggestions to secure the future of this orphanage but why didn't you tell Mr Lyons?" asked Nicholas.

"There are two reasons; the nature of the way we found out that there are money problems and the nature of how we want to get more money for it," replied Natasha.

"I see, well now I'm intrigued," said Nicholas. "When you said you can't tell him about the nature of how the money is made, don't tell me it's something illegal?"

"Technically, no," replied Natasha.

"Technically?" asked Nicholas.

"We think Sam can help you win money from poker," said Gareth.

"I don't play poker to win money," said Nicholas.

"That's because you never do," said Natasha.

"You've got me there," said Nicholas. "But with all due respect, how can Sam help?"

"Whenever we play poker, he seems to know almost every time whether we are bluffing or not," said Natasha.

"So he knows how to read the two of you, his friends, but how could he help me with people he has never met?" Nicholas asked Gareth and Natasha.

"You have to trust us," said Natasha. "Sam just has this instinct I can't explain and in the worst case scenario, you lose the same amount of money you put in every time so there's no risk to it."

"I suppose you're right," he said. "I'll have to come up with an excuse to bring all of you along."

"All of us?" asked Gareth. "You just need Sam."

"That's right, I only need Sam but I'd like you two to come along as well," he said.

"I still don't understand," said Gareth.

"You're going to make me say it, aren't you?" asked Nicholas.

"Say what?" asked Natasha.

"There's a couple I play poker with who have expressed an interest in adopting two children so I'll give you a chance to showcase your adoptability to them," said Nicholas.

"Great, we'll save the orphanage and then leave triumphantly," said Gareth.

"We might not like them," said Natasha.

"Oh I think you will, they're very easy going," said Nicholas. Natasha looked unmoved.

"Come on Natasha, let's at least give them a chance," Gareth told her.

"Fine," she said. "So, now we have the plan in place."

"You're in luck, after my meeting with Mr Lyons, I'm heading straight to my friend's house to play so we can get this done quickly," said Nicholas. "If we're successful, we might have to do it every week."

"Nicholas!" shouted a voice in excitement. He turned round to see Natalie approaching him. Much like the previous time, Nicholas gave Natalie a hug with plenty of enthusiasm.

"Natalie, it's been too long," said Nicholas.

"Don't be silly, it's only been a few days," said Natalie. She looked over to us and saw the cards set out. "I see you have had an influence on these three."

"Yes, they love it," said Nicholas.

"Please don't tell her, please don't tell her, please don't tell her," thought Natasha repeatedly.

"In fact, they have a plan with their new found knowledge of poker," said Nicholas. Natasha's face immediately sunk and I feared the worst as well.

"Don't tell me they are all aspiring to be professional poker players?" asked Natalie.

"No, it's not that," said Nicholas. "It's a plan to raise more money for the orphanage."

"How do they know the orphanage needs money?" said Natalie.

"I don't know," replied Nicholas.

"Wait, the other day, they were in Mr Lyons' room, they must have seen it then," she told Nicholas who looked in shock as he began to stare at us. "But I think it's best we don't tell Mr Lyons about that, okay Nicholas?" asked Natalie drawing his attention back to her.

"But Howard," Nicholas began to say.

"Howard will be happier not knowing about it, after all, there was no harm done and now you say it has inspired these three to come up with a plan to save the orphanage so let's leave it at that," said Natalie who spoke very calmly. Natalie was taking it well so far and seemed enthused but I felt like once she gets to hear the plan, she would shoot it down so that Mr Lyons would suffer.

"I guess so," said Nicholas.

"So, what is the plan?" Natalie asked us. We all sat in silence for a short period wary of what Natalie's reaction might be.

"Well, it's...it's..." said Gareth.

"Oh come on, one of you spit it out," said Natalie.

"We want to go with Nicholas to help him make a lot of money from playing poker with his friends to give as a donation to the orphanage," I said.

"Sounds like a good idea," said Natalie much to the disbelief of all three of us. "The amount Nicholas and his mates play for every week could give us a huge boost."

"Indeed it could," said Nicholas.

"And we want to make it happen," I said.

"But how exactly can you three help?" Natalie asked us.

"These two say that Sam has a great ability to tell when someone's bluffing," said Nicholas while pointing at Natasha and Gareth.

"And you're sure it's not just because they know each other well?" asked Natalie.

"Not according to them," replied Nicholas.

"I could prove it to you right now," I said deciding it was the only way to get them fully on board.

"Alright, let's see firsthand what you can do," said Nicholas.

"I'm in too," said Natalie.

Natasha rounded up the cards and dealt them out to all of us. I made sure on every occasion to use my mind-reading ability; I had to use it over and over again to give Nicholas and Natalie the utmost confidence that I was really good at reading people. A slight doubt entered my mind that maybe, like Mr Lyons and Nurse Scarlett, I wouldn't be able to read the minds of some of his poker friends. After what felt like a long time playing, we could hear movement upstairs which suggested Mr Lyons was on his way down soon.

"He's coming down for me now, do you have enough proof yet?" Nicholas asked Natalie.

"I can't believe it," she said. "They were right; Sam just seems to know every time."

"I think this plan's going to work," said Nicholas.

"Let's hope so," said Natalie. "I want to come with you."

"You do?" asked Nicholas.

"Yes, if these three are going then I'll need to cover for them, what better way of doing that than by joining you?" she asked. "If Mr Lyons noticed, three missing children would be a problem but if I'm gone too, he'll assume I'm looking after them."

"How will I explain it to my friends?" asked Nicholas.

"Well, what's your excuse for these three?" she asked in reply.

"I hadn't thought that far ahead yet," replied Nicholas.

"You could tell them I'm your daughter," said Natalie as Nicholas gave a chuckle.

"Unfortunately not, they've all met my family," said Nicholas.

"If the couple there is going to know we're orphans anyway, you can just tell them that we have to be escorted by someone from the orphanage," said Natasha.

"How will they know your orphans?" asked Natalie.

"Sorry Natalie, I know it's not very professional but there's this couple I play at poker who really want to adopt a couple of children so I was hoping to showcase the twins," he said.

"You're right, it's not very professional," said Natalie calmly. "But if all goes well, we could have a new home for Natasha and Gareth together and make your friends happy too." I was really surprised by Natalie. She was okay with the idea of us being involved with gambling and letting us leave the orphanage unauthorised. I couldn't help feeling there was some kind of ulterior motif behind her actions especially when she insists on coming with us as well. We could hear Mr Lyons making his way downstairs so Natalie and Nicholas immediately threw their cards away from them and stood up.

"Nicholas, this is another thing Howard can't know about, he barely approves of you playing poker in the first place and if he found out you got the children involved, it would mean trouble for all of us," Natalie told him.

"I understand," said Nicholas. "I'm not sure how long I'll be up there but as soon as I'm finished, I'll be back down and we can head off."

"Okay Nicholas, we all look forward to it," said Natalie. Nicholas nodded before heading towards the stairs to greet Mr Lyons once more. This left us in an awkward situation where it was just us three and Natalie with the events of a few days ago in Mr Lyons' room fresh in our mind. I wondered how Natalie would treat us now Nicholas wasn't around. There was a period of silence when Nicholas left as Natasha, Gareth and I were all looking down at the floor.

"I guess you still don't trust me after the other day," Natalie said as she broke the silence.

"Natalie, don't take it the wrong way but I know, just like I know when people are bluffing in poker, I know you want to get rid of Mr Lyons and take control of the orphanage," I told her. Natasha and Gareth didn't dare look up at her.

"I told you I would explain myself before, so I guess now would be the best time to do so," she said. "I don't want you getting the wrong idea of me."

"Just tell me if what Mr Lyons said is true, do you want to get rid of him? I asked her.

"I do," she said. "You wanted complete honesty so here it is."

"And you want to take control yourself?" I asked.

"Yes but this isn't a case of greed," she replied. "I want to take control because I don't think Mr Lyons is doing all he can to save this orphanage, I think he has other priorities that he has moved on to."

"But Mr Lyons loves this orphanage," I said.

"He used to," said Natalie. "I've tried to convince him that the orphanage desperately needs repairs and improvements but he won't listen to me."

"Maybe he's just embarrassed he can't afford to anymore," I said.

"That's what Nicholas' donations are for apparently but I haven't seen him spend any money on the orphanage," said Natalie.

"He might be keeping it in reserve to cover the basic cost of running the orphanage and give the orphanage a few more weeks or months before he finds the solution," I said.

"He's not interested in finding the solution," Natalie told me. "He's putting all of you at risk in this orphanage, your safety is more important than the money right now."

"And you think you putting pressure on him will help him?" I asked.

"I don't want to help him, I want to help the orphanage and, in my eyes, the way I can do that is by taking control myself, I'll improve the orphanage and I'll find a way to keep it running but Mr Lyons is resigned to delaying what would be the inevitable death of the orphanage under his leadership," Natalie told me.

"He may be struggling but I refuse to believe he doesn't care for the orphanage," I said firmly.

"You can believe what you want but I'll tell you how much I care for the orphanage," said Natalie. "Do you remember when I was called Mrs Pullinger before?" she asked.

"No, what does that have to do with anything?" I asked.

"Well, that's how the orphans used to address me around here, just like Mr Thompson and Mr Lyons," replied Natalie. "That was my married name." I still wasn't sure what point she was making but I kept looking straight at her to let her know I was still listening. "The amount of work I had to put into the orphanage meant that my marriage was suffering as a result, I didn't spend much time at home because work always got in the way."

"I'm sorry to hear that," I told her.

"I'm not!" she snapped back. "My ex-husband didn't understand it, he didn't even want a child but the children at this orphanage have been my life and I'm happy I chose them over him because they need me." All three of us stayed silent. "So if you think I'm going to put all this work into the orphanage over all these years and make sacrifices in my personal life just to watch it crumble, or even worse, be accused of wanting it to fail then you are mistaken." It was a passionate response from Natalie which seemed genuine to me.

"Sorry but what did your surname have to do with it?" asked Natasha.

"When I got divorced, I took my maiden name back," replied Natalie.

"Can we ask what it is?" asked Natasha.

"Longhurst, I'm Ms Longhurst," she replied. "I didn't want the orphans to know about it though so I simply told them to call me Natalie instead."

"I'm sure the orphans would have understood it well enough," said Gareth.

"They probably would but they'd understand it too well," said Natalie. "I can't stand here telling kids that they'll go to a home with loving parents if they see the reality that not all couples stay together, I didn't want to discourage them."

"I guess that makes sense," I said to her.

"I think it was the right decision and I haven't regretted any decision I have made in regards to this orphanage and I won't regret trying to take over this orphanage," she said. "You may think Mr Lyons spends a lot of his time working for the orphanage but it's been my hard work that has kept the orphanage running, I have sacrificed everything for this place and I won't let Mr Lyons lead it to a slow, painful death."

"But Mr Lyons funds the orphanage himself, I doubt you'd have that kind of money to run it," I told her.

"I don't have the money but I know plenty of ways to make money for the orphanage and bring in more funding, the problem is all my ideas have to go through Mr Lyons who instantly rejects them," said Natalie.

"Why would he do that?" I asked.

"Politicians and the local council can be a great help to us but Mr Lyons refuses to talk to them, he sees everybody in government as untrustworthy but with the orphanage in this state, he doesn't have the resources to be picky about where the help comes from," said Natalie.

"I can't believe Mr Lyons would be that stubborn," I said.

"Well, he is and that stubbornness will be the ruin of the orphanage," she said.

"So, you're hoping to have him removed by setting him up?" I asked.

"What do you mean setting him up?" asked Natalie in response.

"You wanted to know the code for his office so I assume you plan to sabotage him," I replied.

"No, I don't intend on doing anything unfair or illegal other than trespassing," said Natalie.

"Then why do you want access to his office?" I asked.

"I want to see where the money's going, I want to see how much he's spending and how much he's keeping back, that's just for my knowledge," replied Natalie. "But if I can find some kind of evidence to suggest that he has been cutting corners to save money which, in turn, endangers the safety of the orphans then I'll have him right where I want him."

"That sounds very vindictive and manipulative," I said.

"If Mr Lyons is in the wrong, if he's putting your safety at risk then he is breaking the law, of course if he's doing all he can then I can't really complain," said Natalie. "With that in mind I'd like to ask you for the code, calmly this time." I wasn't sure whether I could trust her with it or not.

"Don't look at me, I don't know the code," I said drawing my gaze to Natasha instead.

"Well?" Natalie asked Natasha.

"What do you two think?" Natasha asked us.

"I think we should tell her, like she said, if Mr Lyons hasn't done anything wrong then he has nothing to worry about," replied Gareth.

"Any objections Sam?" I remained silent. I didn't want to implicate myself in this.

"I'll take that as a no then," said Natasha. "I'll tell you but I don't want these two knowing because it annoys them, especially Gareth, that I won't tell them." Little did Natasha know that I already knew the code from reading her mind but obviously that wasn't something I could give away. Natasha whispered the code to Natalie.

"Thank you Natasha, I won't do it right away but in time, I'll be in that office and I'll prove to you and everyone that Mr Lyons is slacking," said Natalie. "But before that, let's go win some money."

Chapter 9

We weren't sure how long we'd have to wait for Nicholas to finish his conversation with Mr Lyons; Nicholas really liked to chat but Mr Lyons seemed busier than he ever had been so I wasn't sure which one would give out first. Natalie had gone off to run other errands but popped back every few minutes to check if Nicholas had come down yet. The three of us sat in silence for the most part, just waiting and waiting. Eventually, after what seemed like a good half hour, Nicholas came back down the stairs.

"Right, Mr Lyons said he's probably going to be tied down in his office with paperwork for a long time so hopefully, he won't notice a thing, where's Natalie?" asked Nicholas.

"She's around," replied Natasha. "She's been checking here every few minutes to see if you were finished yet."

"I see," said Nicholas who stood in silence looking around the orphanage. Natalie came back to us about thirty seconds later. "There she is."

"Sorry, I was just making sure Mr Thompson was here and not back at his house," said Natalie. "Now, let's not waste any more time." Natalie unlocked the doors and we followed her and Nicholas to the outside. Nicholas led the way to his car which was small and with a basic looking design.

"I thought you said you were rich," I said to him pointing to his car.

"I did say that, I also said that I didn't feel the need to spend all my money on lavish goods, hence I drive around in this car," said Nicholas.

"But you must still treat yourself to a few luxuries?" I asked him.

"I do along with my family but I don't see the need for an expensive car," replied Nicholas. "I am not a man of prestige who needs to show up in a fancy car, I'm a retired man who wants to get from A to B."

"It's a very wise attitude to have," said Natalie. "If Nicholas had wasted away all his money, the orphanage might already be gone."

"I'm sure Howard would have found a way anyway," said Nicholas. "I'm just the easiest option." Natalie didn't respond. We all entered Nicholas' car and almost as soon as the doors were shut and our seatbelts were clipped in, Nicholas began driving.

"What is he doing?" thought Natalie. "He didn't check his mirrors or anything, I should say something." Natalie never did say anything regarding Nicholas' driving. In Natalie's mind, every car journey had to start with a number of safety checks probably instilled into her from her time driving the minibus.

"Gareth and Natasha," said Nicholas as he briefly looked over his shoulder.

"Yes?" they both asked in unison.

"I know I told you about the couple who wants to adopt you but I need to you to act natural," replied Nicholas.

"What do you mean?" they asked in unison again.

"I mean don't try too hard to impress them, they don't know the real reason I'm bringing you two, I just want to plant the idea of adopting you two in their heads," replied Nicholas.

"It would have been easier if we didn't know in the first place," said Natasha.

"Well, you were the ones who had to ask why I wanted to bring you," said Nicholas.

"Yeah but..." said Natasha before stopping. She didn't seem to have a response to what Nicholas had just said so she sat right back and remained silent.

"The couple are called Matthew and Geena; they're both very nice," said Nicholas. The conversation in the car went dead for a little while after that until Nicholas began speaking again.

"Sam, we need to discuss the plan," said Nicholas.

"What's to discuss?" asked Gareth. "The plan is Sam helps you win money."

"Yes but we need a plan for Sam to alert me; a sound, a signal or anything like that," said Nicholas.

"Why don't you just make sure you pick a seat where you're facing me?" I asked. Nicholas was silent for a moment; I thought he was shocked that he didn't think of a plan so obvious but he was actually deep in thought.

"That could work but I have just thought of a better idea," said Nicholas.

"Really?" asked Natalie who had remained silent up until that point.

"Yes, instead of you lot coming round and being left to your own devices, we can just assign each of you as an assistant to one of the players; the twins can have the couple and try to win favour with them, Sam can go with me which means Natalie will be left with the last person, Marie," said Nicholas.

"I don't know Nicholas," said Natalie. "Having Sam help you is one thing but for him to be directly involved in the game, I'm not sure."

"It's perfect!" exclaimed Nicholas. "If Sam is sitting by my side then there is absolutely no way they can think he's cheating."

"He's right," I said. "If I'm making sounds or giving signals to Nicholas, there's a risk that we'd be caught but if we're all playing together then the suspicion will fall away."

"At the same time, I don't want you two to try and lose the game for the others, just let Sam's supposed brilliance shine through," Nicholas told Natasha and Gareth.

"That's going to be awkward if we win though, isn't it?" asked Natasha.

"Well, hopefully Sam's intuition won't be lost just yet," replied Nicholas. "If it is then we wouldn't win anyway regardless if you two were playing or not." I didn't speak too often in the car journey because my mind was fixated on that thought; what if I couldn't read the minds of the people I was about to play against? Even if it was one person whose mind I couldn't read, that could be the difference between winning the money for the orphanage and losing it. Natalie seemed to be getting more and more nervous as the journey went on.

"I still think this is a big risk, why can't you just ask them for the extra money for the orphanage?" Natalie asked Nicholas.

"Because then they'd bring up the fact that over the years, I could have stopped playing poker and put my playing money towards to the orphanage each week instead," replied Nicholas.

"So why didn't you?" asked Natalie.

"When Howard first asked me for extra donations, I thought it would be a short term thing so I kept up playing poker," replied Nicholas. "But now there's been too much time between the start of my extra donations and my continued playing of poker."

"Hmmm," said Natalie sounding unimpressed.

"But I'll tell you what, if we win big this week, I'll cut my playing time down to every other week and pass that on to the orphanage," said Nicholas.

"Or you could just quit entirely," said Natalie.

"It's not my orphanage!" shouted Nicholas which made Natalie jump. Nicholas instantly calmed down. "I'm sorry Natalie, you know I love the orphanage and I want to help my brother but I want to have my own life too, I've been close to death before so I can't just whittle away the rest of my life using my retirement money to fully fund the orphanage."

"I'm sorry Nicholas," said Natalie.

"It's okay," he told Natalie. "Howard never pressured me to make extra donations but he told me about what he needed and I helped where I could but like he said to me, this isn't my fight." Natalie put a consoling arm on Nicholas' shoulder. "So if you tell me that I can make money for the orphanage while having fun playing poker with my good friends then that makes the fight fit perfectly into my schedule."

"I'm sorry Nicholas," Natalie repeated. "I appreciate and always have appreciated all your help towards the orphanage but I guess I have taken it for granted."

"I want to help the orphanage but I don't want to give my life to it," said Nicholas. "I know running the orphanage has taken a personal toll on you and Howard has never settled down either, I've got too much to lose to be fully dragged into your world."

"I don't blame you, it has been tough," said Natalie.

"It's not too late," said Nicholas. "Howard will get the orphanage out of its rut soon."

"How can you be so sure?" asked Natalie.

"I can't say what it is but I know that Howard has a long term project in mind that will bring much more funding for the orphanage so he still needs me in the short term," said Nicholas.

"I thought he told you it was short term a long time ago," thought Natalie who didn't say another word for the rest of the journey. It seemed Natalie can't bring herself to tell Nicholas that she thinks Mr Lyons doesn't have a solution for the orphanage. It is clear Nicholas and I share an admiration for Mr Lyons that isn't matched by everyone else but we both consider him an influential figure. Nicholas puts Mr Lyons on a pedestal as a brother, businessman and as a friend; everything Mr Lyons says is sacred to him. Nobody said a word for the rest of the journey.

As we were driving along, the houses we passed on the street looked nicer and nicer, I was sure Nicholas was bound to pull up to one of these houses any minute but he kept going. Eventually, Nicholas pulled the car into a massive driveway outside a building that was the size of two houses but only had one doorway; it turned out to be a singular, giant house.

"Here we are," said Nicholas.

"Wow, look at this place," said Natasha.

"Wait until you've seen the inside," said Nicholas as he parked the car. Natasha and Gareth's gaze had been firmly fixed on the house ever since we had begun entering the driveway. Gareth and Natasha exited the car first and before I got out, Natalie and Nicholas started talking.

"This isn't where the couple lives, is it?" Natalie asked him.

"No, this is where Marie lives but the couple's house is still very nice," replied Nicholas.

"Good, after what you have said before about not wanting to spoil anyone, it's clear that Natasha and Gareth are in love with the house and the potential lifestyle that comes with it," said Natalie.

"They'll be disappointed when they find out this isn't the house of Matthew and Geena, their house is nice but understated in comparison to this one," said Nicholas.

"Well, at least it might motivate them to put on a good show for Matthew and Geena," said Nicholas.

"And you trust these people, right?" asked Natalie.

"Of course, I have known them for years; you'll see for yourself that they'd be great parents for the twins," replied Nicholas.

Gareth and Natasha looked backed to the car to see myself, Natalie and Nicholas all still inside, they gestured for us to follow them while they were still in awe of the house.

"I'm coming," said Nicholas. "But where's Sam?"

"I'm right here," I replied.

"Oh, I thought you were already out, never mind," he said as we all got out of the car. Gareth and Natasha were trying to look all around the outside of the house, trying to look over the gate to the side and back of the house.

"Come on you two, stop being so intrusive," Natalie told them. They slowly made their way back to the central path which led up to the front door.

"We're already being intrusive, we're all showing up on short notice," said Natasha.

"She's got a point," said Gareth.

"So, if you don't want this couple knowing the reason Gareth and Natasha are here then what excuse do you have for them being here?" Natalie asked Nicholas.

"Don't worry, I've got it under control, I sent a message to each one of them before we left and they were okay with it," replied Nicholas.

"Fair enough, what's our story?" asked Natalie.

"It's a simple one; you and I took them to hospital appointments but you forgot your keys to get back into the orphanage and you now have to wait a while for Mr Lyons to return," said Nicholas. "I know what you're thinking but they know nothing of the orphanage and they don't ask questions, they have no idea you have a structure in place for hospital visits and they think a whole army of staff work at the orphanage so they won't think the other children are being neglected."

"It's a bit flimsy but I guess there's no harm if they don't ask questions," said Natalie.

"Indeed, here we don't like to talk about work or investments; this is our chance every week to unwind from it all," said Nicholas. Nicholas knocked on the door and a woman with curly ginger hair opened the door.

"Come on in Nicholas," she said. "I take it these are your friends you mentioned?"

"Indeed they are Marie," said Nicholas. "I hope it's not too much trouble."

"As long as they don't make a mess or break anything," said Marie in a scolding manner. "I guess you can come in, shut the door behind you," she told us as she headed off leaving Nicholas to lead the way.

"I'm glad she's not one of our potential parents," Gareth whispered to Natasha who tried to repress her laughter. The laughter was soon replaced by silence once again as both Gareth and Natasha returned to their state of awe as we entered through the opening hallway which seemed to stretch for a while. We came to an open area which had a huge set of stairs leading up to the first floor while there were still a number of rooms on the ground floor judging by the number of doors I saw.

"Then again, I'm sure we would've got used to her ways after a while," Natasha told Gareth.

"So wait, this is Marie's house?" asked Gareth. Nicholas let out a sigh.

"Yes, this is Marie's house," said Nicholas. "I was hoping you wouldn't figure it out for a while because this house might have persuaded you to be at your best for Matthew and Geena."

"Well Marie opening the door was a giveaway and then the way she sounded so protective of this house made it obvious it was hers," said Natasha.

"For the record, we would never be swayed by this house or any other if Matthew and Geena were terrible people," said Gareth.

"I wouldn't recommend any children for them if they were," said Nicholas.

"The point remains, we can't just make this work because we want it to, it either works for all of us or it doesn't," said Natasha.

"That's very wise," said Natalie whose mind was filled with thoughts about her ex-husband and Natasha's comment seemed to resonate with her. We followed Nicholas upstairs through a series of corridors; it was like being back at the hospital, until we reached a huge room that was almost empty. The wallpaper was white and the only items in the room were a table and some chairs where Marie and a couple of other people were sitting. Before we walked over to them, Nicholas stopped us.

"I know what you're thinking," said Nicholas. "But I told you we like to take our mind off of things here so

Marie stripped this room of its furniture and decorations so there are no riches on show here."

"Except for your wads of cash," said Natalie.

"Except that," said Nicholas with a wry smile on his face. I looked over towards the table where Marie was sitting along with two other people who I assumed were Matthew and Geena. If it was them, they looked like a very odd couple. Both were skinny but Geena towered over Matthew even as they were sitting down. Matthew's clothes were very plain with smart shirt and trousers whereas Geena's dress was colourful, much like her hair which was a mixture of pink and purple. This was in contrast to the light brown hair of Matthew.

"Ah, here are our extra guests," said the woman I believed to be Geena. "Come on over, don't be shy." We walked over to the table. "Nice to meet you, I'm Geena and this is Matthew." Matthew gave a quick wave but didn't say anything.

"It's nice to meet you too," said Natasha and Natalie almost at the same time, Gareth and I just nodded in Geena's direction.

"And your names?" asked Geena.

"I'm Sam," I told her.

"I'm Natasha and this is my twin brother Gareth," said Natasha.

"Not much of a talker, are you Gareth?" Geena asked

"She does enough talking for the both of us," replied Gareth as he pointed at Natasha.

"I know that feeling," said Matthew who had finally spoken as his eyes hinted towards Geena. Matthew and Gareth both laughed and eventually Natasha and Geena joined in. It was a good start for Gareth and Natasha; Nicholas gave a quick nod in their direction to acknowledge that.

"Twins and they're orphans, if they behave today and if it feels right, we might have to ask Nicholas about the possibility of adoption," thought Geena.

"And Nicholas of course, how are you?" Geena asked.

"I'm very well, my dear," he replied. Geena then looked over to Natalie.

"And Natalie is it? Will you be playing with us too?" asked Geena.

"Not for the kind of money we play with," Nicholas said as he chuckled.

"How much do you play with?" Natalie asked.

"£5000 each," replied Nicholas.

"No, I'm definitely out then," said Natalie. "I don't think Nicholas winning £20,000 once will be enough to save the orphanage but at least it's something," thought Natalie.

"That's actually something I wanted to discuss with you lot, these guys love playing poker and they want to keep learning but obviously they can't play for money," said Nicholas. "One because they don't have any money and two because they're underage."

"What's your point Nicholas?" asked Marie sharply.

"I was thinking that there are four of us and four of them so maybe each one of them could be our assistant in our game today," replied Nicholas.

"I don't see any reason why not, as long as they're good," said Marie.

"Believe me, they are," said Nicholas who tried to look like he was deep in thought. "Let's have Sam go with me, Natasha can go with Matthew, Gareth can go with Geena and Natalie can go with Marie."

"Sounds wonderful," exclaimed Geena. "Come on over, maybe you lot can tell us about the orphanage, we usually tell the same old stories each week here so it might be nice to change up the conversation."

"Well, there's not too much to say," I told her before sensing that could have killed the conversation dead. "But we'll tell you all you want to know."

"Sounds good," said Geena.

We all sat down next to our partners for the game as the cards were dealt out to each team. Matthew and Geena welcomed Natasha and Gareth with a smile whereas Marie didn't really react to Natalie coming over. Nicholas and his friends each took out a huge pile of notes from their wallets and placed it on the table. There wasn't much chat during the first few rounds; Nicholas' friends were trying to assess how helpful their assistant was during this time. Luckily, my fear of not being able to read their minds was unfounded and so I helped Nicholas win the first few bets.

"Well Sam, you must be good because Nicholas never wins anything," said Marie as she and the couple chuckled.

"Yes, it's true," said Nicholas. "But I feel lucky today."

"Regardless everybody seems to be pretty good at poker, I thought Gareth and I almost had it," said Geena.

"Natasha and I were pretty close too," said Matthew.

"Yeah, with a bit more luck, we could have won," said Natasha.

"On any other day, we would have," said Matthew.

"Sam must be Nicholas' lucky charm," said Gareth.

"Or Sam's just better than Nicholas anyway," said Marie with not much hint that she was joking.

"Anyway, how is life in the orphanage?" Geena asked looking around the table.

"It's okay I guess," said Natasha. "We get food and shelter."

"You mean it's boring but safe?" Geena asked.

"Well yeah," said Natasha hesitantly. "Sorry Natalie."

"That's okay, the children have to make their own entertainment around the orphanage," she said as Nicholas made a gesture to her by moving his eyes back and forth between Natasha and Gareth. "Oh yes, and all three of these lot are great at doing that, they're all full of life."

"How do you pass the time then?" asked Geena.

"Oh silly things really, it requires a lot of imagination for Gareth and I to entertain ourselves," said Natasha.

"You sound ashamed of that," said Geena.

"Well, it is a little bit embarrassing to say it out loud," said Natasha.

"Never be embarrassed by the power of your imagination, it shows you have a creative streak in you which will help you when you grow up," said Geena. "Take me for instance, at school I was told to focus on what they called the real subjects but that wasn't my passion, my passion was art and design."

"So what did you do?" asked Natasha.

"I left school as soon as I could and managed to get a role with a design company and I have worked my way up ever since to lead the company," said Geena.

"Sorry Geena, I'd just like to clarify to Gareth and Natasha that dropping out isn't the only option if you have a creative mind," said Natalie.

"Oh of course not but if you really feel it's the right decision to leave, I wouldn't discourage anybody from taking that route," said Geena.

"Really think about it though," Natalie told Gareth and Natasha.

"Sorry Natalie, I'm sure your job is hard enough without me encouraging them to leave school," she said while letting out a nervous laugh.

"It's no problem, it's nice to hear someone tell them they have alternatives and that they're not stuck on one path," said Natalie. "They're both very independent so I'm sure they appreciate it."

"Oh we do," said Gareth before turning to Matthew. "Are you creative Matthew?" That question was met from laughter from Nicholas and the rest of his friends including Marie.

"Matthew's a banker, does that answer your question?" asked Marie who was trying to suppress her laughter.

"And yet, Geena's still with me," said Matthew.

"Of course, I couldn't leave you with no fun in your life," said Geena.

"I think you're all the fun I can handle, you wouldn't believe how much she stands out when she joins me for parties with my colleagues," said Matthew.

"I could say the same about you with my colleagues," she said as they both began laughing again.

"They're both a bit soppy but they're nice people," though Gareth.

"It's not hard to see who the strict parent would be here," thought Natasha.

"This could work," they both thought at the same time. We resumed playing poker which Nicholas and I won again which led to groans before the conversation resumed.

"Sorry Sam, I should have asked you before, what do you like to do?" Geena asked me. Before I could answer, Gareth interrupted.

"He's obviously too focussed on the game, that's why he's winning," he said.

"My hobby is reading books which doesn't really sound very exciting in comparison to what Gareth and Natasha do," I told her.

"It's really not," said Gareth with a wry smile on his face.

"Well, the important thing is you all seem very mature and seem like you'll become good people, the same can't be said for all orphans," said Geena. Natalie immediately cleared her throat and looked right towards Geena. "Sorry Natalie, I did it again didn't I?"

"It's okay; I know some of the stories but my aim at this orphanage is to nurture all the children so they can become a part of a functional family and a functional member of society, it's obviously harder with the background of some kids but these three have given me no trouble," said Natalie.

"That's good to hear, do you run the orphanage?" asked Geena.

"No, I'm the assistant manager but one day I would like to run it," said Natalie. Only Natasha, Gareth and I knew how much of an understatement that was from Natalie.

"So Howard's still in charge, Nicholas?" Matthew asked him.

"Yes, he's still there, I don't think he can ever be separated from that place," Nicholas replied.

"Oh, I thought he might have been leaving it soon so that he can focus on his politics," said Marie.

"Politics?" I asked as Nicholas' face winced

"Yes, Mr Lyons plans to go into politics but he won't leave the orphanage, he plans to do both and put the money he makes from politics towards the orphanage as well," said Nicholas. That explained what Nicholas meant by Mr Lyons' long term solution and I guess Mr Lyons was trying to revive his attempt to get into politics.

"And he hadn't told the orphans yet?" asked Geena.

"I knew he was interested but even I didn't know he was ready to commit himself to it," said Natalie.

"He'll do a great job, everything he touches turns to gold," said Nicholas. "And if he gives money to the orphanage and raises its profile then it is a win-win situation." Natalie stayed silent. "Anyway, let's get back to the poker," said Nicholas.

"Yes, we got a bit side-tracked there but I'm always fascinated to hear people's stories, particularly those of children," said Geena.

"We'll have to bring them again some time," said Nicholas.

"Yes but next time, I'll take Sam," said Marie.

"Not if I get there first," said Matthew.

"I'd welcome that, you're all great company," said Geena. Geena reminded me of Nurse Scarlett, they both always looked and sounded very happy. The only difference being that I could read Geena's mind which confirmed that her mind was only filled with positive thoughts. Altogether, there was a jovial mood at the table. The couple were getting on with Gareth and Natasha really well and Natalie and Marie were getting along as well. Nicholas and I kept playing and kept winning right until the very end.

"All for me," said Nicholas scooping all the money from the middle of the table towards him.

"It's definitely thanks to Sam," said Marie.

"I think Sam has a special talent, I couldn't say that Gareth or myself made any wrong decisions or gave anything away," said Geena.

"It was the same for us two," said Matthew sitting next to Natasha.

"Nicholas was overdue a win anyway," said Marie.

"Exactly, this could be the start of my winning streak," said Nicholas. This was met by mocking laughter from his friends.

"I don't think Gareth, Natasha and Geena have enough imagination combined to picture that reality," said Marie.

"We'll see next time," said Nicholas.

"You mean we'll see when you don't have Sam on your side," said Marie.

"Exactly," said Nicholas. Natalie checked her watch.

"We should get going soon," Natalie told Nicholas.

"Yes, we'll be off...with all this money," said Nicholas as he grabbed some of the notes and waved it in the faces of his friends. Nicholas' friends stood up and began saying their goodbyes to him before turning to us.

"Goodbye," Marie said to us. "Nicholas knows the way out."

"It was nice meeting all of you," said Geena. "You're welcome here any time."

"It's not your house," thought Marie.

"Oh Nicholas, I'd like a quick word with you," said Geena. "Matthew, could you show these three the way out?"

"Right this way," said Matthew as he walked past us and made a gesture for us to follow him. We followed him back through the maze of the house; Gareth and Natasha were still in awe of the house despite having sat in here for a long while now.

"I don't know how you find your way around this place," Natalie said to Matthew.

"It's easy once you have been here enough times but Geena and I would hate to live here," he said.

"So you don't live in a house like this?" asked Natasha in a disappointed tone.

"No," said Matthew. "Our home is very spacious and well-kept like this one but we don't need this many rooms, I don't even know why Marie needs a house this big though."

"Maybe she bought it just because she can," said Natalie.

"It could well be the reason, ever since we have known her, she's always wanted the most expensive things, Geena and I are a lot more minimalistic," said Matthew. "But everyone has different views on spending money whether you have a lot of it or not."

"Very true," said Natalie. Matthew led us to the front door and opened it up for us.

"Here we are, it was nice meeting all of you," said Matthew.

"And you," said Natalie.

"Goodbye," I said.

"Goodbye Matthew," said Gareth and Natasha adding the personal touch to their goodbyes.

"We really hope to see you again," said Matthew.

"I'm sure we'll be back some time," said Sam.

"I look forward to it," said Matthew as he closed the door behind us. We headed towards Nicholas' car but we still had to wait for Nicholas to come out so Gareth and Natasha went back to exploring the outside of the house. Eventually, Nicholas came back outside which led to Gareth and Natasha sprinting back towards his car. Nicholas unlocked the car and we all got back inside it.

"I love those guys," he said. "They're such a bunch of colourful characters."

"Geena seemed to be the only one with any colour," said Natalie.

"Alright, I take it back," said Nicholas. "I meant to say that they all have their own little quirks that make the group dynamic so positive even though none of us are alike."

"What did Geena want to talk to you about anyway?" asked Natalie.

"It's good news," said Nicholas as he started up the engine. "Geena was really interested in coming to the orphanage one day with Matthew."

"That's great," said Natalie.

"To see us, right?" asked Natasha referring to herself and Gareth.

"Yes, to see you," Nicholas said. "I told them how Mr Lyons likes to meet the parents several times and have them meet the kids several times at the orphanage but I can't see any reason he would say no to them."

"You did like them, didn't you?" Natalie asked Natasha and Gareth with a hint of worry in her voice.

"They can be a bit soppy but I'll take that over miserable parents any day," said Natasha. "And they don't seem to want to take all our independence away so I think this could work out well for us."

"I agree," said Gareth.

"Wonderful, I'll let Mr Lyons know as soon as possible," said Nicholas.

Chapter 10

Nicholas drove us straight back to the orphanage as quickly as possible while remaining under the speed limit. It was important that Mr Lyons didn't find out we had been away for a few hours otherwise we'd all be in trouble. As the car came to a halt outside the orphanage, we all jumped out of the car with the exception of Nicholas.

"Aren't you coming back in?" asked Natasha.

"No, I can't go back in there and give him the money straight away, he'll suspect something was up," replied Nicholas.

"He's right," I said. "If Mr Lyons catches us entering the orphanage with just Natalie, we might be able to explain our way out of it but with Nicholas as well, it might be impossible."

"I'll return tomorrow to give Mr Lyons the money," said Nicholas.

"We look forward to it," said Natalie as Nicholas began to drive off. We quickly walked up to the orphanage entrance. Natalie pulled out her keys and opened the doors. "Good afternoon everyone," said Natalie with her head swivelling from side to side on the lookout for Mr Lyons. It was hard not to hear the doors open so it always drew the attention of people when it is opened. The real worry was that even if Mr Lyons wasn't near the entrance area, he might emerge from his office and see who had come in from the top of the stairs. Natalie turned round to us and ushered us inside. The only people in the area were some of the orphans who were preoccupied with their own friends, presumably after seeing that only Natalie had supposedly come through the doors. We hurried inside and made sure to move further inwards in our group to make it appear like we had been settled in one spot for a while.

"No sign of Mr Lyons, that's good," said Gareth.

"And a bonus is that none of the other orphans saw us either though I'm not sure how much they would care about it," said Natasha.

"We can all relax now," I said.

"We just have to stay put and wait for Nicholas to return with the money that we know can make a big difference to this orphanage," said Natalie. "That means no going into Mr Lyons' room over the next few days."

"We won't ruin it," I told Natalie. "We wouldn't want to jeopardise any chance to save and improve the orphanage." Gareth and Natasha were silent but nodded in approval.

"I'm glad we agree, I'll see you three later," said Natalie.

"See you later," we said to her in unison as she wandered off.

"Now what do we do?" asked Natasha.

"You heard her, we wait," Gareth told her.

"Exactly, now we go back to what we were doing before we found out about the money problems; we go back to having fun," I said.

"Most of our ideas for fun involved breaking into Mr Lyons' office though," said Natasha.

"Your idea of fun!" exclaimed Gareth and I together.

"Whatever," said Natasha.

"I think we've had enough poker for one day too," said Gareth.

"Well, we'll have to use our imaginations," I said. "I think we've shown that we can come up with some pretty good ideas." The rest of the day went by very slowly as we found it hard to entertain ourselves. If we didn't have anything to wait for, we probably would have enjoyed it more but, in reality, we were desperate to pass the time until Nicholas' return. We wanted to see what Nicholas' donation would mean for the orphanage and we were impatient to see the results.

The next day was similar; it felt like a chore to try and pass the time before Nicholas' arrival. We sat around near the entrance doors anticipating Nicholas' return although we knew that even though we would see him, we couldn't expect to see work being done to improve the orphanage for at least a few days. We saw Natalie come down the stairs.

"I've just got word from Nicholas; he said he'll be here in a few minutes," Natalie told us.

"Finally!" exclaimed Natasha.

"It's only been a day," said Natalie.

"Yeah and it was one of the longest days of my life," said Natasha.

"Don't mind her," Gareth said. "You know she has a flair for the dramatic."

"Do not," muttered Natasha.

"We just really want this to work out," I said.

"I know you do and I'm grateful for it," said Natalie. "I may think Mr Lyons shouldn't be in charge but as long as he makes some changes to the orphanage with Nicholas' money, I'll have to work alongside him for now."

"You really don't trust Mr Lyons, do you?" I asked her.

"I don't trust him to do everything he can for the sake of the orphanage like I have," replied Natalie. "But as long as he implements some changes now that I know he has the money, I can't be at his throat constantly; it wouldn't be in the best interest of the orphanage if I were to do that." It turns out Natalie meant every word of what she said, her focus really was on saving the orphanage rather than her own desire to be in charge. I felt guilty for viewing Natalie's thoughts of wanting to take control of the orphanage as sinister when, in reality, she feels like she's better suited to lead the orphanage going forward. Suddenly, there was a loud, continuous knock on the door and I snapped out of my focus on Natalie's mind.

"I really hope that's him," I said.

"With knocking like that, I doubt it could be anyone else," said Natalie as she unlocked the doors to reveal Nicholas standing outside.

"Well, hello again," said Nicholas.

"I take it you have the money with you still?" asked Natalie.

"Of course," replied Nicholas patting to a bulk in his jacket pocket.

"You didn't think it was a smarter idea to transfer the money straight to his bank account?" asked Natasha.

"No, I told him not to," said Natalie. "I wanted to make sure Mr Lyons had the physical money in his possession." It was clear that Natalie still didn't trust Mr Lyons.

"Mr Lyons likes a lot of my donations to be put forward in straight cash anyway but it's never usually this much," said Nicholas. It appeared that Natalie still hadn't expressed her discontent with Mr Lyons to Nicholas which I guess was not surprising. Her relationship with Nicholas is strong but she knows that might be ruined if she had a bad word to say about Mr Lyons who Nicholas seems to hold in the highest regard. It doesn't seem as if Mr Lyons has told him about his problems with Natalie, they both seem to appreciate the difficult situation Nicholas would be put in if he knew they were at each other's throats. If it did come down to it, I'd assume Nicholas would be fully on his brother's side.

"Try and find out what he intends to do with the money, if possible," Natalie told Nicholas.

"What do you mean what he intends to do?" asked Nicholas who sounded slightly irritated. "His intention is always to help the orphanage."

"I know that Nicholas, I meant specifics," replied Natalie. "Of course as the responsible owner of this orphanage, he would spend this money on the orphanage but I'd like to know what he will specifically improve, just so I know what to expect."

"Oh of course," said Nicholas without a hint of irritation left in his voice.

"In the past when we have had work done on the orphanage, the people Mr Lyons calls in usually get here reasonably quickly," said Natalie.

"Is he expecting you?" I asked Nicholas.

"Oh yes, he knows I'm here to make a donation but he doesn't know that it's more than usual, I wanted to surprise him," replied Nicholas. "He told me just to head straight up to his room, if he didn't already greet me down here, which it doesn't look like he will."

"Doesn't look like it," said Natalie.

"But should I tell him I won it at poker?" asked Nicholas.

"You could do," Natalie said. "Mr Lyons didn't raise any questions yesterday on the whereabouts of myself, Sam, Gareth and Natasha."

"I'll probably get a telling-off from him about gambling my money in the first place but I can handle that," said Nicholas.

"But does he also know about your losing streak up until yesterday?" I asked.

"Yes," replied Nicholas.

"Wouldn't it be suspicious to him that you won?" I asked.

"No, I don't think he's bothered that much," he said. "He'll probably just congratulate me and make a joke of it."

"Don't forget to tell him about Matthew and Geena," said Natasha.

"Oh, I had actually forgotten that," said Nicholas. "Don't worry, my memory might be bad but I won't forget it in the next half hour or so."

"This could be a very important day, for our future and the future of the orphanage," said Gareth.

"I've got to say I'm very excited for all of you and my brother, I can see how much it means to each of you," said Nicholas.

"It's the only place I've been able to call home," I said. "Even if I were to leave tomorrow, I'd want to see the orphanage do well."

"Don't you worry about that," said Nicholas. "I'll go up soon, hand the money to Mr Lyons and you can expect to see some improvements around here and move a step closer towards keeping the orphanage running in the long term."

"We'll still need to do more but this is a good start though," said Natalie.

"We'll have to wait and see," I said.

"Uh oh, you know what that means for you two?" Natalie asked Gareth and Natasha.

"No," they said in unison.

"You'll have to do more waiting," said Natalie with a smile on her face but Gareth and Natasha didn't react.

"I should go up and see him, give you two a lot less time to wait," said Nicholas. "I'll come back down and let you know what he said."

"See you in a bit," said Natalie. Nicholas patted the bulk in his jacket pocket once more before heading upstairs. "Come and find me when he comes back down if I'm not here," said Natalie as she wandered off. The three of us had a sit down on the orphanage floor. We were in a similar situation to yesterday; we didn't feel the motivation to do anything in particular until we received feedback from Nicholas. Our minds were too focussed on the fate of the orphanage to relax. We couldn't shake the nagging feeling that Nicholas' money wouldn't actually make a huge difference to the orphanage, not having knowledge of the realistic costs of improvements to the orphanage.

The wait for Nicholas' return from upstairs was very brief; it couldn't have been more than fifteen minutes. We spent that time in near silence, not only between us but the rest of the orphans weren't making much noise in that time. The silence was broken by the creaking of the stairs under Nicholas' weight. As soon as Nicholas reached the bottom of the stairs, Natalie began to make her way down from the top. The sound made from Nicholas' steps appeared to have alerted Natalie that the meeting was over. Nicholas headed back over to us in the same spot we were in when he left us.

"Where's Natalie?" asked Nicholas.

"Right there," said Gareth pointing behind Nicholas to Natalie who was halfway down the stairs and gave a wave towards us.

"I could barely hear her come down; her footsteps must be so light," said Nicholas.

"I don't think it's the footsteps that are light," thought Natasha.

"Well, how'd it go?" asked Natalie as she walked towards us.

"It went really well," replied Nicholas. "I showed him the money and even told him where I got it from and he seemed grateful."

"But I thought he has always had a problem with you gambling," I said.

"Well maybe that's just because I always used to lose," said Nicholas as he chuckled to himself. "I couldn't tell if he was joking or not but he told me to keep up my winning streak and donate again if I won."

"If he's happy with that way of making money, that's great news," said Natasha.

"We would have a constant source of funding," I said. "And if you placed confidence in me, we could play for more and more money until the orphanage is saved."

"That would mean we would have to cover up where you three have been next week and every week from then for one day a week," Natalie told us.

"Well, that brings me onto some more good news," said Nicholas. "I told him about Matthew and Geena, he said that he would like to be in contact with them soon."

"You mean they might get to take us to a new home?" asked Natasha.

"Yes although Mr Lyons didn't give a timeframe on when they could come in," replied Nicholas. "That might mean we would only have to sneak all three of you out for a couple of weeks before Natasha and Gareth are free to join us for our poker games."

"Winning at poker seems like a good short term solution but I'm not sure we could keep it up, no matter if it's one or three of you we have to sneak in," said Natalie. "And surely Sam can't win every week."

"You might be surprised," I said.

"Anyway, what did Mr Lyons say about how he would spend the money?" Natalie asked Nicholas.

"Well, he seemed to mirror everything you said," Nicholas replied. "He said the money would be spent on fixing and improving the orphanage's appearance, starting with the loose fixtures around here, rather than the normal running costs."

"That's great to hear," said Natalie. "It's about time the orphanage got fixed up, more than anything; it will raise the mood in here."

"I'd better be off now," said Nicholas. "But I'm sure I'll see you all again soon."

"Goodbye Nicholas, thanks for all your help," I said to him.

"And not just for today but for your donations to the orphanage over a number of years," said Natalie.

"You're very welcome," said Nicholas who gave Natalie a hug goodbye.

He then shook the hands of the three of us children. As I shook his hand, I looked over his shoulder to see Mr Lyons staring down at us from the top of the stairs; he seemed to have a neutral expression on his face and he slowly averted his gaze from us once I had spotted him. As Nicholas exited the orphanage, I looked back to the top of the stairs but Mr Lyons was no longer there. Now, all we could do was wait for a new and improved orphanage over the coming days.

Three days had passed with little incident; there had been no obvious action taken in regards to fixing the orphanage and there was no sighting of Nicholas either. I knew that Natalie was trying to think of a way to somehow bring it up with Mr Lyons without giving away the fact that we know about the money. Gareth, Natasha and I had managed to relax and enjoy ourselves over those few days with the potential for improvements to the orphanage. A few days without seeing any changes had threatened to make us stress out about the orphanage once more but we kept faith.

On the fourth day, I had woken up early and wanted to leave the dormitory as soon as I could as it felt particularly humid that morning. I got up as soon as I heard the key hitting the door, getting changed quickly and heading towards the main area awaiting the call from the dining room for breakfast. Gareth and Natasha remained in their rooms, I wasn't sure if they were awake or not. Natalie saw me sat down near the dining room and headed over to me.

"You're up early," she said.

"Yeah, I couldn't really sleep, it's so stuffy in there," I said.

"I asked Nicholas if he could contact Mr Lyons to find out if he had arranged any work," said Natalie. "However, Mr Lyons has been telling Nicholas that he's getting to it but he is no longer being specific about it."

"I'm sure we'll see something soon," I said to her.

"I hope so," said Natalie as she headed off.

Mr Lyons emerged from the caretaker's cupboard, acknowledged me with a nod and then headed straight past me out the front of the orphanage. The stress of not knowing what was happening with Nicholas' money was the main reason I couldn't sleep. I wanted reassurance that work was being done. And I knew there was only one way to get that information; break into Mr Lyons' office.

Chapter 11

The stress of not knowing what Mr Lyons had planned for the orphanage convinced me that I needed to try and find something in his office to offer a glimmer of hope. I had no idea where Mr Lyons had gone or how long he would be but I decided it was time for me to take a chance. I didn't feel like I could wake Natasha or Gareth and ask them to come with me or indeed Natalie. I know Natalie and I were the ones promoting the value of patience, not poking around Mr Lyons' office so I didn't want any of them to know that I was about to go against that and I didn't want any of them to get into trouble if caught.

Nobody else was up by this point or, if they were, they hadn't got up out of bed. I walked towards the caretaker's cupboard first to check if he was downstairs; he wasn't. The cupboard looked the cleanest I had seen it in a while, the cleanliness of the room is often disregarded by the caretaker since he can choose to go across the road straight to his home if he wants to. I didn't want to raise any suspicion at all from anyone, adult or orphan so the caretaker not being around was a good start. If Natalie caught me, it wouldn't be disastrous but I would rather avoid that confrontation.

I slowly crept my way upstairs. It was impossible to make no noise treading on the stairs but I was confident nobody would have heard me. Most people would probably assume it was Natalie or Mr Lyons anyway. I walked straight past Mr Lyons' office to first check to see if Natalie had returned to her office; the lights in her office were off. I headed back towards Mr Lyons' office door but paused for a few seconds just to make sure that Mr Lyons hadn't yet re-entered the orphanage. I typed in the code of 2404 and the door opened.

As soon as I opened the door up, I heard an audible gasp come from within the room. Natalie poked her head up from behind Mr Lyons' desk.

"Sam, thank god it's only you," she exclaimed with relief. I thought she would have been angry that I was here but instead she was relieved.

"Natalie, you're-" I began to say.

"Doing the same thing that you planned to do," interrupted Natalie. "I told you how frustrated I have felt over the past few years when Mr Lyons has made promises which he hasn't kept and that frustration is in you too."

"I just want to find something to let me know that change is coming," I said.

"I'd like that too," said Natalie. "But the more likely option is that we'll find something to suggest he doesn't intend on making any changes and I'll use it against him."

"How can you prove that he doesn't intend to do something?" I asked.

"By finding out where all this money is going instead," replied Natalie. "I don't think there's anything in the files scattered around here but I have found a drawer by his desk that is locked that I have been working at breaking into since Mr Lyons left his office."

"Don't you think we might be taking this a bit far?" I asked. "If he is genuinely doing all he can then we're just breaking into his office and his drawers for no reason."

"But you are here for a reason Sam, just like me, if you genuinely thought Mr Lyons was doing all he can then you wouldn't be here," said Natalie. I was feeling very conflicted by this point. What Natalie had said about my thoughts and motivation was true but at the same time, I felt like I was betraying a lifelong friend in Mr Lyons.

"I'd feel more comfortable looking through the files that aren't locked away," I said.

"That's fine, you have a closer look around and I'll work on getting into these drawers," said Natalie. It felt like I had to compromise between my curiosity regarding the state of the orphanage and my respect for Mr Lyons; I'd break into his room but I didn't want a part in breaking open a drawer with files he had locked away. Natalie was making a bit of noise trying to open up the drawer while I remained silent. I felt it was important to make as little noise as possible so we could listen out for the front entrance doors opening. I walked around the room picking folders at random to open up and see if it contained any useful information but most folders were just filled with spreadsheets.

"Can't seem to find anything here," I said to Natalie who didn't respond as she continued to work on the drawer so I began to wander around aimlessly instead until I heard a click come from Mr Lyons' desk.

"Got it," said Natalie. "Come on over Sam, these are the files he really doesn't want anyone to see." Natalie picked up the first few files and placed them on the table. I headed over to the table as she began flicking through the files. The first few files didn't look much different from the others; they too were filled with spreadsheets.

"Unless you want to look through hundreds of pages of spreadsheets to find some slight irregularity in his finances, that won't help," I told Natalie.

"There's got to be something, just not in these ones," said Natalie who picked another few files out of the drawer. She flicked through a couple more files all filled with spreadsheets. "No, you're right Sam, there are years and years worth of accounts here, we won't find anything useful in such a short amount of time," said Natalie as she placed her hands over her head and sighed. I decided to look through the rest of the files she had placed on the table. It seemed like an endless supply of spreadsheets until I finally came across a file that had none. Instead, the file was a big collection of letters, many of them sent from the local council.

"Take a look at these," I told Natalie as she removed her hands from her face.

"They're just letters from the local council, not very rare for someone who runs a business," said Natalie.

"Yes but none of them are to do with the orphanage, they're all about Mr Lyons personally as if they are having a conversation with him," I said.

"A conversation about what?" asked Natalie.

"It seems to be discussions about the inner workings of politics, locally and nationally," I said. "Trying to get insight into a political career."

"He tried that before," said Natalie.

"But these are dated from this year," I said. "Don't forget that Nicholas' friends mentioned Mr Lyons was still looking to get into politics." Natalie suddenly stopped her frantic flipping of files and fixated on one particular letter.

"Look at this one here sent to him last year," said Natalie. The letter was handwritten on a scrappy piece of paper with no sender address on it. It read:

'Dear Howard,

I'm sorry to hear about the difficulties the local council have been giving you in your enquiries in regards to a career in politics.

You should have come to me sooner, I could have saved you all the back and forth and mumbo jumbo from the council.

I have personally contacted the council on your behalf and told them that I would be very happy to vouch for you and that I would personally like to help you get into politics.

I understand that the orphanage is very important to you as well so whenever you feel like you're ready to start, I'd like to meet up. I'd suggest that a career in politics and a career as an orphanage owner might be impossible to balance so you may want to consider relinquishing control.

I know you have ambitions of starting your own party one day but as I'm sure you are aware, you're going to need to save up a lot of money for that. I would hope that our two parties could have the support of each other.

Kind regards.'

Where a name should have been was a very messy signature.

"I can't make out this signature," I said to Natalie.

"I'd say with the way the sender is talking it could only be one person," said Natalie.

"Who?" I asked.

"The Prime Minister, I know he has met him," replied Natalie. "You look at the influence he wields being able to take the local council right out of the equation."

"Which would give Mr Lyons a smoother route into politics after he failed a couple of years ago," I said.

"And maybe, a couple of years ago, he couldn't find a way to keep the orphanage running while also having a political career," said Natalie.

"But surely, he could make enough money from politics to continue funding the orphanage while leaving someone else in charge," I said.

"Not if he wants to form his own party like the letter suggested," said Natalie. "He wouldn't be able to afford both."

"Unfortunately the letter doesn't really tell us anything new, we were aware he wanted to get into politics but he hasn't done that yet nor has he sold the orphanage," I said.

"We'd best keep looking," said Natalie. I decided to take a look in the drawer myself. At the very back of the drawer, I saw a first aid kit that looked bigger than ones I had seen the caretaker use.

"I think we should take a look at this here," I said.

"It's just a first aid kit," said Natalie.

"I haven't seen any first aid kits this size and if he needed to use it for himself, why would he keep it locked away instead of it being ready to hand?" I asked. "If he suddenly felt weak, he'd have the hassle of unlocking the drawers and having to drag all the files out the way to get it out of the drawer."

"You raise a good point there Sam," said Natalie. I shook the briefcase around and there was no sound of anything rattling inside. I opened it up to find a number of documents inside. "These all look like medical reports."

"Maybe Mr Lyons isn't well; maybe he's losing his capability to run the orphanage but he's too proud to admit it," I said as I began to worry for the health of Mr Lyons.

"We'll see," said Natalie who didn't sound convinced. None of the reports had any names on them at all, no names of patients, doctors or nurses or even the hospital it took place in. "They look like medical reports from a distance but up close, it's not laid out very professionally at all, I can't believe these would have come from a hospital."

"But why would Mr Lyons have a pile of anonymous medical reports that might be faked?" I asked.

"I have no idea," replied Natalie.

"Mr Lyons knows Nurse Scarlett; maybe he wanted to keep his medical history a secret and used her help to do it," I said.

"I doubt Mr Lyons would go to these lengths to conceal his own medical history," said Natalie. "And no nurse would risk their career by forging reports for the sake of concealing an illness for a patient."

"He must want to hide something though given how well concealed these files were," I said.

"Well, let's find out then," said Natalie as we both began to read the reports. There was no frantic flipping through this time; instead we studied each report in detail. The bulkiest report had the title *'A Study into the Human Brain and its Potential to Perceive Brain Wave Signals of Another.'*

"That just sounds like gibberish to me," I said.

"Perceive brain wave signals," said Natalie.

"What does it mean?" I asked.

"Well, from what I understand, the study suggests that the brainwaves of two different brains could be linked, maybe they mean empathy," said Natalie.

"Empathy?" I asked.

"Yes you know, when your mind puts you in the shoes of another person, you feel sorry for them because you understand how they're feeling," replied Natalie.

"Understand how they're feeling," I repeated.

"Are you alright Sam?" Natalie asked. "You seem to be stuck in a trance of repeating the last few words I say." I didn't want to believe it but the words Natalie used made me realise it was obvious what the study was about though I'm not sure Natalie would believe me.

"The ability to read minds," I said.

"What?" asked Natalie who sounded shocked.

"It's a study about the ability to read minds," I said.

"To become a magician or what?" asked Natalie.

"No, it's not based on any kind of trick," I replied.

"How do you know?" asked Natalie.

"Because I can read minds," I told her. "I've been able to since birth." Natalie was left speechless and she didn't seem to believe it but she looked deep in thought.

"Is that why you won every time at poker?" she asked.

"Yes and that's how I knew no matter what you told me, you did want to remove Mr Lyons," I replied.

"If all this is true, then why can't you read Mr Lyons' mind and find out what he has been up to?" asked Natalie.

"I've never been able to read his mind, I don't know why that is but I can with almost everybody else, when I want to," I replied.

"You mean you can control it?" asked Natalie.

"Yes, I have the choice of reading someone's mind or not," I replied.

"And you never said anything about it to anyone?" asked Natalie.

"I'm not sure what I could say without sounding crazy especially in the eyes of Mr Lyons, a person whose mind I can't even read," I replied.

"Well maybe this study, if it really is a look into mind reading, can explain why that is," said Natalie. The first page of the study was just a huge diagram of a human brain with a number of labels pointing to different sections of the brain. One of the labels identified and pointed to the cerebral cortex and it was highlighted. A note written below the diagram said:

'Previous studies of brains suggest the supramarginal gyrus located in the cerebral cortex would be the most likely area of the brain to give humans this ability-further research needed. 6th June 1997.'

We went on to the next page without saying a word to each other. A small note read:

'The only way progress can be achieved in this area of research is to study a live brain that may already possess this ability. 31st July 1997.'

"So they needed to monitor the brain of someone who was alive and had the ability to read minds," said Natalie.

"That means the people running the study already knew that mind-reading was possible otherwise they wouldn't assume they could find someone who has the ability," I said.

"This study wasn't set up to find out if it was possible, they wanted to know how it worked," said Natalie. Natalie turned to the next page.

'A subject who had this ability has been identified and is to be referred to as Subject 1. However, the subject can no longer replicate the ability that they have shown in the past. Surgery may be the only option to try and rediscover their hidden ability. 1st September 1997.'

"It seems like they found someone who used to be able to read minds but no longer could," I said.

"That sounds like a very invasive surgery, to experiment on the brain of Subject 1 to try and get their ability back," said Natalie. "I can't believe any person would let the surgery be performed on them for the sake of research."

"Maybe they wanted to get their ability back," I suggested.

"If you lost it, would you want it back?" Natalie asked me. I stayed silent and went onto the next page.

'The surgery was a success!-

The operation on Subject 1 can be deemed a success.

The operation was carried out and any potential damage to the brain was avoided, early signs show.

Subject 1 has been kept unconscious for several days while their brainwave activity is monitored.

Although Subject 1 has lost their ability, stimulation of the supramarginal gyrus should lead to heightened activity in the brain which may provide us with results not expected of a normal brain wave pattern.

However, we do not expect that Subject 1 will regain their ability to read the minds of others but we are confident the data gathered as a result of this operation will be invaluable for us.

Having worked on the brain during the experiment, we do not believe that it is possible for any subject to relearn this ability.

Subject 1 is expected to make a full recovery. 30th September 1997.'

"I can't believe they actually went through with the surgery," I said. "Even if they told Subject 1 that they would be okay."

"It doesn't look like they keep up the same level of optimism for Subject 1's health," said Natalie as she looked over to the next page.

'Side effect for Subject 1!

Subject 1 has woken from this procedure displaying a few symptoms that indicate damage to the brain.

Work in and around the supramarginal gyrus appears to have affected the mental capacity of Subject 1. Fortunately, Subject 1 motor skills seemed to be unaffected.

It is expected that a loss of mental capacity is only a temporary side effect of the operation. 1st October 1997.'

'Subject 1 leaves hospital!-

Having been monitored for several weeks, we are satisfied that it is safe to release Subject 1 to allow the subject to rest at home.

We have decided we will not learn anything new from any more readings of Subject 1's brain waves but the results of the experiment and scans are very promising indeed.

The experiment and resulting scans lead us to believe that the supramarginal gyrus is the correct area of the brain to study in future; this means no further surgery is needed on any future patients monitored.

If more operations do need to take place, we hope that we can soon have access to equipment that will make procedures less invasive.

The subject may still feel weak but displayed promising signs that they have returned to their regular mental capacity.

Subject 1 is not advised to return to work for several months to ensure a full recovery. 23rd October 1997.'

"So, Subject 1 survived the ordeal," I said.

"And apparently, all they had to do was rest and then they could get on with their life," said Natalie.

"Subject 1 went through all that without getting his ability back, I'd be pretty annoyed if I was them," I said.

"They might have been too mentally fatigued to really think about it, they probably had no idea how they ended up in a hospital bed for the first few days," said Natalie.

"It seems like they didn't really need to do the operation to stimulate the brain," I said.

"Their main motivation must have been for Subject 1 to relearn the ability; he might have demanded the doctor try anything he could in order for that to happen," said Natalie.

"This makes for some really grim reading, I don't see why Mr Lyons has it," I said.

"He obviously had some kind of interest in this study," said Natalie.

"I wonder how much progress they made," I pondered.

"I can't believe this study exists about mind-reading," said Natalie. "But then you said you can read minds?"

"That's correct; it's an ability I have never lost unlike Subject 1," I replied.

"So it does exist then?" asked Natalie. "It isn't a case of a madman cutting people's heads open because they think mind-reading exists?"

"No, to have that kind of commitment to it, they would surely have to know it existed," I replied.

"There are more reports below," said Natalie.

"Let's hope they didn't have to experiment on anybody else like they predicted," I said.

"I'd hope not, it looks like the rest of these reports involve children," Natalie told me.

It read:

'Six babies at the nearby hospital have been identified as potential mind-readers according to abnormalities in their brain waves.

Throughout their early years, the brain wave patterns of these six children will need to be constantly monitored to provide us with data which will help us understand their ability.

The parents have been informed that the babies will need regular check-ups at the hospital but have been told it is just precautionary.

We hope the data provided by these six will allow us to discover the secrets of mind-reading and provide knowledge of how to unlock this ability in all humans. 5th February 1998.'

"They didn't just want to learn about it, they wanted to find a way to allow everyone to have the ability to read minds," I said.

"I'd imagine it would be a very popular procedure, maybe this was all one big research project to develop a drug or procedure that can allow humans to read minds and sell it on at a huge price," said Natalie.

"But how would society manage and how would people cope with each other if everybody could read each other's minds?" I asked.

"I'm not sure they thought that through, they would have only been interested in the money," replied Natalie.

There were a number of reports on these children dating from 1998 to 2002 with mixed results.

'Two years into the study, the six children have been evaluated regularly.

Unfortunately, three of the children's brain waves now show a normal pattern.

Another two have left the area and are now treated at a different hospital so no more data can be compiled on them.

There is one remaining child who has retained their abnormal brain wave patterns so they will continue to be monitored. 5th February 2000.'

Natalie flicked through a few more reports which all said the same thing about abnormal brain readings when it came to the one remaining child. Then, we saw a different, more detailed report.

'It has come to our attention that for the last three years, the one remaining child with this ability has been in the care of numerous foster parents but has failed to settle down in any home.

From what we can see, this is the only difference between this child and the remaining three who lost their ability; the three children living with their parents have lost this ability but the other child hasn't.

This could suggest that a child's potential to learn and keep this skill can alter depending on the environment they live in. 6th March 2001.'

"That child wasn't me, was it?" I asked as I began looking at the dates. "I know Mr Lyons said I was born in 2003 but it all just seems to match up so well, me not having parents and possibly jumping from foster home to foster home." I wondered if that was why he wouldn't let me leave the orphanage.

"No, I was here when you arrived in 2003," said Natalie. "You came in here almost as soon as you were born, I had no idea why."

"So, there's at least one other person in the world who still has this ability," I said.

"Assuming they didn't eventually lose it which, according to this report, they didn't," said Natalie continuing to flick through the files. "Here's something from 2003 though."

"What does it say?" I asked.

"Take a look," Natalie told me.

'Assuming the potential to maintain an ability to read minds from birth is linked to nurture, it is necessary to find

a child born with this ability and to be out of the care of parents to move this research forward.

The likelihood of these two events combining will be very rare. 4th April 2003.'

"They were looking for either an orphaned child or a child removed from their family with mind-reading abilities," said Natalie. "That sounds like a more fitting description of you." I looked over the page to the next report.

"This one's dated 16th June 2003, my birthday," I said as we began reading.

'A child born today has been identified as having the potential for possessing mind-reading abilities but has been born to two parents.

'Another child with normal brain readings has been born an orphan. The father was already deceased and the mother died in childbirth.'

"That's me," I said. "I was told at the hospital that my father died before I was born and my mother died in childbirth.

"But why would you have normal brain readings if you could also read minds?" asked Natalie. I had no response; instead I continued reading down the page. It continued:

'There is too much risk of this child losing its ability or moving away to a different hospital where we can no longer keep track of them.

The parents of the baby who may be a mind-reader haven't seen their baby in the flesh yet so as to not recognise the face shape.

The orphaned, normal child will go in place of this special child who must be brought up under strict conditions. 16th June 2003.'

"I don't understand," I said to Natalie who looked deep in thought. I noticed a piece of scrap paper with a hastily written note on it which read *'None of this would be possible without Nicholas Lyons.'* I didn't want to believe that Nicholas could be involved with this research too. Just then, we could hear the footsteps of someone coming upstairs and by the sound of it, it was Mr Lyons heading back to his office. I immediately put down the piece of scrap paper. "Natalie, we need to clear this up and get out of here."

"No, we don't have to go anywhere," she told me. "I think we need to have a word with Mr Lyons."

Chapter 12

I was desperate for Natalie and I to leave but she insisted on standing and waiting for Mr Lyons.

"Natalie, why are we still here?" I asked her.

"I told you, we'll need to have a word with Mr Lyons about this," she replied.

"Can't you speak to him afterwards?" I asked.

"If we do, he'll deny it," said Natalie. "We have to confront him with the evidence right in front of our face."

"I still don't understand, I don't understand any of it," I said. "I still don't know what you mean." I was feeling so flustered by the dread of being caught by Mr Lyons that I couldn't focus on reading the mind of Natalie to find out what she was up to.

"You'll see when he gets here," Natalie told me. By this point, Mr Lyons was just outside the door and I heard the click of the door as the code to enter the office was entered. Mr Lyons opened the door quickly probably having already seen our outlines through the window to the office. He entered in silence. I didn't want to look at him but Natalie was looking dead ahead at him.

"Natalie, Sam, how could you break into my office?" he asked calmly. "I'm really disappointed in both of you, especially you Sam." I kept my head down.

"I don't think us breaking in is the real issue here, is it?" asked Natalie waving the report we had just been reading in her hands.

"I think it definitely is the real issue, you two are going through all my personal files," said Mr Lyons.

"I'm sorry sir," I said.

"It's alright Sam, I forgive you," he said. "It's clear that you're here against your will."

"Well I...I..," I began to say.

"It's okay Sam," said Mr Lyons. "Just be on your way while I talk to Natalie." Natalie was remaining silent, unwillingly to reveal what the real issue was so I was curious enough to stay and find out.

"Actually sir, I came in here of my own accord," I told Mr Lyons. "And I want to know what you and Natalie have to talk about so I'll stay."

"You accuse me of manipulating Sam and doing things against his will?" Natalie asked Mr Lyons. "But you've been doing it his whole life."

"What nonsense are you spouting?" asked Mr Lyons. "I have looked after Sam all his life; I have given him a home from the very beginning."

"You told him that I was plotting against you," said Natalie.

"You were plotting against me!" exclaimed Mr Lyons.

"But you told Sam about it so that Sam could admire your honesty while distracting him from the questions he has asked over and over again without getting an honest answer," Natalie told him.

"I have told Sam many times that I really can't reveal anything about his family," said Mr Lyons. "I thought he had come to terms with that and I still don't see what Sam's family has got to do with you two breaking into my office."

"We don't trust you!" exclaimed Natalie.

"Oh, 'we' is it?" asked Mr Lyons. "Sam, tell me that you don't trust me and tell me why you're here." I was trying to look anywhere besides Mr Lyons' face. "Look at me!" I immediately looked up directly at his face.

"I just had doubts about how much was being done to help the orphanage," I said hesitantly.

"Do you trust me?" Mr Lyons asked very slowly.

"I'm not sure," I said. "I used to trust you fully but now I can't help but think the arguments Natalie makes against you add up." Mr Lyons didn't respond.

"Sam definitely won't trust you after this," said Natalie who once again waved the report round in her hand.

"He won't trust me because of some medical reports?" asked Mr Lyons in a derisory tone.

"Sam may not fully understand these reports because he doesn't want to believe it's true of someone like you," said Natalie. "I was hoping you would have given up this charade as soon as you saw me with this report in my hand."

"I'm still waiting for this big revelation," said Mr Lyons.

"These files, these procedures into the studying of mind-reading are all your doing," she said.

"That's not true; I will admit that I have been supporting the research because I'm curious but I have never put money into it at the expense of the orphanage," said Mr Lyons.

"I could almost believe you were just a donor in this whole thing but the last page we read made me think otherwise," said Natalie. "The experiment on Subject 1 and the scans on the children were bad enough but you really took it to a new low." The confidence from Mr Lyons' face had drained; where before he was making derisory remarks towards Natalie, he was now staring at her with a soulless, stony expression.

"Wouldn't it be better he didn't know?" asked Mr Lyons.

"Will someone please tell me what I'm missing here?" I asked.

"Natalie, think about this," said Mr Lyons.

"This is your last chance to tell him before I do," Natalie told Mr Lyons. Mr Lyons didn't respond so Natalie turned to face me. "Sam, Mr Lyons stole you."

"Stole me, what are you talking about?" I asked.

"The report said that the child with abnormal brain waves, you know the sign that suggests that they can read minds, was born with both parents alive," Natalie said. "But it just so happened on that same night that there was an orphaned child who could be swapped with you so no parents could freak out over having their baby stolen." I was in shock but I realised Natalie was right, I didn't want to believe it but everything she said made sense.

"Tell me if that's true!" I shouted at Mr Lyons who let out a huge sigh.

"Yes, it's true," said Mr Lyons. "And I don't regret it one bit." That comment from Mr Lyons made me even angrier than before.

"I could have had a normal life with parents but instead you took me away from all that and you don't regret it," I said.

"That's right, I don't regret it," said Mr Lyons. "By keeping an eye on you, I've been able to finish the research I started all those years ago."

"And you gave no thought to anyone else?" I asked.

"I gave plenty of thought to everyone else; I swapped you with an orphaned child so nobody would be upset and who is to say you would have had a better life outside of the orphanage, you've enjoyed your time growing up here so I see no problems," said Mr Lyons.

"I can see plenty of problems with that but it's not just involving me," I said. "The fact you sunk your time and money into this research tells me that's it more important to you than the orphanage just as Natalie said."

"The orphanage is still running as far as I can see, you think it would still be standing after all these years if I'd put all my money into the research?" asked Mr Lyons.

"You've spent enough on the orphanage to keep it alive long enough for you to monitor my brain scans," I said. "I think it's safe to assume that was the purpose of those scans on my hospital visits."

"But Sam, the cost of research ended with your birth," he said. "You're entitled to a free scan at the hospital so what else do you think I spent the money on for the past thirteen years?" I didn't have an answer for him. I'm sure he was hiding something else but he made a point I couldn't contend with.

"Forget the orphanage right now Sam, even if he has been doing all he can to save the orphanage, it doesn't excuse the horrible crimes he has committed against you," said Natalie.

"I needed you Sam, my assumption that caring parents had an adverse effect on a child's ability to read minds was correct," said Mr Lyons. "It's something to do with the voices you hear as a baby."

"Go on," I said.

"I think when a child hears the same two voices over and over again, the focus on those voices drowns out all others which include the voices they hear in their heads," said Mr Lyons. "If you isolate that child instead, they have no central point of focus allowing them to fulfil their ability to mind-read so orphans are the ideal target area for this."

"And it was a coincidence that you owned an orphanage?" I asked.

"It truly was," replied Mr Lyons. "When I set up this orphanage, I knew mind-reading existed but I had no idea it could thrive under these circumstances."

"Did you learn about it from Subject 1?" I asked.

"Oh yes Subject 1," he said. "That's a person I have known for a long time and when I first knew them, they could read minds which started my curiosity."

"But then they lost it so you manipulated them to take part in an experiment to get it back," I told him.

"It was nothing to do with manipulation; I was curious to see how their mind works and they wanted to see if their ability could be retrieved," said Mr Lyons. "Subject 1 was more than compliant in the whole thing; their contribution helped me take a huge step forward in this research."

"And how is Subject 1 nowadays?" I asked.

"They are as healthy as they ever were," he replied. "Sure maybe the procedure makes them a little bit slow at times but they're happy enough with everything and they set the research going forward."

"The unpermitted research on the babies you mean?" I asked.

"Yes we picked out six with abnormal brain readings at birth but I believe every baby is born with some potential to mind-read but those with abnormal brain readings are much more likely to develop it," he replied.

"What makes you think that?" I asked.

"Because it's an ability of your brain you can unlock," he replied. "Sure, you have it to the extreme where you can read minds but there's something called intuition."

"I don't see what that has to do with anything," Natalie said.

"Everybody has an intuition, a gut feeling about people they meet, that comes from the same area of the brain," he said. "Twins; people believe them to have an understanding of one another's thoughts, maybe they do." It made sense to me given that I knew Gareth and Natasha always knew what the other was thinking.

"That goes against your theory about the attention of loved ones taking away that ability though," I told him.

"When they are born, twins can't understand each other but they still want to communicate so maybe they communicate that way until they can speak," said Mr Lyons. "Like I said, it never truly goes away from anyone; people have intuitions all the time and perhaps it's more pronounced with twins."

"How can you speak about all these things you've done and show no remorse?" Natalie asked him.

"I have nothing to show remorse for," replied Mr Lyons. "Nobody has been harmed by my actions; Subject 1 not only gave me an understanding of how it works but they also inspired my theory as to why people with mind-reading abilities might lose their talent."

"You keep talking about this like you're the only one involved," I said.

"Well, of course there were others," said Mr Lyons. "A mercenary of a doctor who agreed to carry out my work and another one who turned a blind eye as we used his room at a private hospital."

"More people you manipulated," said Natalie.

"The only manipulation involved in that was money, I can't help it if people are so weak-minded that they will do anything for money," said Mr Lyons.

"A mercenary happy to cut a person's head open," said Natalie.

"They're a doctor; that's what they do," said Mr Lyons. "Granted we could have done with some better medical equipment but we had to make do with what the private doctor left us."

"Well I hope it was all worth it," said Natalie in a scathing tone.

"Oh you have no idea," said Mr Lyons. "These years of research have shown us a way to block our minds from being read and presented us with a way to unlock mind-reading capabilities in anyone's mind."

"So that's why I could never read your mind," I said.

"Precisely, the only physical part the private doctor played in this whole scenario was inserting a tiny chip into our skull to block people like you out," he said as he pointed at me.

"I was never interested in reading minds for the sake of being nosy, I only wanted it for situations like this to learn the truth from you," I told him.

"Yes, I've seen it," he said. "You think you're using it selflessly to help others in need but, in reality, you're using it to paint yourself as this great reader of people to enhance your own self-worth." I wasn't sure how to respond to that. Mr Lyons seemed to be answering every question with a degree of honesty, Natalie and I may not view it the same way he does but he was giving his opinion. He isn't denying our accusations but instead simply trying to downplay them with his point of view. However I knew that Mr Lyons has taken this honest approach before with me and I couldn't shake the feeling that there was still more he wasn't telling us. I still couldn't think of a response to Mr Lyons' accusation.

"At least Sam isn't harming anybody with such an ability, I dread to think what you want it for," Natalie told

Mr Lyons. "I doubt it's just for your curiosity to be fulfilled." That was when it clicked with me; Mr Lyons had been speaking honestly about the way he sees his actions but he hadn't revealed what his plan was if he ever found a way to allow himself to read minds. I began to think about his possible motivations while Natalie and Mr Lyons continued talking.

"First and foremost, I'd want to do all I can to save the orphanage and I can think of certain situations where mind-reading would come in handy," said Mr Lyons.

"I don't believe for one minute you want to save this orphanage, we know Nicholas gave you money to make improvements and you haven't done anything," Natalie told him.

"As I said, the cost of research ended years ago and that was a calculated investment, where else could this money possibly be going?" he asked. "You don't see me turn up to work in a new car every week and a fancy new suit so the money isn't being spent on me."

"Then what is it?" asked Natalie.

"Nothing, it's just a reflection of the world we live in," replied Mr Lyons. "Every time Nicholas and I put money into this orphanage, the cost of keeping it running seems to rise and rise."

"Maybe I'd believe you if I ever saw the accounts in this place," said Natalie.

"That's not where you are best though, is it Natalie?" he asked. "You don't want to be doing spreadsheets, calling people up left, right and centre; you want to be involved with the children as much as possible."

"I do but this isn't about what I want which I have let Sam know already," said Natalie. "It would be greedy for me to take over from you for the sake of raising my own profile but it would be even greedier of me if I allowed the orphanage to fail under your control because I didn't want to get bogged down in paperwork."

"Sam, you've been very quiet over there," said Mr Lyons. I was still deep in thought; I had been fully focussed on the papers on Mr Lyons' desk. "You see, Sam knows that no matter what side projects I have, my primary focus has always been this place."

"You seem to keep ignoring the fact that you stole him," Natalie said.

"Sam likes to portray himself as selfless so he should be happy that a child had parents, a child who otherwise would have grown up an orphan," said Mr Lyons. "And besides, you've been happy here, right Sam?"

"I have been happy here," I replied directing my focus back to him. "And maybe I've learnt things about life that I wouldn't have learnt elsewhere, at least not so soon."

"Exactly, everybody wins from this scenario, why can't you accept that Natalie?" he asked.

"But," I continued. "The fact you could kidnap a child for this research tells me that you have some big plans with this ability."

"I've been completely honest with you like you asked," said Mr Lyons.

"You've been honest in telling us what you've done and why you think you're in the right," I said. "But that doesn't come across so much when you try to string together answers about how you are doing all you can to save the orphanage."

"How many times do I have to repeat myself?" he asked. This was the first sign of Mr Lyons becoming irritated by our questioning. Up until this point, he had been very calm and measured in his response no matter how much we berated his decisions.

"You see, that question strikes a nerve," I said. "You're happy to tell us honestly about the past, information that could get you arrested, but whenever we bring the future up, you get more and more agitated."

"That would be because I can't tell the future," said Mr Lyons with a tone of derision.

"Once again, you avoid the question and go on the defensive," I told him as I looked back down to his desk. My eye suddenly caught a glimpse of the letter we had read early from the person we assumed was the Prime Minister. "Just like a politician," I said.

"What are you talking about now?!" asked Mr Lyons angrily.

"When a politician comes across a question they don't want to answer, they avoid it," I said. "You even went to the trouble of admitting your past crimes to get us to stop asking questions."

"No I-" began Mr Lyons.

"But now I see it, you've wanted a role in politics for a long time now and you tried it before but the responsibility of running an orphanage got in the way."

"You better watch what you're saying," said Mr Lyons who was becoming more and more irritated.

"And you needed to save up a lot of money over the years to get involved," I said.

"Preposterous!" exclaimed Mr Lyons before calming down. "You'd be surprised how little money you need to get started in a political career."

"For a normal political career, maybe so," I told him. "But you want to run your own party and I bet that requires a healthy injection of cash, the kind of cash someone who was no longer making any money wouldn't have."

"Come to think of it, that first attempt you made to get into politics coincided with the downfall of this orphanage," said Natalie. "That was the start of my uphill battle to keep the orphanage running while you were preoccupied with yourself."

"Say what you want about my commitment but where do you think this orphanage would be if it wasn't for me?" Mr Lyons asked Natalie. "You can talk about your dedication and your morals but what good is that if you don't have my money going into this orphanage?"

"We can get donations from elsewhere but you wouldn't be interested in that, would you?" asked Natalie. "Nicholas is the only donator who will pay you in cash with no receipt and no questions asked because he trusts you as his brother."

"What are you implying?" asked Mr Lyons.

"You don't have to make a record of Nicholas' donations so there's no proof you even got it," replied Natalie. "That means that there can be no questions asked as to why donations have been transferred away from the orphanage to other projects, like your political career." The irritation written on Mr Lyons' face had turned to anger as a result of our constant questioning, scowling at both of us.

"Well done; you've managed to put all the pieces together," he said. "I'm impressed that you have hassled and hounded me enough to suss me out."

"It's all true then, what we just said?" I asked.

"Yes but you knowing the truth won't change anything," replied Mr Lyons.

"Right now the truth is the most important thing," I told him.

"Well, if that's the case then let's go through the whole truth if it's so important to you two," said Mr Lyons.

"It must be hard for you to know where to begin when everything is a big lie," said Natalie.

"You already know most of the truth now anyway," Mr Lyons told her. "Yes, I have been using Nicholas' donations over the last few years to fund plans for my new political party while doing the bare minimum to keep the orphanage running."

"I can't believe after all this time at the orphanage that you are ready just to chuck it all away for your own good," said Natalie.

"What happened to the selfless man who sold his company to build an orphanage twenty five years ago?" I asked.

"That man spent the first ten years of his time at the orphanage sheltering orphans in order for them to still have a good life, to keep them off the streets and make sure they grow up to become functioning members of society," said Mr Lyons.

"You're talking as if they are part of some kind of prison system here," said Natalie.

"Sometimes it is like that," said Mr Lyons. "Some children go off the rails when they don't have their parents around and some of those get better with foster parents while others don't."

"You still can't talk about them like that!" exclaimed Natalie.

"But you know it's true," replied Mr Lyons. "My brother and I both made successes of ourselves despite our upbringing under foster parents but there were more stories of failure than stories of success when it came to the orphans who passed through here."

"It's not fair to compare you and Nicholas to everybody else, not everyone grows up to be a successful businessman," I told him.

"Of course, our success would be hard to emulate but that's not the kind of success I'm talking about," said Mr Lyons. "For me, success for these orphans would have consisted of staying in one place, not being returned by foster parents because the kids were too broken to function normally."

"So you gave up on them when they returned to you?" asked Natalie.

"No, I did all I could to try and fix their problems which I thought I had done and sent them out to a new home," said Mr Lyons. "Even if they never returned to me again, it wouldn't be the last I would hear of them."

"What do you mean?" I asked.

"You wouldn't believe the number of stories I hear about some of the orphans who at one point had been under my care," replied Mr Lyons. "So many of them became drug addicts or criminals and those who stayed away from that were just unstable in general, failing to settle down into a job or into a family."

"That wasn't the case for all of them though," said Natalie.

"It felt like it was to me," said Mr Lyons. "I lost faith in all orphans from then on."

"You turned your back on all the orphans because of the actions of a few?" asked Natalie.

"They were all destined to turn out the same way," replied Mr Lyons. "If they left here they'd end up on the streets, if this place closed down they'd end up on the streets, what difference does it make?"

"Those options mean you aren't prepared to give the orphans who want to do well the chance to prove you wrong," said Natalie. "For the last fifteen years, you've let this orphanage gradually get worse and worse to punish the orphans for what the previous generation had done."

"It didn't go downhill straightaway, I'm sure you and Sam remember the nice meals we used to have," said Mr Lyons. "With Sam here, I could finally put an end to the money I had to spend on this research."

"You mean once you stole me?" I asked.

"If that's how you want to describe it, yes," he replied.

"That's the only way to describe it!" exclaimed Natalie.

"So you began your research before you'd lost faith in the orphanage?" I asked.

"Absolutely, I was curious about it before I even began running the orphanage," replied Mr Lyons. "And Subject 1 gave us a good head start on the research."

"I can't believe Subject 1 would have agreed to the operation," I said.

"Oh they didn't really, I mean I never asked," said Mr Lyons nonchalantly. "Subject 1 knew nothing about any of it but I knew they had had the ability to read minds."

"You performed surgery on them without them wanting to," said Natalie. "That means you always were a monster, never mind what happened after you'd lost faith in orphans."

"Subject 1 couldn't know anything about it or my involvement in it so we had to perform surgery even if we could have got the information through other means," he said.

"You had to give Subject 1 a reason to wake up in hospital with no knowledge of what had just gone on," I said.

"It was the easiest way to keep everybody happy and to stop people asking questions," said Mr Lyons. "Subject 1 was none the wiser as to what happened other than an emergency medical procedure."

"Your justification for everything you've done seems to be based on the fact that everybody is happier living a lie," I said.

"In most cases people are," said Mr Lyons. "It's better to live in blissful ignorance than to be devastated by the truth, like you must be now."

"I'm shocked by the truth but I can deal with it, I'm glad I won't spend my whole life looking up to you because of it," I told him. Mr Lyons simply rolled his eyes at me.

"Anyway, enough of this bashing of my character, don't you want to hear the rest of the story?" he asked.

"You suddenly sound like you're more than happy to tell us," I replied.

"Anyway, we stole you, as you call it," said Mr Lyons. "We studied your brain activity for years on end to find a way to gain the ability for myself but I wasn't entirely sure what I would plan to do with it for a few years."

"You mean you went through all that and you didn't have a particular plan for the ability?" I asked.

"I knew it would be a useful ability to have in all walks of life; I just needed to decide which path I was going down," replied Mr Lyons. "And politics was my decision."

"You've been to a lot of events with politicians over the years and you despised them, I don't see why you would want to get a role in politics yourself," said Natalie.

"You're right, I do despise them," said Mr Lyons. "That's why I wanted to set up my own party to knock these elite politicians off their perch."

"What makes you think your party could become the main party?" asked Natalie.

"These politicians get up to a lot of dodgy deals which they shared with me in confidence at these events but I know there's more they're hiding," replied Mr Lyons.

"The mind-reading," I said. "You're going to expose their secrets."

"We all know politicians aren't honest but nobody can hold them to account," said Mr Lyons. "I won't expose their secrets if they do what I say."

"Blackmail!" exclaimed Natalie. "Your list of crimes gets worse and worse."

"Well I haven't done that yet," said Mr Lyons.

"Not every politician breaks the rules," I said.

"But every person in the world has secrets," said Mr Lyons. "Whether it's regarding politics or not, legal or illegal, someone will have something I can hold against them."

"You're going to discredit your opponents without doing any work yourself by manipulating them," I said.

"If in a debate, a politician really wants me to avoid mentioning a certain topic; they'll have that thought constantly running through their head," said Mr Lyons.

"By topics you mean their secrets," I stated.

"Sam, you make everything sound so sinister," said Mr Lyons. "I meant government topics; if a politician really has no feasible plans for a certain area of government then I can and try and suss it out of them or blatantly shout out how unprepared they are."

"That still doesn't make it right," I told Mr Lyons.

"Why not?" he asked. "If I shout out their thoughts, the politicians are in trouble and if I pressure them into admitting their mistakes then I'd be responsible for the rise of honest politicians."

"It's not right to use people's own secrets against them, even if they are committing a crime," I said.

"But I thought you said that people shouldn't have to live a lie?" asked Mr Lyons.

"People can choose to live a lie rightly or wrongly but if you force people like me to live a lie then you are the one in the wrong," I replied.

"There's no room for morals in politics, I've met a lot of politicians over the years and morals are the least of their worries," said Mr Lyons. "I could be the most influential leader of this country in a very long time."

"What would your party actually do to make things better?" asked Natalie. "Or is this just an ego trip?"

"Like I said, first we would clear out the corrupt politicians to gain power for ourselves and then I'd make jail sentences tougher for all criminals," he replied.

"Tougher for the orphans who became criminals, you mean?" I asked.

"That's a part of it," replied Mr Lyons. "But this country has gone too soft in general."

"Even if your views were right and accepted by all, the end doesn't justify the means," I said. "Your political career will be built on the legacy of a stolen child and an orphanage you ran into the ground."

"I don't have to justify anything to you," he said.

"Why would you tell us all this anyway?" asked Natalie.

"I didn't want to tell you but you kept asking," replied Mr Lyons. "I didn't want you knowing the truth for your own good."

"For our own good?" I asked.

"Yes because I no longer need you Sam," he replied.

"So that's why you told me I could finally be adopted," I said.

"Indeed, I no longer need you or Natalie around," he said.

"You can fire me but that won't stop me coming after you," said Natalie.

"It's a pity; if you hadn't asked the questions, I would never have had to send you away," he told us.

"What makes you think we're going to leave?" asked Natalie.

"I'll call the police on you," he replied.

"What's to stop us calling the police on you?" asked Natalie.

"You can call the police if you want to but I doubt they'll believe your story because they trust me," he replied. "They're going to think you're crazy when you try to explain the crimes I have committed."

"They won't trust you when they see those files," said Natalie.

"The files will be long gone by the time you can convince the police to search my premises," said Mr Lyons. "They don't hand out search warrants easily you know."

"I don't care how long it takes, you'll still be a sitting duck if the police get suspicious of you," said Natalie.

"If you say so much as say a word to them, I'll have them arrest you first which will give me time to sort myself out," said Mr Lyons.

"Why would they arrest me?" asked Natalie.

"They might be interested in hearing about how you and Nicholas took three orphans and made them gamble," he replied.

"You knew?" I asked.

"Of course, I know that Nicholas always goes to play poker with his friends the same time every week," replied Mr Lyons. "So when I couldn't find the five of you the other day, I knew exactly where you went."

"You can't prove it!" exclaimed Natalie in a panicked tone.

"That's where you're wrong," he said. "The thing about rich people is that they are so paranoid about their possessions that they'll have security cameras set up everywhere all around the home, I'm sure a few of those will have caught you and you can't ask Nicholas' friends to lie, can you?"

"But..." Natalie began to say.

"Yes?" asked Mr Lyons. Natalie didn't say a word; she knew that Mr Lyons had us right where he wanted us.

"Exactly, so Natalie you are fired!" he shouted at her while pointing to the door. Natalie looked around; she desperately wanted to think of a way to stop Mr Lyons but she couldn't.

"You'd better go Natalie," I told her. Natalie nodded very hesitantly towards me.

"Are you sure you weren't happier with the lies?" he asked us. "Now, Natalie has lost her job and Sam, your lifelong trust in me has been shattered." Natalie and I both remained silent; we were both very despondent given how the tide had turned. Natalie walked slowly towards the door trying to hold back tears. As she got to the door, she looked back at Mr Lyons one last time.

"If you hurt them," she said.

"I won't harm them," he said.

"Sam, we will find a way," she said to me as she walked out the door.

"I won't harm them," repeated Mr Lyons as he closed the door behind Natalie. "But when you're all gone from here, the streets will harm you," he said looking directly at me.

"Natalie's right, we will find a way," I told Mr Lyons who responded with a snort of derision.

"Just remember if you try anything, I can have Natalie and Nicholas placed under arrest," he said. "I know you're resourceful so maybe you'd get your hands on a phone somehow but I'm here to remind you to not do anything stupid."

"I won't," I told him calmly. "Yet," I whispered under my breath. I didn't have any kind of plan in my head but I knew I couldn't let this be the end.

"Good, then go back to your normal routine," he said as he opened the door and held it open for me to walk out. I didn't say another word to him, I looked up at him once and there was no sign of remorse on his face, he was proud.

Chapter 13

I spent the next few days at the orphanage in a self-imposed isolation. I worried about telling Gareth and Natasha what happened for fear of them being punished so I told them I wasn't feeling well and stuck to my book. I was surprised that Mr Lyons hadn't set a punishment for me; perhaps the agony of concealing the truth from my friends and ignoring them was punishment enough. I hadn't seen or heard Natalie come in at all during this time while the orphanage was getting dirtier and dirtier. The only work that was done on the orphanage was changing the locks on the doors presumably to keep Natalie out. As I sat on my bed reading the book, there was a knock on the dormitory door.

"Come on Sam, you can't still be ill," shouted Gareth through the door.

"I am," I said weakly.

"Ill enough not to talk?" asked Natasha. I didn't have an answer for her. This led to Gareth and Natasha opening the door and charging towards me. I placed my book down by the side.

"What are you up to?" asked Gareth.

"Just catching up on my reading, our days have been very busy recently," I replied.

"You always find time for your reading," said Natasha.

"But you've never gone to such lengths to ignore us in favour of it," said Gareth.

"Believe me, there's a good reason for it," I told them. "I just need to work something out."

"And we can't help you work it out?" asked Natasha.

"Wait, it's not about those scans at the hospital is it?" asked Gareth. "Don't tell me you got some bad news from that." I had spent three days in isolation and hadn't worked anything out so I decided it might be best to tell them everything to see if they can help.

"No, I didn't get any bad news from the scan," I said. "But you are on to something with the scan."

"I'm already confused," said Gareth.

"So, you're feeling down because of the scan even though there are no bad results from it?" asked Natasha.

"I'm down about the reason that I have to have the scan in the first place," I said. Gareth and Natasha looked at each other with blank expressions.

"I think we're going to need a bit more," said Natasha.

"Well, did you ever wonder why I seem to be the only one who has that scan at the hospital?" I asked.

"We've wondered a lot of things about you; why you've never been able to meet potential adoptive parents, why Mr Lyons took a shine to you and why you're treated different in general," said Gareth.

"Well, all that links together for the same common reason," I said as I took a deep breath.

"Come on Sam, don't leave us waiting," said Natasha.

"Here goes," I said. "Ever since I was young, I have had the ability to read people's minds if I choose to." Natasha and Gareth stood silently; it was probably the last thing they were expecting to hear me say.

"You can read minds?" asked Gareth hesitantly.

"I know it sounds crazy but it's true," I replied.

"Sure sounds crazy," said Natasha.

"That's why I never intended to make friends here at the orphanage; I didn't want to be friends with people if I could read their minds," I said.

"So, you've been reading our minds all this time," said Natasha.

"I can control it," I told them. "So I've tried to read your minds as little as possible but there has been the odd occasion."

"So, when we play poker," Natasha began.

"Yes, I was reading your minds," I said. "But I only did that while we were learning to play and when we playing to win money for Nicholas."

"That explains why you were so sure then," said Gareth.

"At least we know now before we were old enough to play with our own money," said Natasha.

"I was never going to play you two for money and I didn't feel good about taking it off Nicholas' friends but when the orphanage needed money, it was the best option," I told them.

"You don't have to feel sorry for Nicholas' friends, that money meant nothing to them," said Natasha.

"It still doesn't seem right," I said.

"So you have this supposed ability and you're not going to use it to your advantage?" asked Gareth.

"I will and have at times but if it puts me at an unfair advantage against someone who doesn't deserve it than I'll tend not to," I replied.

"Well, it's a good job someone like you has it, I could imagine it would mean trouble for others," said Natasha.

"That's exactly what I'm worried about," I said looking to steer the conversation towards Mr Lyons before Gareth spoke up.

"How about some proof then?" asked Gareth.

"Proof?" I asked in response.

"Yeah, showcase your ability to us," replied Gareth.

"How do you want me to do that?" I asked.

"It's simple; I'll think of a completely random word and you tell me what I'm thinking," replied Gareth.

"Okay then, go ahead," I said. I could see in Gareth's mind he was changing his word of choice every few seconds trying to think of the most obscure word possible before finally settling on one.

"Automaton," thought Gareth.

"Okay, have you got a word?" I asked Gareth. Gareth nodded.

"I'll count you two down," said Natasha. "Both of you say the word at the same time."

"Got it," I said.

"3...2...1," said Natasha.

"Automaton," Gareth and I said in unison.

"Whoa," said Gareth.

"You two better not be pulling a trick on me," said Natasha.

"We would never think of it," said Gareth.

"Why don't you give it a go then?" I asked Natasha.

"Very well, let's see now," said Natasha as she began thinking of a word.

"Caramel," thought Natasha.

"3...2....1," said Gareth.

"Caramel," said Natasha and I together. She looked to Gareth in disbelief.

"Now do you believe me?" I asked.

"Well, we have seen magicians who supposedly read minds; they seem to have a way of making it appear as if they are doing it," replied Natasha.

"Those magicians read minds in very specific ways but I'm sure if they could really do it all the time, they'd probably be successful gamblers or men in higher positions of power," I said.

"But still," began Gareth.

"Here's something else I learnt," I said to them. "You two should be able to read each other's minds if you really try."

"I doubt that," Natasha scoffed.

"Everybody's brain has the potential, as unlikely as it may be, to read minds from an early age and though not many develop it, twins have an inherent ability to know what the other is thinking nonetheless," I said.

"So, your brain is different from ours?" asked Gareth.

"Yes," I told him. "But I know you two are always thinking the same thing and half the time you say the same thing as well."

"We've spent all our life together and have the same hobbies so we're bound to say something similar," said Natasha.

"How did you learn about this anyway?" asked Gareth.

"It turns out Mr Lyons knows about it and he has an interest in it, he's done years of research," I replied.

"So that's why he's always liked you and kept you here," said Natasha.

"Yes but the way he got me here in the first place is the bad news, I don't want to tell you at this moment why but let's just say we were wrong about Mr Lyons," I said.

"Why can't you just tell us?" asked Natasha. "We can handle it."

"I'm worried Mr Lyons will punish you, that's why I've put myself in isolation," I told them.

"Punish us for what?" asked Natasha.

"He knows about the poker," I said.

"And why would he tell on us?" said Natasha. Before I could respond, there was a knock on the door.

"Sam, a word," came the voice of Mr Lyons through the door.

"You two stay back, I don't want to involve you in this," I told Gareth and Natasha.

"You still haven't told us what," said Gareth.

"It's better you don't know right now, just don't trust Mr Lyons," I said. I walked over to the door while Gareth and Natasha headed to the corner.

"All alone in here Sam?" asked Mr Lyons who had a sinister smile on his face.

"Yes," I replied.

"Good, then if you'd like to follow me," said Mr Lyons who was talking very calmly. I decided to follow him so I could draw him away from the room so he wouldn't know I was talking to Gareth and Natasha.

"What are you going to do to me?" I asked him as we walked towards his office.

"Sam, once again you make it sound so sinister," said Mr Lyons. "I'm making your wish come true." I had no idea what he was talking about but I didn't trust his tone of voice. We went up to his office and there was a man waiting outside, the man was wearing all black with a hooded top and sunglasses covering his eyes.

"Who are you?" I asked.

"Meet your new father," said Mr Lyons as the hooded man nodded. "He's here to take you away to a new home; his wife is waiting in the car." I was speechless.

"You'll love it at our place," said the hooded man in a deep voice who was just looking down at the floor. I didn't trust Mr Lyons or the man. While Mr Lyons could get rid of me by sending me away to a home, I doubted that was his intention especially since the man was being so secretive.

"The paperwork has already been sorted, off you go," said Mr Lyons who led us towards the front doors. I couldn't imagine it would all be sorted so quickly. I knew I couldn't do anything until the doors were open so I had to play along. Mr Lyons opened the doors and as soon as I saw the rays of sunlight burst through the doors, I immediately ran past him and the hooded man. I looked back to see the hooded man beginning to run towards me while Mr Lyons closed the doors, he didn't care if I went with the man or not, as long as I was out of his way.

"Stop!" shouted the hooded man whose voice had suddenly become a lot less deep. "Just turn around for a second," he said. I had no intention of stopping until another figure dressed exactly like the man stepped out of a car and held me back.

"Get off me!" I shouted trying to wriggle free.

"Calm down Sam," said a familiar female voice. The woman took off her sunglasses and put her hood down; it was Natalie. "You didn't think the other day would just be the end of me, did you?" I didn't know what to say.

"Thank god you got him," said a male voice. I looked round to see that it was Nurse Lewis who had been chasing me.

"I don't blame you for running," said Natalie. "I wouldn't trust a man looking like that, no offence," Natalie told Nurse Lewis as she let out a small giggle. It was good to see her spirit wasn't completely broken from the other day.

"We couldn't let Mr Lyons know who we were, even though he probably wouldn't remember me anyway," said Nurse Lewis.

"Maybe not but I'd have thought he'd have recognised Natalie, disguised and all," I said.

"He never saw Natalie," said Nurse Lewis.

"For a long time, Mr Lyons has been so lax with doing all his checks of parents even to the point of meeting them both or taking their ID," said Natalie.

"Natalie told me what happened so we met up and we prepared a plan to get you out of there," said Nurse Lewis.

"It's great for me but what about the others?" I asked. "They're still with Mr Lyons who will gradually run the orphanage into the ground."

"We had to get you out because you know the truth which puts you in the most danger," said Natalie.

"But he let me leave," I said.

"Yes, that must mean he no longer needs you so he must be nearly finished with his work," said Nurse Lewis. "Natalie told me everything, it's a fascinating and tragic story, can you really read minds?"

"Yes, I can," I told Nurse Lewis. "And Mr Lyons wants to be able to as well."

"So he went to those terrible lengths?" asked Nurse Lewis.

"Indeed," replied Natalie.

"It's hard to get my head round it all, how he could have just nicked a child from under the hospital's nose is beyond me," said Nurse Lewis. "And all that money for the orphanage that he's spent for himself, it just infuriates me."

"We can worry about that later, what we need now is a plan," I said.

"We should talk through a plan when we get back to my house," said Natalie.

"Yes, we shouldn't stay outside too long," said Nurse Lewis.

We all got into Natalie's car and she soon drove us away. I noticed a woman sitting in her car who must have been there the whole time we were talking. She immediately started up her car. The car was a fair distance away so I couldn't make out the face and they seemed to be wearing a hat but as it drove away, I did see a flash of red from the side of the hat. It felt like I was being paranoid but nobody had got in or out of that car while we were talking on the street and the car only moved when we did. The car journey to Natalie's house was a quiet one, Natalie and I were worried about the orphanage and it appeared Nurse Lewis cared a lot as well.

Natalie pulled the car up outside a small house on a quiet street. The front lawn was covered with overgrown grass. We followed her to her front door as she opened it up. The house was very small and cramped with narrow hallways made narrower by boxes of old junk stacked up against the wall.

"Oh Natalie," said Nurse Lewis.

"Don't say it," Natalie told him while she looked rather embarrassed. "I know it's a mess."

"It's not the mess I'm worried about; it's what it represents," said Nurse Lewis

"What do you mean?" asked Natalie.

"I know this isn't you; you like everything to be neat and organised," replied Nurse Lewis. "That orphanage really has been killing you."

"It's not the orphanage that's the problem; if Howard had done his fair share of work I could have had a healthy balance," she said. "But now I have had to sacrifice the cleanliness and comfort of this house to keep the orphanage running against Howard's best wishes."

"Well, we'll find a way to get Mr Lyons out of power and then we'll find a way to lower the workload," I said.

"If Howard leaves, it will only increase the workload," said Natalie. "But that's not a problem; at least I know my hard work won't be undermined by Howard."

"You don't have to do it all on your own," said Nurse Lewis.

"I do," said Natalie. "When we take Howard away, there won't be enough money to get the people in required to fix up the orphanage so I'll have to gradually sort things out myself."

"I hope it doesn't come to that," said Nurse Lewis. "And besides, Nicholas will still help you."

"You mean he'll help us when we overthrow his brother?" asked Natalie.

"He will if he learns the truth," replied Nurse Lewis.

"What if he's in on it too?" I asked as I recalled the note I had read previously. "All I know for sure is that Natalie really does care about the orphanage; I'm sorry I had accused you before."

"All is forgiven Sam, Howard knows how to manipulate people and spin things in his favour," said Natalie.

"That's right, there's no point thinking about what Howard has done," said Nurse Lewis. "Instead we just need to focus on how to stop him from doing anything else."

"Nurse Lewis, if you don't mind me asking, why are you here?" I asked him. "This isn't your fight."

"I can't say no to Natalie," said Nurse Lewis. "At the hospital, we've always discussed the orphanage and she's told me about how Mr Lyons has been ruining the orphanage but I never imagined he's been doing it so intentionally, I just thought she meant he was doing a bad job."

"I went straight to Nurse Lewis after Howard kicked me out, I just wanted to tell somebody but he insisted on helping me which is when we came up with the plan to get you out of there," said Natalie.

"At one point or another, I've treated all those kids at the orphanage besides you so I can't let Howard ruin their lives, not now that I know about it," said Nurse Lewis. "The danger to Natalie and the orphans make it my fight whether I like it or not and we both think you can help."

"We need a plan, how much time do you think we have?" asked Natalie. "Howard said his research was complete, it might be any day now that he decides to just close the orphanage and be done with it," said Natalie.

"Howard never saw us so he won't be rushing things along," said Nurse Lewis.

"Someone saw us," I said.

"What do you mean?" asked Natalie.

"A woman was watching us from her car, I'm sure of it," I told her.

"Did you see her face?" asked Nurse Lewis.

"No and she was wearing a hat so I couldn't see her hair, just a flash of red," I said as a thought suddenly dawned on me. "Just like Nurse Scarlett."

"Nurse Scarlett?" asked Nurse Lewis.

"Natalie said we can't trust anyone associated with Mr Lyons and now I think of it, that red hair was reminiscent of Nurse Scarlett's hair," I replied.

"So you think Nurse Scarlett was watching us from her car?" asked Natalie.

"I think so," I told her.

"Well, Nurse Scarlett and Howard do have a long history together," said Natalie. Nurse Lewis looked deep in thought before he began speaking.

"That night at the hospital, Nurse Scarlett told Howard about you and he was more than willing to take you rather than send you somewhere else first," said Nurse Lewis.

"So he could take Sam and always keep an eye on his progress," said Natalie.

"Except I was never the orphaned child," I said.

"Of course!" exclaimed Nurse Lewis. "As soon as Natalie told me, I wondered how in the world Howard could steal a baby and know which one to steal, I never figured out his link to the hospital."

"But Nurse Scarlett knew," I said. "She knew which baby was born as an orphan and which baby would have had an abnormal brain reading and born to parents."

"Only she could have swapped them at birth," said Nurse Lewis.

"And she did it right under the nose of the hospital," said Natalie.

"She even involved me," said Nurse Lewis.

"I guess she needed a witness that there was an orphaned child who needed a home, you weren't to know I was switched with another baby," I told him.

"I can't believe she'd be involved with something so despicable," said Nurse Lewis. "Why would Nurse Scarlett do such a thing?"

"Let's go find out," replied Natalie.

"You mean you want to go see her at the hospital right now?" asked Nurse Lewis.

"If it was her in the car and if she is on Mr Lyons' side, which I don't think there is any doubt, then she would have let him know as soon as she saw us," I told him.

"Exactly, we don't have time to think of a plan now," said Natalie.

"The only plan we can have now is to confront her and Mr Lyons may be there too," I said.

"If he knows about us, he'll want to cover his tracks as soon as possible," said Natalie.

"But what about his threat to call the police on you?" I asked.

"Do you think he'd call the police at a time where all his secrets are at their most likely point of being exposed?" asked Natalie. "He'll be in a rush."

"And besides Natalie won't be scared of the police," said Nurse Lewis as he chuckled.

"Well, what are we waiting for?" asked Natalie who ushered us towards the door.

Chapter 14

We got in Natalie's car and headed towards the hospital. The strong afternoon sun from when we left the orphanage had faded as the sky became cloudy. There was no telling how quickly Mr Lyons would act. If it was Nurse Scarlett in the car and her intention was to help Mr Lyons then he would probably be taking swift action to cover his tracks.

"Are you sure we should be doing this?" asked Nurse Lewis.

"What do you mean?" asked Natalie. "Of course we should!"

"I'm just thinking about the safety of you two," said Nurse Lewis. "Mr Lyons is intent on ruining the orphanage and even if we stop him, the orphanage might be beyond saving."

"Like I've said before, we'll find a way," I said.

"The important thing is taking the orphanage out of Howard's hands while it's still running," said Natalie.

"What did you mean about looking out for our safety?" I asked Nurse Lewis.

"You two have escaped the orphanage and it's great you're drawing yourself back in to save it," said Nurse Lewis who paused for a brief moment. "But what if it goes wrong, we confront Mr Lyons but he gets away and then he does call the police, which would punish you two as well as the rest of the orphans."

"If we do nothing, then the orphans would suffer anyway, I wouldn't be able to live with myself knowing that I didn't try to help," said Natalie.

"I can't help but wonder why he would let you two leave the orphanage when you know the truth," said Nurse Lewis.

"It's like you said, with the threat of the police, he had a stranglehold over us," Natalie told Nurse Lewis.

"And Mr Lyons wouldn't have counted on Natalie being able to associate herself with someone from the hospital," I said. "Now we have access to the hospital, he knows he's at risk of exposure so he won't call the police on us."

"So, I'm the difference maker?" asked Nurse Lewis with a smirk on his face.

"Yes, I guess you could say you're the difference maker; you're keeping us protected from the police," replied Natalie.

"You're welcome," said Nurse Lewis still smirking.

"Although you keep up with that cheeky smirk on your face then we might need the police to protect you from me," said Natalie in a serious tone before turning to face Nurse Lewis and smiling at him.

"Oh Natalie, even now, I see you've still managed to retain your wonderful sense of humour," said Nurse Lewis.

"You need a sense of humour to get through life," said Natalie. "I had hoped I could have shown the orphans more of this side of me."

"What side?" I asked her.

"A more relaxed side, everything's falling apart and yet I seem to be as relaxed as I can remember," she replied. "When I first joined the orphanage, I wanted to chat with as many orphans as possible but unfortunately with the workload I had to carry, the only time I got to talk was to tell them off, I was always the bad guy for Howard."

"It's okay," I said to Natalie.

"It's true, isn't it?" she asked.

"Believe me, the orphans appreciate everything you've done so far," I said. "You're right; they don't see you as a friend but more like a parent, we need you to tell us off to guide us, Mr Lyons just wanted us to leave." Natalie was silent.

"Sam's right, Natalie," said Nurse Lewis. "We'll take the orphanage away from Howard and we'll find a way to get you more involved with the orphans."

"Thanks you two, I appreciate it," said Natalie. Almost every question about the future of an orphanage without Mr Lyons was answered with 'we'll find a way.' The truth is, none of us know what that way entails but I have faith that somebody who wants the orphanage to succeed will find a way, if we didn't believe that, there was no point in us trying to confront Mr Lyons. After a short break in the conversation, Nurse Lewis picked it up again.

"So wait, if we're not afraid of the police being called on us, why don't we call the police on Mr Lyons and Nurse Scarlett?" asked Nurse Lewis.

"There are a number of reasons Lewis," said Natalie. "Firstly, we don't know if Nurse Scarlett or Mr Lyons is actually at the hospital."

"And we don't know for sure yet that Nurse Scarlett is involved, however likely it seems," I said. "The only doubt I have is that Mr Lyons' accomplice was a doctor, at least in regards to Subject 1, which might be Nurse Scarlett's only saving grace."

"Exactly, we need to know where they are before we call the police," said Natalie. "If we call them and tell them to go to the hospital when neither of them is there, then they'll probably accuse us of wasting police time."

"And that discussion with police could delay us by quite a bit and we really have no time to lose," I told him.

"And they won't believe us if we call them up again," said Natalie.

"Alright, you made your point," said Nurse Lewis as the conversation went silent for the rest of the journey. We arrived at the hospital car park just a few minutes later but the public car park was completely taken up as Natalie drove round slowly.

"We can take my space," said Nurse Lewis directing Natalie towards the staff parking.

"You actually have your own parking space?" asked Natalie.

"Yes, that's what you get for years of service in hospitals," replied Nurse Lewis.

"Good, that's going to save us time," said Natalie. "I was afraid I was going to have to park anywhere, block everybody and get fined."

"It's like you said, I'm the difference maker," said Nurse Lewis.

"Okay yes, you definitely are now," said Natalie. She drove the car into the spot and we all jumped out as soon as the engine stopped. Natalie and I rushed ahead but Nurse Lewis was moving slowly by comparison as he looked back and forth.

"Nurse Scarlett's car is there," said Nurse Lewis. Natalie stopped and scanned the car park herself.

"No sign of Howard's car," moaned Natalie.

"Yet," said Nurse Lewis. "There's no way he would have already reached the hospital ahead of us and collected any evidence from here."

"I hope you're right," said Natalie.

"I'm sure he is," I reassured her. "Either way, Nurse Scarlett should help us find him." We rushed through the hospital doors.

"Lewis, we can't keep you away from this place, can we?" asked one nurse.

"It's a personal matter Raven, I just needed to come back to look at some files involving the family of these two," replied Nurse Lewis.

"Okay then, don't work too hard," said Raven.

"Thanks," said Nurse Lewis as the three of us walked past her and went beyond the waiting room to the maze of corridors. Nurse Lewis led the way in and out of corridors heading towards Nurse Scarlett's room; even though the lights were on, the corridors all still appeared very dim.

"Nurse Lewis!" shouted a voice from behind us. We looked round to see a young man who looked incredibly nervous.

"What's the problem Robbie?" asked Nurse Lewis calmly.

"I need your help," Robbie said. "I'm sorry, I can see you're not dressed for work but I can't find anybody else to help me."

"He's in the middle of-" Natalie began to say before Nurse Lewis put up his hand towards her.

"It's okay Natalie, you two go on ahead, I'll join you shortly," said Nurse Lewis as he walked towards Robbie.

"But we don't know where we're going," said Natalie quietly.

"I think I know," I told her. "Every time I'm here, I walk towards Nurse Scarlett's room."

"Well, lead on," said Natalie. I hadn't meant to suggest to Natalie that I completely knew where I was going; after all, I only told her that I thought I knew. I felt a lot of pressure about getting my directions to Nurse Scarlett's room right. I didn't want to waste time trying to picture each corridor I had previously turned in to but I didn't want to rush my way through the hospital and end up taking us in the wrong direction. I wasn't heading through corridors with much confidence so our pace had slowed down.

"How can you tell where we're going in a place like this?" asked Natalie. "I know you said you've made this trip a few times but still."

"I just need to look out for certain things," I said. I saw the sign with the faded words. "Like this for instance, that sign has always been faded for as long as I can remember." We headed past the sign and I kept my eye out for the next unique identifier. It still involved me tentatively looking round corridors to work out if we were still on the right track, I was fairly confident we were.

"Well, what's next?" asked Natalie.

"Soon, we should see an old, broken chair discarded in a corner," I told her.

"That doesn't seem like a rare thing," said Natalie.

"You haven't seen the dust on this one, it's hard to miss," I said. We walked on a little bit further and turned into another corridor.

"You mean this one?" asked Natalie pointing towards a chair covered in dust and cobwebs.

"Yes," I replied. "I told you it's hard to miss."

"Well, it's a good job for us they never fix anything around here," said Natalie.

"We've got more important things to do," said a voice from behind us. It was Nurse Lewis.

"You caught up to us quickly," said Natalie.

"Well, when you know exactly where to go and in a hurry, it's not hard," he said.

"Either way, Sam was doing a very capable job of leading us," Natalie said.

"Maybe so but I'd much rather Nurse Lewis took over," I told her.

"Come on then," said Nurse Lewis who went ahead of us. I saw the plaque on the wall with the hospital build date which meant I knew we were getting close to Nurse Scarlett's room. I began to worry about what we would do if Nurse Scarlett wasn't there or if we wrongly accuse her of being involved which, in a way, I wanted to believe but I was torn. If she was innocent then it would mean we would have wasted our time at the hospital.

We reached the door to Nurse Scarlett's room. Nurse Lewis looked at us both but didn't say a word, he just nodded towards us and we nodded back as Nurse Lewis opened the door. As we entered, I could see a stack of files and a few syringes on Nurse Scarlett's desk. Nurse Scarlett had been stood by a cupboard before she sprung back towards her desk as we entered the room.

"Oh, hello you lot, what a pleasant surprise," said Nurse Scarlett politely and with a smile on her face which I was taken aback by.

"Cut the act Scarlett," said Natalie.

"I don't know what you mean," said Nurse Scarlett who appeared to be very calm.

"Want to explain what those files are there?" asked Nurse Lewis.

"Oh, I was just sorting through my files, just reorganising," replied Nurse Scarlett.

"Then you won't mind if I take a look," said Nurse Lewis.

"No!" snapped Nurse Scarlett as she thumped her hands against the files. "I'm sorry about that; it's just that I like to do things my own way and don't want anybody changing it."

"Or is it because you're hiding something?" asked Natalie.

"What would I be hiding?" asked Nurse Scarlett who started to look irritated with the smile fading from her face.

"Maybe something about Sam, mind-reading and kidnapping," said Nurse Lewis.

"You lot really aren't making a lot of sense," said Nurse Scarlett. "Sam, tell me what's happening, you know you can trust me right?" she asked as the smile returned to her face. I was hesitant to look at her face as I realised that was how she defused any situation.

"Don't be fooled Sam," said Nurse Lewis.

"Sam," said Natalie.

"Don't worry, I can handle this," I told Natalie and Nurse Lewis. "What I know is that I can read minds," I said to Nurse Scarlett.

"Really?" asked Nurse Scarlett sounding surprised. "Well, you can look into my mind and tell these two that I'm not involved with whatever they're talking about."

"I can't read your mind," I said.

"You can't, you just said you could," said Nurse Scarlett. In this moment, I had to decide whether to keep up this soft interrogation or go right in and accuse her myself.

"I can't read your mind," I repeated. "Just like I can't read Mr Lyons' mind."

"Well, if it's true, that helps no-one right now," said Nurse Scarlett.

"That's where you're wrong," I told her. "The fact that I can't read either one of your minds gives me all the help I need."

"I still don't follow," said Nurse Scarlett.

"I know Mr Lyons is guilty of several things which he has freely admitted to me," I said. "But I wasn't sure if you were involved or not...at first."

"Involved in what?" asked Nurse Scarlett. "I can't imagine Mr Lyons doing anything illegal in the first place but if he did, it wouldn't involve me."

"Mr Lyons is interested in my mind-reading abilities so he stole me from my parents that night at the hospital," I said. "He wanted to keep an eye on me and use me for his research so he needed help from someone in the hospital."

"Even if that were true, you still haven't explained what that's got to do with me," said Nurse Scarlett.

"Mr Lyons' research led him to discover a way to block people from reading his mind, that's why I can't read his," I said. "And I highly doubt that you just stumbled across a way to block people from reading your mind without you knowing."

"You're the help from the hospital," said Nurse Lewis. "You were the one to let Mr Lyons know about Sam in the first place."

"But I...I," Nurse Scarlett stuttered as she looked on the verge of crying.

"You and Mr Lyons are both the same; you both use kindness to those who feel isolated to manipulate people into your way of thinking and hide the truth," I said. "I'm ashamed that I had bought into it too."

"But I...I," repeated Nurse Scarlett before the look of sadness on her face turned to anger. "You just had to keep pushing, didn't you?"

"So you do admit it," said Natalie.

"Sam, the work is done, if you had never known about any of this you would be happier, right?" asked Nurse

Scarlett. "Mr Lyons could have all the knowledge he wanted about mind-reading, you would have been adopted by an actual family and you would have left with a high opinion of everyone you'd met."

"Right now, I won't be happy until I know the orphanage is in safe hands," I told her. "If the only piece of information I knew at this point was that Mr Lyons wanted to close the orphanage then that's enough for me to make it my own business."

"That's because Sam actually has a conscience," said Natalie. "He never stopped looking for ways to save the orphanage and once he found out the truth, he wanted to save me too."

"Well, now you know the truth, the man you have looked up and considered a father figure your whole life was using you," said Nurse Scarlett. "You know your past and the fate of the orphanage so your misery goes well beyond the closing of an orphanage and all because you wouldn't stop asking questions."

"I've learnt that asking questions is how you find out the most about people, even more so than mind-reading," I told her. "I'm glad I know the truth, I can handle it, and I told Mr Lyons that from the very beginning, no matter how sordid it is."

"You should have stopped asking questions once I'd revealed your parents' death," said Nurse Scarlett. "That's why Howard wanted me to leak it to you."

"I've got to admit, that was very convincing," I said. "I really believed you had made a genuine mistake when you let slip about the night I was born."

"As if I would do something so foolish," said Nurse Scarlett.

"What you don't realise after all that is that you and Mr Lyons did make a mistake by feeding me that false information," I told her.

"Oh really?" she asked me condescendingly.

"If I had been told about how the ones you called my parents had died early on, I probably would have stopped asking questions," I replied. "But when Mr Lyons wouldn't tell me, even though there was nothing gruesome or unbearable to hear, it kept me curious for a long time," I continued. "I might not have even constantly talked to Mr Lyons if I had been fed that story and never got myself entangled in this struggle."

"Struggle is the right word...for you," said Nurse Scarlett. "It doesn't matter how much you know, nobody will believe a word you're saying."

"You're right, unless we have proof," I told her looking to the stack of files on her desk which she edged even closer towards.

"If nobody is going to believe us then I guess you can tell us why you did it," said Nurse Lewis. Nurse Scarlett let out a sound of derision.

"Fine, if that's how you want to play it," said Nurse Scarlett.

"Take your time; we know you're waiting for Howard to arrive here anyway," Natalie told Nurse Scarlett who scowled back at her.

"I've known Howard for a long time throughout my whole medical career and he is a friend who has always been there for me, during the good and the bad," she said.

"The bad, like stealing a baby?" Natalie asked angrily.

"Calm down sweetie, we're not at that bit yet," she told Natalie. "I mean the bad times long before this ever happened, when I first knew him, I was working as a doctor in another hospital."

"You were a doctor?" asked Nurse Lewis.

"Yes and what a stressful time that was," she replied. "I couldn't handle the pressure of long, stressful shifts so to cope with it, I turned to drugs and working at a hospital, I had a lot at my disposal."

"I still don't see what this had to with kidnapping a baby!" shouted Natalie.

"Once again, calm down Natalie," she said. "I was soon found out and they struck me off the medical register so I'd never work as a doctor again."

"If that really happened to you, you wouldn't be working in a hospital in any medical capacity," said Nurse Lewis.

"That's where Howard comes in, he supported me throughout both personally and financially," she said. "He made sure I got the best treatment money could buy and it worked for me and he used his influence to get me a role as a nurse so that I still had some kind of medical role."

"Why did he take an interest in your life?" I asked her.

"We were friends long before that," she replied.

"But why would he go to all those lengths just to get you back into a medical role?" I asked her. "Why not just help you with treatment so that you could get back to a normal life?"

"Well I-" she began.

"I'll tell you why," I interrupted. "Because Mr Lyons knew you were isolated and vulnerable, he knew he could manipulate you."

"No!" she shouted.

"And at first, you thought it was okay when he asked you to give him information on babies with irregular brain patterns, no harm done," I said. "Until that plan developed flaws so he had to take it to a new level."

"You don't know what you're talking about!" shouted Nurse Scarlett.

"He hatched a kidnapping plan and you couldn't say no because you knew by this point, he had the power and knowledge to end your career all over again," I told her.

"Howard never bullied me into making that choice, I was happy to go along with it because there was no harm done," she said. "Yes, we stole a baby from its parents but they'd never have to know that."

"Just like Mr Lyons, you seemed to be obsessed with the idea that everyone is happier not knowing," I said.

"That's because I believe it to be true," she responded. "There were no parents left heartbroken by a missing baby and we never had to go to extreme measures to make sure we got an orphaned child so my conscience is clear."

"I can't believe what you're saying, you're delusional," said Nurse Lewis.

"If you think Howard did all of that for you out of kindness, then you are mistaken," said Natalie.

"You can believe what you want but I know that Howard will always look out for me, I don't care if there's some ulterior motive as long as he keeps looking after me," said Nurse Scarlett who suddenly went silent. We could hear heavy footsteps heading towards the door; the door opened and Mr Lyons appeared through it.

"Ah, I see everybody's already here, how embarrassing of me to arrive late," he said. "Natalie, it's so nice to see you again."

"Go to hell!" Nurse Lewis shouted.

"And you, it's nice to be able to actually see you this time," said Mr Lyons.

"Go to hell!" repeated Nurse Lewis.

"Easy now, we're all calm here now, right?" Mr Lyons asked before moving towards the desk and picking up one of the syringes with a clear liquid. "We wouldn't want to get all worked up and end up on the end of one of these."

"You wouldn't kill us," I said.

"Kill you?" asked Mr Lyons. "I wouldn't think of it but too much of this would render you helpless for a while."

"What about that one there?" I said pointing to a syringe with a blue liquid.

"Oh, that one's for me," he replied. "The result of all my work."

"You mean-" I began.

"Yes," Mr Lyons interrupted. "This will allow me to read the minds of other people; I'll take one now and then I'll be off."

"Did you get everything from your office?" asked Nurse Scarlett.

"No, we still need to go back," he replied.

"Why wouldn't you do that first?" she asked.

"Don't worry, I have my reasons, now give me a dose of this," he said to her as he handed her the syringe with the blue liquid.

"We know where you're going next, what makes you think you can get away from us?" asked Natalie.

"Let's just say your actions will become easily predictable to me," he replied.

"No!" shouted Nurse Lewis as he charged towards Mr Lyons. Mr Lyons easily pushed him aside given the big size difference and Nurse Lewis hit his head hard on one of the drawers.

"Lewis!" exclaimed Natalie as she ran over to check on him. Nurse Lewis looked dazed and let out a small groan while Mr Lyons chuckled.

"Now do it!" he shouted towards Nurse Scarlett.

Nurse Scarlett drove the syringe into the arm of Mr Lyons. Almost instantly, Mr Lyons placed his hands over his head as he began to groan.

"The voices!" he shouted swaying side to side. "They're everywhere!" It seemed to me that Mr Lyons had gained the ability to read minds but he didn't have the ability to filter them so he was being bombarded with constant noise. Nurse Scarlett placed all of the files on her desk into a big bag and filled up a smaller bag with the syringes left on the desk.

"Come on, we need to go!" she told him putting her arm under his to assist him in walking. They went past us and went out the door with Nurse Lewis still suffering from the blow to the head. After twenty seconds, Nurse Lewis sat up.

"We need to go after them, help me up," said Nurse Lewis weakly. Natalie and I both hoisted Nurse Lewis to his feet at which pointed he ushered us aside. "Don't worry, I can handle myself." We headed out the door as Natalie and I rushed ahead. We looked back to see that Nurse Lewis hadn't been keeping up with our pace although he wasn't moving really slowly. Since we weren't entirely sure where the exit was, we had to drop back to his pace.

"Sorry," he said.

"There's no need to apologise," said Natalie. "You've helped us this much so far and we need you to help us see it through to the end." Nurse Lewis nodded and continued onwards. We weren't sure how far ahead Mr Lyons and Nurse Scarlett were but we knew they couldn't be too far ahead because Mr Lyons was struggling with his movement as well.

Myself, Nurse Lewis and Natalie eventually found our way out of the hospital. The sky was pitch black and the rain was now falling heavily. As we got outside, we saw Mr Lyons disappear around the corner in Nurse Scarlett's car. It was clear that Mr Lyons was still feeling some adverse effects to the drug, slouching in the passenger seat. I could see the faces of Nurse Lewis and Natalie sink but only for a few seconds as they knew we had to act fast.

"Quickly, get in the car," said Natalie as she scrambled around in her bag looking for her keys.

"Stay calm Natalie, we know where's he going and we will catch him," Nurse Lewis told her as he put a reassuring arm on her shoulder. I didn't need to read Natalie's mind to know that she was in a blind panic, to know that she had the future of the orphanage and the orphans on her mind. She knew the importance of stopping Mr Lyons and making sure he is held accountable.

Natalie pulled her keys out of the bag and, at that moment, we all hopped in Natalie's car to return to the orphanage, I got in the back leaving Nurse Lewis in the passenger seat up front. Natalie started up the car and we drove away instantly, she wasn't concerned with safety checks this time. It was clear to see that the events of the past few days had affected Natalie's usual calm and measured approach and this showed in her driving. She swerved in and out of cars and continued to pick up speed and yet, she seemed calmer in a car than she ever had been before. I knew Natalie was in complete control of the car and she would calculate the risk of each swerve and overtake in her head and come to the correct decision so I wasn't worried.

"Howard's secret is exposed so he's not going to leave any evidence behind at the orphanage," I told her. "But why would he tell us that so explicitly?"

"What if he's lying?" asked Nurse Lewis.

"He wasn't," said Natalie. "His car wasn't anywhere in this parking lot and the only files in the car were from Nurse Scarlett but the most incriminating files are still at the orphanage."

"I'll call the police," said Nurse Lewis.

"What will we tell them though?" I asked. "We can't really say there's a mind-reader on the loose."

"We can tell the police that the children are in danger from a drugged-up man, we can try and explain it to them afterwards," Natalie said. "Right now, all we need is for them to turn up." Nurse Lewis dialled 999 but Natalie beckoned him to place the phone closer to her on the dashboard. "Put them on speaker, I want to talk to them," Natalie told Lewis. Lewis obliged.

"Hello, emergency service operator. Which service do you require? Fire, Police or Ambulance?" asked the man on the other end of the phone.

"We need the police please, we need them to come to the Lyons Orphanage as soon as possible," Natalie told them.

"Okay, may I ask who is calling?" asked the operator.

"My name is Natalie Longhurst, assistant manager of the Lyons Orphanage," she said.

"Ms Longhurst, we had a warning from Howard Lyons that you would call, he told us that you were no longer under his employment and that you would try to harass him," the operator told her. There was a moment of silence. Natalie gave a huge sigh as if she was defeated, the lengths Mr Lyons had gone to discredit her and protect himself and it was also startling how influential his word was against anyone else. "Hello?" asked the operator. "Are you still there?" Natalie turned to face me; she didn't look beaten in my eyes, she looked determined as she turned back round.

"Yes, I'm still here!" Natalie shouted. "The children at the orphanage are in serious danger, if I'm lying, the police can arrest me when they show up but if you want to take that chance with the safety of the children, then you'll have to live with that regret for the rest of your life!" Natalie then snatched the phone off the dashboard and ended the call before the operator could reply. I had never seen this side of Natalie. "Maybe they will turn up or maybe they won't but we will stop Howard either way," Natalie told us.

"Don't you think you should have stayed on the line to get a definitive answer?" asked Nurse Lewis tentatively.

"I'm fed up of sitting around waiting for help," she said. "I took Howard's word for it that he would be implementing improvements on the orphanage which never came, I sat back and allowed him to run the orphanage into the ground just because he was in charge and had access to the donations from his brother," Natalie suddenly paused. "We need to let Nicholas know, you can use my phone," Natalie told Nurse Lewis as she pointed to her bag and Nurse Lewis retrieved the phone and began to search for Nicholas' number and rang him up. There was no answer.

"He's not responding," said Nurse Lewis. "I'll have to leave him a voicemail and hope he gets it." No response from Nicholas at a crucial point didn't help to shake the feeling he was in on it as well. Nurse Lewis waited on the phone for a few seconds so that he could leave a message. "Hi Nicholas, my name is Lewis and I'm here with Natalie and Sam, if you receive this, we need you to come to the orphanage immediately, there's no time to explain." Nurse Lewis then ended the call.

"So, we don't know if the police are coming and we don't know if Nicholas is coming?" I asked.

"No," replied Natalie. "We'll do it without them if we have to."

"But Mr Lyons might be a bit dangerous in his current state, there's no telling what the drug could do to his mind," I said.

"It's a chance we will have to take, if not, Howard will get away with everything and he's been doing that under my nose for far too long," said Natalie. The reality of that statement hit me hard. For everything I have discovered about Mr Lyons, what he has done to me and what he has put my parents through, to think he could get away with it unsettled me. We needed true evidence of his misdemeanours to get anybody in authority to believe us otherwise he could just leave this life behind him and start fresh in politics with mind-reading powers in hand.

Chapter 15

We finally arrived at the orphanage but there were no police cars in sight and no sign of Nicholas either but Mr Lyons' car was there. As we got out the car, I looked at the front doors of the orphanage, the silver of the lion-head knockers were lit up by a small orange light just above the entrance; one facing upright, the other on its side. The black of the doors made it appear as if the lion-head knockers were simply floating. The front doors were very likely locked by Mr Lyons and only he had the keys to get into the orphanage.

"I should have mentioned that Mr Lyons changed the locks so any keys you have definitely won't work to get inside," I told Natalie.

"If he thinks locked doors will stop us after all we've gone through, he had better think again," said Natalie. Natalie ran up to the entrance just to check that it was locked; it would have been embarrassing if it wasn't. She pulled at the front doors with all her strength but it wouldn't budge, Nurse Lewis also joined in with the pulling. However, the front doors were sturdy and all the nearby windows were high up and well-enforced. Natalie's optimism was looking a bit misplaced at this point.

"Well, what do we do now?" asked Nurse Lewis.

"There's more than one way to get inside," said Natalie. "There's an entrance to the kitchen from the side." We followed Natalie round the side of the building and Natalie pointed at the overgrown plants and bushes that covered the majority of that side of the orphanage. "There's a door behind all of that which leads into the kitchen," Natalie explained. As I looked closely, I could just about see a door through all the overgrowth.

"I never knew that was there," I said as the three of us edged our way through the overgrowth to get to the door. We had to endure the irritation of the stinging nettles as I went deeper than I had before. Natalie's determination meant she was leading the way without hesitation and she was taking the brunt of the stinging nettles.

"Why didn't Howard change the lock for this door?" asked Nurse Lewis.

"He completely forgot it was here," responded Natalie. "This back area of the kitchen and exit hasn't been used in a long time due to the overgrowth."

"And Howard never sorted it?" I asked.

"Of course not, Sam's seen the lack of improvements in the orphanage so this was the least of his worries," said Natalie. Natalie reached the door and inserted the key. I could hear the door unlock but it was still very stiff. It took a few barges of the door from Natalie to push it open, at which point she stumbled through the door into a dirty, old room full of kitchen equipment that had seen much better days. This room was well-hidden at the back of the kitchen, it looked like nobody had been anywhere near it for a long time. We walked through to the main kitchen, which wasn't exactly spotless, but looked much nicer than where we had just been.

"It's a massive fire hazard to not have an exit out of the building directly from the kitchen but no matter how much I asked, Howard would do nothing to help," said Natalie. "I thought the people who carry out our safety checks would have raised the issue with him but it is clear that he had influence over them too." We exited the kitchen, went through the dining area and into the central area. Almost all of the orphans were in bed but Gareth and Natasha were still awake. I ran over to them and hugged them both.

"It's good to see you two again," I said.

"I thought you were gone," said Natasha.

"It's a long story," I said.

"Still can't tell us?" asked Natasha.

"There's no time," I replied which brought a sigh from Natasha. There really was no time to explain anything as much as I wanted to.

"Gareth, Natasha, what are you two doing up?" asked Natalie.

"We were just making the most of being able to stay up," said Gareth. "Mr Lyons saw us and he didn't seem to mind so we stayed here."

"Where did Mr Lyons go?" asked Lewis.

"He's still up in his room, we would have seen him if he had left," said Natasha.

"I want you to go and wake the rest of the kids up, bring them here and wait with Nurse Lewis and try to find the caretaker," said Natalie. "If you hear a police siren, I want you to get all the kids outside when that happens, you got it?" It was clear Gareth and Natasha looked confused but they could sense the worry in Natalie's voice and then they looked over to me; I gave them a nod to indicate that they should follow Natalie's advice.

"Go on you two," I told them.

"Okay," they said in tandem as they both ran off.

"Lewis, you'll need to try and get the doors open, there should be plenty of tools in the caretaker's closet," she said as she pointed him in the direction of the closet.

"You can count on me," Nurse Lewis told Natalie. At this point, Natalie and I made our way to Mr Lyons' office to confront him. We made our way up the creaking steps alerting Mr Lyons to our position. As we approached the door, we could see the outlines of Mr Lyons and Nurse Scarlett standing completely still as they anticipated our arrival. At that point, Natasha came rushing up the stairs to join us.

"We've got the kids awake and Nurse Lewis is working on the doors," said Natasha. "So, with that in mind, I came to join you to find out what's going on and to let you know I haven't seen the caretaker anywhere all day."

"You shouldn't be here, we were wrong about Mr Lyons, he's in a dangerous state at the moment," I told her.

"But I want to know what's happening and if it involves me being able to help the orphanage, then I want to do all I can," she said. "What's the point in having friends if you don't want their help in difficult times?" At that moment, we could hear a police siren nearby and heard a car stopping. There was a huge sense of relief that the police had actually turned up.

"The police are here now!" Natalie shouted to Mr Lyons through the door and then she turned to me and Natasha. "We just need to keep him in there until the policemen get here," she told us.

"But I want to confront Mr Lyons," I said as we heard Nurse Lewis' continued attempts to open the doors. "Also, it may take a while for the policemen to get in here."

"Okay, let's do it now," she said as she turned to us. In all this time, Mr Lyons and Nurse Scarlett were still standing, waiting for us. They weren't frantically running about to collect any incriminating evidence from his room. Then it occurred to me that Mr Lyons could read our minds so he knew we were still in a bind. Nonetheless, we had to do what we could to delay him or even apprehend him ourselves. I entered the code '2404' to open the door and we walked into Mr Lyons' office.

"Come in," he beckoned to us with Nurse Scarlett by his side.

"The police are here and your only way out is through the front entrance, give it up," said Natalie. Mr Lyons chuckled.

"From what I can hear, the policemen aren't getting in any time soon unless you intend to physically overpower me yourselves and let's not forget, I'll know exactly what you'll try to do." Mr Lyons had an incredibly confident look on his face while Nurse Scarlett was at his side smirking.

"As you can tell, Mr Lyons has all those thoughts in his head under control," said Nurse Scarlett.

"Like Natalie said, some time tonight you will be stopped, it just depends how long you want to delay the inevitable," I told him.

"Where is the caretaker?" asked Natasha.

"You mean the caretaker who cares more about the money than the work?" asked Mr Lyons. "I gave him a month's paid holiday just a few days ago, he deserves it." It didn't surprise me the caretaker would take the offer but he must have thought something suspicious was occurring when he got this offer from Mr Lyons.

"The police are here," said Natalie once again.

"Well, all the police know is that there's some kind of commotion at this orphanage but they don't know specifics, do they?" he asked as he pointed to his head and then pointed towards Natalie, mocking her. "I can walk out the front doors, tell the police the culprit is still inside and be on my way."

"Nobody is going to believe Natalie did anything wrong, she's the one who called the police," I said. Mr Lyons still had a huge smile on his face. He walked over to one of his drawers and pulled out some forms.

"Of course Natalie did nothing wrong, after all, I've signed paperwork to give her full authority for the orphanage starting from yesterday," said Mr Lyons, waving the pieces of paper in her face.

"What?!" exclaimed Natalie.

"Surely you know about this Natalie, after all, you had all this paperwork on your desk signed by you," said Mr Lyons. "It contained everything you needed to take control except my signature, well now you have it," he said as he pointed to the bottom of the page which contained two signatures. I assumed one was his and the other one was Natalie.

"I wanted you out even before I knew the truth about you so of course I did my research on how to gain ownership from you," Natalie told him. "Some of the documents on your desk helped point me in the right direction to compile those forms you're holding."

"And now it's paid off for you," said Mr Lyons. "Now, I can't have a political opponent bring up my failed orphanage because you were in charge."

"That means you're not allowed to be here so the policemen will have every right to arrest you," said Natalie.

"The policemen won't know it until I'm long gone so as far as he's concerned, there is nothing wrong with me being here," said Mr Lyons.

"But you mentioned a culprit," said Natasha.

"That's right, I did," said Mr Lyons as his expression changed from a smile to a scowl. Mr Lyons took a syringe filled with clear liquid from Nurse Scarlett's bag and drove it straight into Nurse Scarlett's arm. Nurse Scarlett let out a piercing scream before turning to Mr Lyons with a sheer look of confusion on her face as she started to sway before finally collapsing in a heap.

"What did you do to her?!" asked Natalie.

"Relax," said Mr Lyons whose expression had changed back to a smile. "There's your culprit, a nurse with a lot of connections to the orphanage with a secret history of drug abuse posing a threat to the children and you let it happen under your management," Mr Lyons said as he pointed to the signatures again. I realised it had been dated from a few days back which would mean Mr Lyons could deny responsibility about the events of today. "Oh well," he said letting out a loud sigh.

"That's why you drew us back here," said Natalie. "That's why you didn't bring all the evidence with you to the hospital."

"We still won't let you leave," I said. "Nurse Scarlett deserves to be arrested but we can't let you get away with all this."

"Why not?" asked Mr Lyons. "Natalie will get over the public outcry about this happening under her regime, Nurse Scarlett was the one who took you from your parents Sam, why not let her take the punishment rather than trying to convince people that I'm at fault?"

"We wouldn't waste our time trying to convince the police you're a criminal, we know you've got a lot of sway with officials," said Natalie. "That's why we can't let you leave with the evidence." At that point, we heard the code being entered from behind the door and Mr Lyons' brother Nicholas appeared. It felt like we were sandwiched between the two brothers with Nicholas' considerable stature blocking the entrance to the office door.

"Nicholas, did you get our message?" asked Natalie.

"You mean the phone he left right here with me?" Mr Lyons asked as he picked up a phone from his desk. "No, no new messages came through while you were in the bathroom."

"What's going on Howard?" Nicholas asked. "Why have I returned to find these three here and Nurse Scarlett on the floor?"

"Natalie and Sam have been trying to set me up for something and they used Nurse Scarlett to try and sabotage my career as an owner and a politician," said Mr Lyons. "Natalie wants to take control of the orphanage, the orphanage I've dedicated my whole life to and they want to snatch it away; that's why I needed you here."

"Nicholas, he's lying!" I said. Nicholas looked back and forth between us and his brother.

"Oh come on Nicholas, I know they asked you to do things behind my back but I forgive you," he said. "They were just using you to try and undermine me, why do you think they were so interested in where your money was going?" Nicholas was trying to respond but he was stuttering over his words. I could read it in the mind of Nicholas, there was doubt but Mr Lyons could also read his mind and for someone who was already a master manipulator, this put us at a huge disadvantage.

"But I thought they had the orphanage in mind," Nicholas said.

"We do!" exclaimed Natalie. "Your brother wants to be done with the orphanage altogether and there's a reason for it."

"No!" shouted Nicholas as Natalie's accusation seemed to set off a spark in him. "My brother loves this orphanage." Before we knew it, the giant hands of Nicholas had a hold of both Natalie and I while Natasha was simply being pushed along by the sheer girth of Nicholas. I struggled as much as I could but deep down, I knew with the strength of Nicholas that I had no chance of wriggling free.

"Now tie them to the chairs and tape over their mouths," Mr Lyons said as he pointed to three chairs and some ropes. It was clear that Mr Lyons wanted to make this look like a hostage situation where Nurse Scarlett was at fault for all of it and he needed Nicholas' help to restrain us. Mr Lyons came over to restrain Natalie while Nicholas was strong enough to subdue both Natasha and I at the same time.

At that moment, there was a crash that came from downstairs followed by the onrushing footsteps of the other orphans. I could only assume at least one of the doors were now open which meant the orphans could be rounded up outside and the police could get in. The problem now was that we were tied up and the only people who know the code to this room are in the room already.

"Nicholas, I need you to help me pack up all these folders and files around the office, then we can leave and let the police sort this mess out," Mr Lyons told Nicholas.

"Okay, but what are the police going to do to them?" asked Nicholas.

"What do you care, they are criminals and they are trying to discredit all my work!" shouted Mr Lyons. I really wish I was able to talk to Nicholas at this point because he knew something didn't quite add up but with only his brother's voice in his head, there wasn't any way he was going to be talked out of it. Nicholas reluctantly starting grabbing files and folders from around the office, carefully stepping over Nurse Scarlett each time he passed her. At that moment, I saw a couple of outlines on the other side of the door. One was clearly Gareth but the other figure beside him didn't look like anyone I'd known before.

"Open up, police!" I heard a man shout through the door. Mr Lyons turned round to face them.

"One police officer? They sent one police officer?" asked Mr Lyons who chuckled away. Nicholas looked at him with a look of confusion on his face.

"Why are you laughing at a time like this?" asked Nicholas.

"I'm laughing at the state of the policing around here, I called them up and told them about this ongoing disturbance and they think it's not serious enough to send more than one officer," replied Mr Lyons. Those words incensed Natalie who wriggled in her chair and made muffled sounds. Not only was Mr Lyons lying but he was mocking each of us, including Nicholas. I could see Gareth standing by the keypad to the door met with several buzzes to say his attempts had failed.

"This is Officer Barrett, please open the door!" shouted the officer.

"There's no longer a problem, officer, my brother and I now have everything under control and have apprehended the culprit," said Mr Lyons.

"Well, let me in," said Officer Barrett.

"Just a minute, I need to do some tidying up, your patience will be rewarded when I am in a position of power," Mr Lyons told the officer. I looked into the mind of Officer Barrett. I could see that he was nervous but he was also unfazed by Mr Lyons' offer. He knew that he would simply have to wait for Mr Lyons to be finished before he gains access to the room and after that, he wasn't sure what he was expecting to see or who even to arrest.

"Sir, if anyone is in danger or hurt, I need to get in now whether the people are innocent or not," said Officer Barrett sticking to the line of duty.

"Just a minute," repeated Mr Lyons. At that point, I could see Natasha making a gesture to Nicholas for him to come over, she wanted to say something. Nicholas peeled off the tape from around her mouth.

"Gareth, the code is..." Natasha began to shout before Nicholas immediately put the tape back around her mouth.

"What is it Natasha?!" asked Gareth. Mr Lyons looked round in disgust.

"Nicholas, leave them alone and get back over here, we can't afford any slip-ups with them now when they're so close to being caught," Mr Lyons told Nicholas. Nicholas didn't say a word, nodded and continued to pack folders away.

"2404, 2404, 2404," was being repeated in the mind of Natasha whose expression had sunk having been so close to letting Gareth know the code to get him and the officer inside. Natasha now realised that what I had said about the mind-reading is true and she believed what I had told her, that twins knowing each other's exact thoughts isn't a myth, there's a reason for it. She was repeating it over and over in her mind in the hope that Gareth could learn the code to enter.

I could see through the window and I could tell by the lack of buzzing that Gareth had stopped trying to enter the code, he had the same thought about the potential for mind-reading. Nurse Scarlett regained consciousness but she was still very woozy and just managed to prop herself up against one of the corners of the room.

"Nicholas, keep an eye on her too, even though she won't be going anywhere fast," Mr Lyons told Nicholas who had stopped dead in his tracks in regards to packing away Mr Lyons' items. He was fixated on the files that had been packed in the first aid kit, beginning with the scrap paper that had his name on and moved on to the reports we had read previously. "Nicholas, don't worry about that, give it here," he said as he attempted to snatch the file from him. Nicholas pulled it away and kept Mr Lyons at a distance, not even Mr Lyons' considerable frame could overpower Nicholas so he was powerless to stop him reading. Nicholas' face was a mixture of confusion and anger.

"What is this?!" shouted Nicholas as he swung the file around to show Mr Lyons. "Why is my name at the start of these files?"

"That's just the report I kept from when you had your stroke," Mr Lyons replied.

"Howard, I may struggle with memory but I'm not stupid, I read the whole report," said Nicholas as he began to well up.

"Nicholas I...." began Mr Lyons.

"Don't!" shouted Nicholas who had another quick flick through the file. "What has this got to do with me?!" he asked.

"Nothing at all," insisted Mr Lyons. That seemed to infuriate Nicholas who grabbed Mr Lyons and held him against the wall.

"What's all this about Subject 1, mind-reading and experiments on the brain?" asked Nicholas as he shook Mr Lyons about.

"You really don't remember do you Nicholas?" asked Mr Lyons. "You don't remember something very special about your childhood."

"I remember we had great foster parents but you never liked them," said Nicholas.

"There was a reason for that," said Mr Lyons. "When we were young and growing up in the orphanage, you told me about your ability to read minds, I didn't believe you until you gave me several examples."

"I was only three years old when we were in that orphanage; I don't remember anything I said at that point," said Nicholas.

"Well, you could read minds until we got adopted," said Mr Lyons. "As they showed you more and more attention and your bond got stronger with them, you seemed to lose your capacity for mind-reading."

"So then why is this note about me bundled together with these medical reports for random people?" asked Nicholas.

"Once I started my business and had some spare money, I wanted to investigate if other people shared your power with the help of Nurse Scarlett and the first person was Subject 1," said Mr Lyons. "That note shouldn't still be in there; it was written as a tribute to you for starting my curiosity in this area."

"A tribute?" asked Nicholas.

"Because I didn't think you would survive your stroke," replied Mr Lyons. Nicholas loosened his grip on Mr Lyons.

"You never had a stroke," said a weary voice coming from the corner, it was Nurse Scarlett who was barely conscious but managed to speak. "He's lying to you, you're Subject 1," she said as her head drooped back down.

"Don't listen to her, Nicholas," said Mr Lyons who tried to wriggle free. Instead Nicholas tightened his grip again.

"Tell me the truth or I'll open that door right now and let the police handle all of you!" shouted Nicholas. I could see from Mr Lyons' expression that he knew there was no way out without telling Nicholas the truth, Nicholas was no longer buying Mr Lyons' vague answers to his questions and suspicions. By this point, I don't think Nicholas trusted anybody in the room, not even his own brother, but he wanted to work out where he fitted into all that was going on.

"Okay," said Mr Lyons calmly. "Nurse Scarlett is right, you never had a stroke, your scar and memory loss is the result of an experiment where we examined your brain, I wanted to learn how I could get any brain to unlock such power," he explained.

"You experimented on me?!" asked Nicholas furiously.

"Well Scarlett did with her knowledge as a doctor," said Mr Lyons. "And for such a dangerous experiment, you should be grateful memory loss is your only problem and it all worked out with your company still."

"That company was my life!" shouted Nicholas. "You stole that away from me."

"You helped set me on my path of research without the need for any more medical operations, just the monitoring of children's brains, and the research has come to fruition tonight, you made it all possible and for that, I thank you." Nicholas was left speechless. He loosened his grip of Mr Lyons and sat down right on the spot he was currently standing. He looked in complete shock. The problem now was that Mr Lyons' files were all gathered up and he was ready to leave. That is when the door buzzer made the noise which indicated the code was correct. Gareth and Officer Barrett entered.

"I bet you're glad we got involved now," Gareth said while looking at me.

"Mr Lyons, sir, please stay there while I piece everything together and I promise everything will be resolved," said Officer Barrett.

"That's alright officer, I know a rookie like you wants to make sure everything is correct," said Mr Lyons condescendingly as he immediately tried to dash past the officer. The officer got in his way and tried to hold him back but the police officer was nowhere near the size of Mr Lyons.

As Mr Lyons began to overpower the officer, a needle containing the blue liquid used for mind-reading was plunged into his arm. Nurse Scarlett had mustered the energy to get herself to her feet and drove it in. With another syringe worth of the drug, it seemed the voices crept back into Mr Lyons' head without him having any filter. Nicholas had composed himself and began to free Natalie, Natasha and myself. Officer Barrett had turned his attention to Nurse Scarlett who was slumped over the desk. His pre-occupation with her allowed a disorientated Mr Lyons to run past him and out the office door.

Officer Barrett grabbed his walkie-talkie. "I need backup at the Lyons Orphanage and we'll need an ambulance," said Officer Barrett speaking into his device who was becoming increasingly nervous as he realised the seriousness of the situation.

"Nicholas," I said. "You stay here and make sure Nurse Scarlett doesn't get away, we'll go after Mr Lyons." Nicholas was still shocked but nodded his head. All three of us as well as Gareth and Officer Barrett ran downstairs to catch up to Mr Lyons. We saw Nurse Lewis standing at the entrance.

"Lewis, where's Howard?" asked Natalie.

"He saw me standing here so he ran towards the kitchen instead," said Nurse Lewis.

"I have a plan," I said. "Nurse Lewis, go round to the side of the orphanage where we found that entrance, the rest of you go catch up to Mr Lyons in the kitchen, I'll be there in a minute."

"Okay," said Officer Barrett who sounded baffled at being told what to do by a teenager like me but he could tell there was something big going down so he agreed and went off. I walked outside where the orphans were gathered.

"Everyone, the orphanage is in serious danger of falling apart thanks to Mr Lyons, we need to stop him so follow me," I said. There were confused murmurs amongst the crowd but they slowly began to come back inside. "Wait here," I said as we entered the dining room, prompting one of the orphans to hold the door to the kitchen open so they could hear what was going on.

As I entered the kitchen area and headed towards the exit at the back, I saw Natalie, Officer Barrett, Natasha and Gareth all standing a few paces behind Mr Lyons. It was plain to see why they were keeping their distance as Mr Lyons had picked up one of the sharpest knifes in the kitchen. Mr Lyons may have evil intentions but he's usually very cunning in his plans and actions to cover his tracks, the drug had driven him to an erratic decision like this. Any damage he could do with a knife, he wouldn't be able to talk his way out of. He was holding the knife with one hand while trying to find an opening through the bushes that covered the exit. This was even harder for him because every few seconds, he put the hand he was using to try and take apart the overgrowth across his face as he was still suffering.

"That's enough, Howard!" I shouted at him.

"That's still Mr Lyons to you," said Howard.

"Calling your elders 'mister' or 'sir' is a show of respect, I no longer have any respect for you," I said.

"No-one will respect you when you end up on the streets after this wretched place closes!" he shouted. Howard was becoming more and more disorientated; he was flailing the hand he held the knife in very carelessly. The orphans waiting by the kitchen entrance could hear every word of it, I could tell from the collective gasp that came from them as Howard made that exclamation.

"Well, no-one will ever respect you in any walk of life ever again," I said. "A millionaire, a child snatcher and a man who uses donations for his own financial gain."

"It wasn't always like that!" He shouted. "I had to change it!" At that moment, Howard closed the door leading out to the overgrowth, stood up straight and tightened his grip on the knife; he had regained some of his composure. "I'll soon have these thoughts flowing into my mind under control so I'll have no distractions when it comes to escaping, your policeman can't overpower me and Nicholas isn't here, what can you do?"

"Soon isn't soon enough for you," I told him.

"What are you talking about?!" asked Howard.

"You said you almost had those thoughts under control, well I'm about to change that," I said as I looked behind me at the orphans who had gathered just outside the kitchen. "Everybody, I know it will be hard but I want you to think about your saddest thoughts and memories, think of the anguish you've suffered being orphaned, your cries, the cries of anguish from your parents as they met their fate, anything," I told them. They all still looked bemused about the whole situation but I could see they were deep in thought with their eyes firmly closed. After a few moments, Howard went back to clutching his head as the voices flooded in.

"Shut up!" he shouted at the voices. As I was looking back and forth between Howard and the orphans, I realised I should have been thinking too. Just as I started to think and reflect, the only real drama I could think of occurred very recently so I thought of Nurse Scarlett's wail of pain when Mr Lyons plunged the syringe into her. I looked over to Howard who dropped the knife and was now writhing around in agony on the floor. This allowed Officer Barrett to move forward and restrain him. With all the wriggling, Officer Barrett was struggling to keep Howard's arms still but he eventually managed to place the handcuffs on Howard.

"It's okay, you can stop now," I told the other orphans. They opened their eyes, many with tears running down their face. "I'm sorry I asked you to do that but you've helped us achieve a great deed."

"But Mr Lyons is being arrested, what will happen now?" asked Natasha.

"I don't know but Mr Lyons didn't have the best interests of the orphanage in mind as you could hear so it was important we stopped him," I said. "I can't explain how but your thoughts really helped." I decided to walk through the crowd of orphans as quickly as possible because I could hear plenty of quizzical noises from them so I didn't want to stick around to answer questions. I could hear more sirens arriving as I walked upstairs to check on Nicholas and Nurse Scarlett. As I walked in, Nurse Scarlett was standing but she didn't look very steady on her feet. In fact, it seemed as if Nicholas was keeping her on her feet.

"I stayed and watched her, just like you asked," said Nicholas.

"Thanks Nicholas, I know it must be tough for you but now you can see that Howard was guilty," I told him.

"I know," said Nicholas. "I looked through some of his other files as well; I can't believe the heinous things he has done with my money, I should have questioned him harder on why I rarely saw improvements to this orphanage."

"That's all in the past now, the important thing is he will no longer take money from you, he will no longer be in charge of the orphanage and he can't affect everybody's future with his politics," I said.

"I'll keep up my donations to the orphanage, I don't care about my money but I do care how it is used when I give it away, this is one Mr Lyons who still cares about this orphanage," said Nicholas.

"That's very kind of you but we will still need to find more money from somewhere else," I said.

"I'm sure you'll find a way, you always do," said Nicholas. At that moment, Officer Barrett knocked on the door and I let him in.

"Mr Lyons is being taken away in a police car now, are either of these two guilty?" he asked me as he gestured towards Nicholas and Nurse Scarlett.

"Yes, Nurse Scarlett needs to be treated at hospital first but she was a part of Mr Lyons' misdemeanours from the beginning," I said. Nicholas looked relieved that only Nurse Scarlett was mentioned.

"I'm not sure I understand any of this but I can justifiably arrest Mr Lyons for wielding a weapon, however it seems like there is more to the story," said Officer Barrett.

"Oh believe me, there is," I told him as I gestured towards the files that Howard had tried to pack away. "Make sure you take this with you, Howard might be close with some of your colleagues so I only trust you to take it."

"Howard's deeper crimes are exposed in there and I think Nurse Scarlett will be more than ready to let you know all about it after what he did to her," said Nicholas.

"But what can I arrest her for right now?" he asked.

"That's simple," said Natalie who had emerged through the door. "She's trespassing on my property and I'd like to press charges," she said with a smirk as she grabbed the paper Howard had waved at her earlier, confirming her as the new owner. Officer Barrett took Nurse Scarlett away as she was escorted in the ambulance by police.

Natalie went around the orphanage making sure all the orphans were rounded up and sent back to bed. She let Gareth and Natasha stay with me for a little while longer.

"It's good to have you back," said Natasha.

"Turns out you were right, I can read Natasha's mind," said Gareth.

"I still have to try it on you sometime," Natasha told Gareth.

"I'd have thought that would have kept you occupied once I told you about it," I said.

"To be honest, we didn't believe you so we didn't try," said Gareth.

"We were still thinking about how to save the orphanage," said Natasha.

"I'm sure we can work something out now that Mr Lyons won't be taking money away from the orphanage," I said.

"But you might not have to work it out; they might be able to track down your parents soon and you'll be gone," said Natasha.

"Well, there aren't many clues in the paperwork but it could help find them," I said.

"That's the spirit," said Natasha.

"But this orphanage is a part of my life and whether I'm here or not, I won't rest until the orphanage is saved," I told her. "And Nicholas' money alone should keep the orphanage running for a bit longer."

"Nicholas doesn't look too good right now," said Natasha pointing to the outside of the orphanage entrance.

"I'd better go see him," I said. I headed outside the orphanage and stood with Nicholas as he looked on.

"I'm sorry about what happened tonight Sam, I tied you, Natalie and Natasha to chairs, you could have got them to arrest me too," said Nicholas.

"It's okay Nicholas, I know Howard has been an important part of your entire life and that bond you shared was hard to break," I said.

"But still, I believed Howard through everything until I saw indisputable proof," said Nicholas.

"It was the same for me too Nicholas," I said. "I believed Howard for a long time that Natalie was in the wrong because I couldn't see the full picture, I misinterpreted Natalie's thoughts because Howard had convinced me."

"So, you really can read minds then?" asked Nicholas.

"Yes but I could never read Howard's mind; that's what led me astray," I said.

"Is it not strange to constantly be in someone's mind?" asked Nicholas.

"It is but I'm good at controlling and filtering it," I said.

"So that's how you know who's bluffing in poker, I could do with that ability," said Nicholas.

"I don't intend to make my way in this world by cheating at poker but if at any point in the future we desperately need money for the orphanage, I'll do anything," I said.

"Otherwise, just for fun, right?" asked Nicholas.

"Yes, just for fun," I said with a smile as the ambulance and police cars left the scene.

Chapter 16

Three months had passed since the arrest of Howard Lyons and Nurse Scarlett leaving Natalie in charge to keep the orphanage running. The news of his arrest garnered national media attention although no-one is reporting the whole truth. The media portrayed Howard as insane for believing that people might have mind-reading abilities and paid more attention to that than the kidnapping. Nurse Scarlett was portrayed as a helpless pawn, that she was a woman who had lost her way in life and was hopelessly devoted to Howard. While there may be some truth to that, Nurse Scarlett knew exactly what she was doing and showed no remorse for her actions.

I don't think a single journalist believes there is any truth in Howard's suggestion and his research is seen as a diary of his insanity rather than actual medical research. His case for not being insane can't have been helped by his claims that he could hear voices in his head. If the research files weren't being kept as evidence, I'm sure they actually might be of use to people in the medical profession just to find out more about the brain. They might explain whether Howard now has a permanent ability to read minds or if he had to keep taking the drug to keep it up. I'm happy that Howard has been rightfully arrested for his horrendous crimes but I can't shake the feeling that people want to label him as insane and focus on his obsession with mind-reading rather than his crimes to do with kidnapping me and keeping donations for himself.

Howard had predicted the orphanage would fail without him. Even though I feared that could've come true, it would have failed with Howard anyway. Ironically, his actions have helped to keep the orphanage running without his money or influence. The national media coverage of his actions gained a lot of exposure for the orphanage. The potential political allies and rivals of Howard were quick to sever any links with him and pledged to provide donations to the orphanage, both monetary and material donations.

The orphanage looks brand new; the walls have been repainted with lots of light blue and pink to balance out the traditional boy and girl colours. The open area of the orphanage was kitted out with new furniture and a variety of books, board games and magazines and nothing is loose or wonky. The local companies as well as the politicians were quick to donate what they could, having heard about the state of the orphanage and the risk of closure.

I sat alone in the dining room as I had become accustomed to over the past month since the school term restarted. The food had improved dramatically, it wasn't fine dining but at least the food had some taste and shape to it. The kitchen staff hadn't changed but it is easy to tell they are in good spirits, the kitchen and dining room is colourful now and they have decent ingredients to use. I saw Natalie heading over towards me. Natalie looked refreshed in her role as head of the orphanage. There was a worry that the amount of catch-up work she would have to do and the effort she would have to put in would've taken a toll on her. However, she's got herself some help from volunteers, so much so that although she works every day, she doesn't have to work into the early hours of the morning each night.

"Good morning Sam," she said with a gleaming smile on her face. "All ready for another day at school?"

"I suppose," I replied.

"You're not tired of it already, are you?" she asked.

"No, it's just the early mornings I'm tired of," I replied.

"You'll get used to it," she said. "Besides if it wasn't for early mornings, you'd barely spend any time in this orphanage during the week."

"I like it here in the orphanage especially with all the changes but I prefer to spend the majority of my time with

Gareth and Natasha during school and the extracurricular activities the school offers afterwards," I said.

"I still think you should try and start to make new friends here, you've told me you don't want to go to foster parents because your real parents are out there somewhere but it might be a long time before they are tracked down," said Natalie. Knowing that I have birth parents out there makes me hesitant to join another family so I'd like to stay at the orphanage until my birth parents are found or I'm old enough to leave.

"I'm not worried about that, like I said, I'm happy here and I'm happy with my current arrangement; to socialise during the day and come back here for dinner, reading and bed," I told her.

"I can see you're enjoying your independence," said Natalie.

"And I have you to thank for it, I realise now that Howard was always very restrictive and I thought we had a mutual trust," I said. "But for you to trust me to stay after school and come back here in my own time means a lot to me."

"Well, you've earned it, after all you have done for the orphanage, I want you to have as much freedom as possible," said Natalie. "You have the freedom to stay at this orphanage as long as you want to."

"Through good and bad it has been my home and the fact that it's starting to feel good around here again means I'm in no hurry to leave," I said.

"How are Gareth and Natasha doing?" asked Natalie.

"They've been doing great the last month, they tell me they have settled in well with Matthew and Geena and believe me, I know it's true," I told her as I pointed towards my mind.

"That's a relief, I know everyone was so excited about it happening but nobody could tell for sure how well it would work out," said Natalie. "You don't miss them?"

"Seeing them during and after school is enough for me," I replied. "And that way, they can't distract me from my books in the evening; it took me long enough to finish reading Of Mice and Men."

"Well, now there's plenty more where that came from," she said. "Did you like it?"

"I did although the way it ended makes me think twice about how Howard said I should look to replicate George and Lenny's relationship," I replied.

"Despite that, he is right though, good friends can become more important than family," said Natalie. "You saw the bond between Howard and Nicholas and how that came to a screeching halt."

"How is Nicholas?" I asked.

"He seems to be fine now; he still plays poker, apparently he actually wins a few times now and he still donates to the orphanage," replied Natalie. "He's doing a lot of work outside the orphanage as well looking for other donors and volunteers for the orphanage which I'm grateful for." Natalie's face suddenly began to look sombre. "I hope he doesn't feel he has to do all this work just to make up for his brother's mess."

"I'm sure he's okay," I said. "Besides, he said his brother robbed him of his work well now he has a chance to work on something else."

"I guess you're right Sam, you've seen Charlotte come in a few times haven't you?" she asked.

"Yeah, she's one of the volunteers," I replied.

"Well, she's Nicholas' daughter and she couldn't wait to volunteer here, it's so nice to meet so many helpful people now that Howard is out of here," she said. "We've still got a lot of work to do but I'm confident with the discussions I have had with people that I can build this orphanage back up again with a healthy number of staff and volunteers."

"What about Nurse Lewis?" I asked. "I haven't seen him in months."

"He's doing well, the bump to the head he took that night went down quickly and now he spends a lot of time at my place....to help me clean it up of course now that I have enough free time to actually live in my house," she said.

"I'm glad to hear it," I said.

"Anyway, I'll let you get on Sam, I'll see you in the evening," she said as she walked off. I soon finished my breakfast and headed back towards the dormitories. I could see the caretaker Mr Thompson doing the usual rounds of the orphanage in the morning; he had managed to keep his job since any other options are limited at the moment. I assume it was because he is good at his job even though Natalie can see he doesn't have a passion for the orphanage or children. Whenever I see Mr Thompson disgruntled, he always composes himself and the same thought runs through his mind each time.

"Work is work," he thinks to cheer himself up. I realised it was wrong to demonise him because his sole motivation for this job is money; at least he has a motivation which doesn't harm anyone else. The survival of the orphanage isn't set in stone but I can relax at night knowing that everybody working here is committed to doing their best in order to maintain and improve the orphanage. So instead my focus turns to ways in which I could track down my birth parents if somebody doesn't track them down for me. I'd imagine there might be a clue in all of Mr Lyons' files that were seized but I'm sure they'll gloss over my kidnapping and focus solely on his interest in mind-reading. I think the people stopped caring because they weren't allowed to identify me.

Despite my intention to track down my birth parents, there is a hint of trepidation in regards to meeting them and things not going to plan. Like Natalie had said, Nicholas and Howard were brothers tied by blood and it didn't work out well for them. Gareth and Natasha are happy with Matthew and Geena so far and they have no family link. I had also viewed Howard as a father figure, without having any blood connections, and he was not trustworthy. Through all that, all I can say is that family or not, there are good people and bad people in the world so I have to be wary; family isn't everything.

I'm very happy to stay at the orphanage as long as I need to; I want to see the changes, the improvements taking place. This place has always been my home and feels like home, which I can embrace even more if the orphanage improves. I've gone this far in my life without parents so it's not so much that I need to go live with my parents but I feel as if I need to see them, just so I know and they know about everything that has gone on.

I couldn't help but draw my mind back to the research of Mr Lyons. The legacy of the research may be tarnished with Howard's crimes but it is still a piece of interest to me to see everything he learned. The research mentioned one other child born a few years before me who supposedly kept his or her mind-reading ability. So that means there is at least one person out there with the ability and who knows about the ones he lost track of.

I changed into my school uniform which fit almost perfectly; a rarity among the rest of my clothes. It's the time when I can wear something that isn't baggy and worn out. I think Mr Thompson's least favourite part of the day was the school morning run with children of different ages going to different schools over different distances.

Mr Thompson has to set up camp by the orphanage entrance each school day between 7.30am until 9am. For those in secondary school, they are trusted to leave at what time they choose and leave on their own. Luckily, all the juniors in the orphanage were based in the same school and it included a short walk accompanied by Mr Thompson. I always made sure to leave nice and early just in case there was a problem with buses. I'd usually always arrive at school with plenty of time to spare but it was nice to not be in a rush and it gives me more time to hang out with Gareth and Natasha. I exited the orphanage to bright sunshine, although there was still a chill in the air, and headed towards the bus stop. I'd often see a few other pupils there so it was nice that my uniform fit, otherwise I'd really stand out when next to the others.

I entered through the front gates of the school and arrived with plenty of time to spare. I waited around in an open area referred to as The Quad hoping to see Gareth and Natasha; I'd see them most mornings but sometimes they would only just arrive to school on time leaving no time to chat. I saw a familiar, dark blue car pull up at the gates of the school carrying Gareth and Natasha; it was Matthew's car. I had seen the car's interior before which looks luxurious and makes the outside of the car look cheap in comparison. I think that summed up Matthew and Geena's philosophy of how they spend their money. I haven't seen any indication so far that Gareth and Natasha have been spoilt by them although they do like to rub a few of their luxuries in my face from time to time. Gareth and Natasha exited the car and quickly headed towards me.

"How are you Sam?" asked Gareth.

"I've been good," I replied.

"Ready for another day at school?" asked Natasha.

"More ready than last year," I replied. "This year, I get to have breakfast that actually resembles food at the orphanage." Gareth and Natasha laughed.

"Yeah, actual food must be a nice change," said Gareth.

"I'm sure you would know that more than I do with your new home," I said.

"Well yeah but we wouldn't want to rub it in your face if we had nice breakfast and you still had slop," said Natasha. "Now we can just rub in the fact that our breakfast is probably generally nicer than what you have."

"Probably so but at least it's proper food now," I said. "I bet you have some nice meals throughout the day."

"We do but there's always a compromise," said Natasha. "Matthew and Geena like to cook us tasty but basic meals, if we want the more fancy meals, we have to help them prepare it."

"They give us the basics but the luxuries come with hard work," said Gareth.

"My heart weeps for you," I said. After a brief pause, the three of us burst into laughter. I was pleased that Gareth and Natasha's principles hadn't been compromised by their move to a wealthy family and I was pleased that Matthew and Geena wouldn't enable them to. "We don't exactly have luxuries at the orphanage but it's looking and running a lot better than what it was before."

"I'm sure you'll get some luxuries soon, we have to work hard for ours but you've already put in the hard work which hopefully will entitle you to some future luxuries," Natasha told me.

"Yeah, your hard work saved the orphanage; it's only a matter of time before you get your reward for it," said Gareth.

"It isn't entirely safe yet," I told Gareth. "The only reward I want is for the orphanage to continue running during and beyond my time there."

"But you got rid of Mr Lyons, that was the main thing and you already said things were improving," said Gareth.

"We all helped to get rid of Mr Lyons," I said. "Natalie has been rewarded with ownership of the orphanage, you've been rewarded with a new family and I've been rewarded with a place to stay as long as I need to."

"You still deserve more though," said Natasha.

"Maybe I do, maybe I don't," I said. "I don't deserve to have friends like you but I've got you anyway; friends who helped me through my struggle with Mr Lyons."

"We don't deserve you as a friend," said Gareth. "Like you just said, we helped you but you were the one who got everything in place to take down Mr Lyons."

"Okay then," I said. "Let's just agree that no-one automatically deserves anything and no-one is entitled to anything, let's be happy with how things have turned out and see what happens next."

"Sounds good to me," said Gareth.

"And me," said Natasha. The three of us gathered for a hug before heading inside the school building. It was great to see from the conversation we just had that there is a mutual respect and appreciation between the three of us. Natalie was right; blood has nothing to do with families. The three of us had bonded together through good and bad times and we are all grateful to have each other in our lives; if I never find my birth parents, I can take solace in the fact that from now I will always have a family.

Lightning Source UK Ltd.
Milton Keynes UK
UKOW03f0607030417
298192UK00001B/29/P